SOME THINGS I NEVER THOUGHT I'D DO

Pearl Cleage

ONE WORLD
BALLANTINE BOOKS • NEW YORK

A One World Book
Published by The Random House Publishing Group

www.ballantinebooks.com/one/

Library of Congress Cataloging-in-Publication Data
is available upon request.

ISBN: 0-345-47826-6

Text design by Holly Johnson

Manufactured in the United States of America

First Hardcover Edition: September 2003
First Trade Paperback Edition: April 2004

10 9 8 7 6 5 4 3 2 1

For Michael Jondré Pryor Lomax,
who made me start thinking about grandsons in the first place;

For Deignan Cleage Lomax,
who allowed me to be there for the miracle;

And for Zaron W. Burnett Jr.,
whose name should be on the cover.

FREEDOM AND LOVE MAY BE THE MOST
REVOLUTIONARY IDEAS AVAILABLE TO US.

Robin D. G. Kelley

I GUESS I'LL SEE YOU NEXT LIFETIME.

Erykah Badu

ACKNOWLEDGMENTS

Special thanks to Kristin Cleage Williams and the other members of my expanding family for their love and support. Thanks also to my friends and neighbors, including Jondré Pryor, Karen and A. B. Spellman, Walt Huntley Jr., Cecelia Corbin Hunter, Ingrid Saunders Jones, the Honorable Shirley Franklin, Valerie Boyd, Michael L. Lomax, Zaron W. Burnett III, Ray and Marilyn Cox, Lynette Lapeyrolerie, Tayari Jones, Meghan V. Underwood, Jill Nelson, Tina McElroy Ansa, Donald Stone, Jimmy Lee Tarver, Marc and Elaine Lawson, Debra Thurmond, Granville Edward Freeman Dennis, the Broadway and Burnett families, Bebe Moore Campbell, Don Bryan, Ouida and Andrew Collins, E. Lynn Harris, Travis Hunter, Carolyn Monteilh, Maria Broom, Curtis and Barbara Jackson, Watt Hackett, ROOTS International, the Shrine of the Black Madonna, Nia Damali and Medu Bookstore, and the hardworking brothers and sisters at the Post Office and the Publix who always find time to ask me how my work is going. As always, thanks to Denise Stinson, Howard Rosenstone, and Nancy Miller for taking care of business, and to Bill Bagwell, because a deal is a deal.

1

I HAVE REALLY SCREWED UP NOW. This man is actually sitting behind that great big desk telling me he's going to take my house. The house I was born in! The house my mother was born in! He must be crazy.

I know I'm the one who borrowed against it. I know I'm the one who didn't make the payments on time. I know *all* that. That's the first thing they teach you in rehab, to accept responsibility for the stuff you did when you were a stomp-down dope fiend, *and I do*, but I never thought they would actually take the house. What good is trying to reform if you have to spend the rest of your life paying for the stupid things you did when you still got high and didn't give a damn?

Of course, I don't say all that to this little weasel-faced white man who probably has no life at all outside of this windowless office where he gets to bring up your file on his computer and then swivel it around so you can see all those missed payments and bounced checks, daring you to deny them.

He clearly does not want to hear my tale of woe. Having your heart broken and thinking cocaine can fix it does not qualify as an appropriate topic for discussion with your banker. I know this from experience, so I skip the explanations and start right in on the serious begging.

Please, I say, *I'm okay now. I just got a good job. I'll have enough to bring everything current if you can just give me a little more time.*

He ignores me. He's heard all this before. He knows the house has been in our family for three generations. He knows I was born there. He knows my grandparents got married there. He knows it is more than a house. That it is an essential part of our family history, our memories, our dreams. He knows it is a sacred trust passed from one woman in our family, to the next one, and the next one, and, finally, to me.

He knows all this because I have told him many times. I want him to understand that losing this place is not an option. I'm not going to greet my mama in paradise and tell her I snorted up *her* mama's house because I wanted a man who didn't want me. If I tell her that, I'll have to tell her that during that same amazing eighteen months, I also lost my credibility as a journalist by sleeping with all the editors I wasn't doing drugs with, missing deadlines like it was a sport, and, in the last few months before I finally went into rehab, behaving badly at several important Washington social events, culminating in the unforgettable evening when I cussed out a congressman, spilled a drink on his wife, and wrecked my car all in one forty-five-minute period.

But that was *then*. This is *now*. I've been clean for almost six months, and as soon as I get paid from this new job, I'll pay the weasel what I owe and he can go swivel his screen at some other poor fool. All I need is a ninety-day extension. *Just three months,* I hear myself still begging. *I'll be able to bring everything current. I promise!*

The weasel raises his eyebrows to let me know he doesn't buy it for one second. He glances down at the screen again, and I mentally prepare myself to segue from begging to groveling. I'm ready to roll around on the floor and tear my hair, if that's what it takes. I'm the one who messed everything up, but I'm also the one who is going to make it right. Starting with this house.

The weasel is still staring at the screen. He better hope whatever he needs to see there to give me my ninety days shows up in the next sixty seconds because I am *this close* to dragging him across that desk and whipping his smug little ass until somebody comes to pull me off him. *This close.*

Then he sighs deeply and looks up. *Sixty days,* he says, like it's killing him. *I'll give you sixty days.*

And I want to say, *It's not even your money, so why are you acting so shitty in a moment that is already shitty enough without your adding a single thing?*

But it's not his fault. I wouldn't even be sitting here if I hadn't done the things I did. The reason he's acting like he's doing me a favor is because he *is* doing me a favor. They could have taken the house two months ago, and no amount of world-class begging could have stopped them if the weasel hadn't let me slide. Being mad at him is a waste of time, and if I've learned anything, it's that time is all you've got.

Thank you, I say, standing up to go before he can change his mind. He stands up and reluctantly shakes the hand I offer. He's giving me that disapproving stone face like he's Robert Young on *Father Knows Best* and I'm Kitten trying to hide a bad report card.

I'm at the door when he calls my name, and my first reaction is to keep walking like I don't hear him, but that would be gutless, and courage is one of the things I'm supposed to be working on, so I stop and half turn back toward him. *Yes?*

Good luck, he says with a smile that's almost human.

Thanks, I say, smiling back, even if he is my banker. *I'm going to need it.*

2

Aunt Abbie says I don't need luck because I now have a visionary adviser. That's what she calls herself these days. A *visionary adviser*. She even had little blue cards printed up that say *Abbie Allen Browning, V.A.* Her long-range plan is to open her own salon where she can receive people and offer her visionary advice for a small fee.

When she first told me this, I laughed and asked her if she was going to use a crystal ball or tarot cards, and she said I sure did have a smart mouth for somebody who just got out of rehab, and she was right. It was, after all, one of Aunt Abbie's visions that brought her here at the exact moment when I needed her the most.

The day I got out of rehab, I caught a cab home, hoping I wouldn't find a padlock on the door and an overgrown yard with a FOR SALE sign sticking up in the middle. Getting *myself* together had been my full-time job for the last few months. Now it was time to get my *business* straight, if I wasn't already too late. Figuring out how to get the house out of hock was the first item on the agenda.

When the cab pulled up in front of the house, I started to tell the guy he'd made a mistake. The grass was neatly trimmed and the house itself looked freshly painted and generally spiffed up. I paid the driver, got out with my suitcase, and just stood there for a minute. Before I could come up with a plausible reason for the unexpected changes, the front door opened and my aunt Abbie walked out to meet me. She's sixty if she's a day, but she moves with the physical confidence of a woman half that age.

"Welcome home, dear," she said, picking up my suitcase and giving me a quick hug. "Come inside before you catch your death."

I followed, literally speechless with amazement. I hadn't told anybody I was going into rehab, much less when I was coming out. Aunt Abbie and I had hardly communicated at all since my parents' funeral almost two years ago, and we had never been especially close. I always liked her, but she hadn't ever been around much. The youngest of my father's three sisters, she was the baby of the family, but by far the most independent one. She traveled a lot, got married a lot, divorced a lot, and always carried the scent of patchouli in the multiethnic clothing she invariably wore.

She was fond of long skirts, silver bracelets, and those flat black Chinese shoes with flowers embroidered on the toes. She had never been an artist, but she had always looked like one. She liked the company of creative people and among her husbands had been a writer, a painter, and a cellist, who also played guitar. As far as I knew, at this point in her life she was traveling solo.

She held the door open for me, and I stepped inside my own house like I was visiting. The place had been transformed. When I checked myself into rehab, I know I left the house a wreck from my unmade bed to a sink full of dirty dishes. I felt a wash of shame at anybody finding the place in the state in which I'd abandoned it, but I was running for my life. *Neatening up* was the last thing on my mind.

But there was no hint of disorder here today. The place was spotless, smelling of furniture polish and patchouli. The rugs had been shampooed, the windows were sparkling, and the furniture had been brushed and plumped to within an inch of its life. There was a fire burning in the fireplace and fresh flowers in a huge vase in the center of the dining room table. The place looked better than it had in ages.

I looked at Aunt Abbie. "Did you do all this?"

She laughed. "Don't look so shocked. I had a couple of months and I did hire some guys to do the outside painting and the rugs, but otherwise, a little at a time was all it took. Nice, huh?"

"It's beautiful. How did you know I was getting out today?"

She shrugged and set my bag down at the foot of the stairs. "I just had a feeling."

"How long have you been here?"

"Since Christmas. I thought you might come home for the holidays."

That was a month ago! "How'd you get in?"

She smiled. "Your mother gave me a key years ago. I had married a fool who was trying to be abusive and she was worried. She wanted me to have a place to go if I ever needed to leave in a hurry. Since they were on the road so much then, she just gave me my own key."

My parents hadn't been actively on the road for thirty years before they passed.

"When was that?" I said, still trying to make sense of everything.

She thought about it for a minute then shrugged again. "1972? '73? Somewhere around in there."

"Thirty years ago?"

She looked surprised at my surprise. "At least. I never married a fool after I turned thirty. That's what your twenties are for."

My head was spinning, but I had to admit, it was a lovely homecoming, however she got here. It was good to come back to somebody who was glad to see me.

"Thanks," I said.

"Welcome home," she said, and we hugged again. *Family.* "Now come on in here and let's have some lunch and catch up."

That was six weeks ago, and when I look back, I can't imagine how I would have made it without her. She listened to the story of how I got to rehab with a look of concern, but no censure. I had the feeling that she had had her share of broken hearts and bad judgments and that there was very little that went on between consenting adults that would shock or surprise her.

She let me tell it all as we watched the fire die down to a pile of glowing orange coals. Then she looked at me and said calmly, "So what are we going to do now?"

The fact that she said *we* almost made me burst into tears. *We* meant I wasn't alone in the world. That somebody was around to help me figure out how to undo the messiness I'd made. *We* meant she had my back. How she got here was beside the point. All I really needed to say was *thank you*.

I understand that now. From encouraging me to go see the weasel and work something out, to convincing me I was strong enough to take the job Beth Davis was offering, to agreeing to house-sit while I was in Atlanta, Aunt Abbie had helped me play to my strengths by treating me like she was unaware of any weakness. If I was actually able to pull this off, go to Atlanta for a couple of months and make enough money to rescue the homestead, I had Aunt Abbie to thank for it.

So I decided to stop by Union Station on my way home from my successful negotiation with the weasel and buy her a big bunch of flowers. The vendors outside the main entrance always have such a wonderful variety of brightly colored bouquets from which to choose. This used to be one of my regular stops in the old days when I was still working downtown. Money is going to be a little tight until I get my finances settled, but as impulse purchases go, flowers are always worth more than whatever you pay for them.

Buying flowers is not just a way to bring home beauty. It's an expression of confidence that better days are coming. It's a defiant finger in the face of those naysayers who would have you believe your fortunes will never improve. Well, this afternoon, I was flushed with enough confidence to justify not simply a mixed bouquet, but the tropical selection, heavy on purple, orange, and blossoming birds-of-paradise.

The smiling vendor wrapped the flowers in pink tissue paper and tied them with a curling strip of white ribbon while I watched the travelers rushing into the big front doors of the train station, heading to their own adventures, oblivious to their fellow adventurers striding along beside them with equal fervor.

I love trains. Overnight in a sleeper is, in fact, my favorite way to travel. Amtrak runs the Southern Crescent from D.C. to Atlanta seven nights a week, and I'd be booked on it for my trip if sleeper accommodations weren't so pricey. They're not as expensive as a first-class airline ticket, which is now about the cost of a year's tuition at a good junior college, but they're a lot more than I can afford right now.

Coach seats are, of course, a lot cheaper, but also a different experience entirely. Spending twenty-seven consecutive hours, including the nighttime hours, with a bunch of people you just met is only romantic in the movies. In real life, it's crying babies, communal bathrooms, and strange-smelling food somebody brought from home and wants to share.

I hate to fly, especially these days when collective paranoia is booked on every flight along with the passengers, but ultimately, it gets down to a choice between two and a half hours of white knuckles or twenty-plus hours of hearing the snores of sleeping strangers. This time, flying won out, but I wasn't looking forward to it.

When I walked in the house, Aunt Abbie was in the kitchen already rinsing out a vase and filling it with water and just a pinch of sugar to keep the blooms fresh.

"I knew you could do it," she said, taking the bouquet from me without even asking how it had gone with the weasel. "They're lovely! My favorites!"

I had to smile. "Weren't you even a little bit nervous that he might turn me down?"

She snorted at the absurdity of such an idea. "Not a chance. That little man is in no position to stand against the flow of things."

"What things?" I asked, watching her deftly arrange the flowers in the vase and carry it to the dining room table. She placed it dead center and then smiled her approval.

"Just lovely. Did you get them at the train station?"

"Yes. The flow of what things?"

"I thought so," she said. "I saw these birds-of-paradise earlier and I knew they would be the ones you'd pick!"

Having a conversation with Aunt Abbie was like learning how to swim. You could hang around on the edges of the pool if you wanted to, but sooner or later, you were going to have to take a deep breath and plunge on in.

"You were at the train station today?"

She nodded, making a minor adjustment to the largest of the blooms. "I had to pick up your ticket."

"I'm flying, remember?"

"Not anymore," she said, handing me an Amtrak ticket folder. "You're leaving tomorrow evening at seven-thirty."

That was the southbound Crescent all right, but she had obviously forgotten my recent rantings about the problematic nature of coach-class train travel. "I'm flying Delta, day after tomorrow, at noon."

"Look at the ticket," she said.

I pulled it out. One way, deluxe bedroom accommodations, all the way to Atlanta.

"But, I can't afford this," I said, wishing I could.

"My treat," she said. "Happy Birthday."

I looked at her. "My birthday is in August."

She grinned at me. "Merry Christmas, Happy Kwanzaa, and welcome to the new millennium! You're missing the point, dear. It's a gift."

I laughed. "Do you have a secret bank account you're not telling me about?"

"It's no secret," she said. "It won't cover near what you need on the house, or I would have offered it up long before now, but a first-class train ticket to celebrate a job well done?" She shrugged gracefully, releasing a little whiff of patchouli from the folds of her Chinese kimono. *"Piece a cake!"*

"You amaze me," I said. "Thank you."

"That's because I'm amazing," she said. "And you're very welcome."

I looked at the ticket again and noticed it was one way. I couldn't resist teasing her a little. "So how come you didn't make it round trip? Don't you want me back when it's over?"

"Of course," she said, still smiling, taking my arm and leading me into the living room. We sat down on the couch, side by side. "But you won't be coming back by train."

"Oh?" I said, amused by her certainty. "How will I be traveling?"

"By car," she said, immediately. "Definitely by car."

"Maybe not," I said. "By then, I'll have enough money to buy my own first-class ticket."

She was looking at me with a funny expression.

"What's wrong?"

She got up, stirred the fire into life, and turned back to me. I had a sickening feeling. She had that "I'm ready to tell you something serious as hell whether you're ready for it or not" look on her face.

The suspense was killing me.

"What?"

She came back to sit beside me. "You remember when I told you I had a vision about your needing some assistance and that's why I came here?"

I nodded.

"Well, there's more to it than that."

"More to the vision?"

"More to *everything*. That's why I knew that little banker wasn't going to turn you down. It's much bigger than that."

I was swimming around in the conversation as best I could, but I was barely keeping my head above water.

"Hold it!" I said. "Start at the beginning."

She patted my hand gently. "That's just what I'm talking about. Where is the beginning? The *real* beginning?"

This was getting us no place fast. I decided to double back and try again. "Start with the visions."

"All right," she said, curling up and tucking her feet under her long skirt. "That's as good a place as any. Ever since I went through menopause, I've been having visions."

"What kind of visions?"

"All kinds. Big things, little things. I can't determine any of that yet. Right now, all I can do is recognize them and write down what she says."

"What *who* says?"

"Whoever is speaking to me through these visions. They're more auditory than visual, although sometimes I do see images, but they're usually fleeting."

"And how long have you been hearing these voices?"

She heard the skepticism in my voice, and she did not appreciate it.

"I don't hear voices," she sniffed. "I have *visions*. There's a difference, although you're still too full of estrogen to understand it."

The way she said it, the hormone sounded like an active blocker of both intelligence and intuition. I wanted to tell her that at thirty-four, my estrogen was probably already on the wane, but I didn't want to piss her off even more.

"Sorry."

"Don't be sorry," she said. "Estrogen is fine, but it definitely blocks a lot of female magic, especially the stuff having to do with being able to see the past and the present and the future as all part of the same bolt of cloth. As long as you can have babies, you can't really focus on this stuff. You've got to have time to let your mind wander for it to come through. Especially the voices. Which is why I've only been hearing them for about five years. It's like as soon as the hot flashes went away, I could hear things coming through on a whole different wavelength."

It sounded a little crazy, but I do believe in the existence of untapped wells of female gifts and magic, and menopause could as easily be a font of special wisdom and spirituality as the time of diminished powers and depression people sometimes want us to think it is. If my vibrant, self-sufficient, patchouli-smelling aunt said she had a postmenopausal vision that brought her to my door, I wanted to hear *all* of it.

"I believe you," I said. "It's just hard to talk about this stuff without feeling a little self-conscious."

"It's just like oral sex, dear," she said. "It seems silly at first, but you'll get used to it. Just try to keep an open mind," she said with an encouraging smile. "Ready?"

"Ready."

"Here's the deal. There's a man in Atlanta who's been looking for you across time."

"*What?*"

"Oh, wait! That shouldn't come first. I should talk about the journey first."

I felt my head sinking beneath the waves. "What journey?"

"To Atlanta." She stood up suddenly. "Wait a second. I need to get my notes."

She hurried out of the room on her little satin mary janes and up the steps to the second floor. I heard a drawer open and close, and she returned quickly with a well-worn reporter's notebook. She flipped it open and smiled her relief.

"All right! This will make it easier for me to tell you exactly. I was right! The journey comes first. And she specifically says it's a journey you don't want to take." She looked up at me. "That's how I knew you had to go to Atlanta. Because you truly didn't want to."

I nodded like any of this made sense. It didn't.

She consulted her notes again. "A journey . . . okay. I did that one. Here! You must complete a task for a fallen friend."

That sent a little chill through me. I was going to Atlanta to do a project about the life and work of a good friend of mine who died in New York last September. I had loved him and lost him, but he had saved my life, and I owed him one.

"Go on."

"And the third thing is—*don't laugh*."

"I'm not laughing."

"The third thing she said you have to do is rescue a damsel in distress."

"*I'm* the damsel in distress," I said.

Aunt Abbie gave her head a little impatient shake. "You can't be the damsel in distress. You're the *shero*."

"I am?"

"Of course. If you can't be the star of your own story, what's the point?"

She had me there. "What am I rescuing her from?"

Aunt Abbie flipped a page of her notebook. "My notes don't say, but since she used the word *damsel*, I'd say some kind of dragon wouldn't be out of the question."

"A fire-breathing dragon?"

She chuckled. "Of course not. A *symbolic* dragon, dear."

That didn't make me feel much better. Dragons of any kind tend to make me nervous.

"What about the guy?" I said.

"What guy?"

"The one who's been searching for me across time."

She flipped a few more pages. "He's in Atlanta, like I said, which works out nice, and he'll know you as soon as he sees you, but you probably won't recognize him except for his eyes."

"What about his eyes?" I had a sudden flash of *Rosemary's Baby,* with those weird yellow orbs the devil left behind.

"They're blue."

"He's a white man?" I almost shrieked.

"I didn't say he was white. I said he had blue eyes. The exact words she used were, 'He has the ocean in his eyes.' That's lovely, don't you think?"

"How many black people do you know with blue eyes?"

"It's not the color that's important," she said gently, trying to calm me down. "He had to have some way of being sure you'd recognize him. He's convinced he just missed you the last time around and he's determined not to let it happen again."

"But why blue eyes? Why couldn't he just be real tall or something?"

She frowned. "Because you could make a mistake and end up with Rick Fox and then where would you be?"

I resigned myself to blue eyes. "What else does it say about this guy?"

"*She.* What else does *she* say." Aunt Abbie corrected me gently, but firmly.

"My apologies. What else does she say?"

"She said he sings an ancient song."

I rolled my eyes. "That's all I need. A blue-eyed brother who sings Gregorian chants."

She ignored me. "And he's not who he appears to be."

I groaned. "He's a con man, too?"

13

"I didn't say anything about his being a con man." She was scanning the page again. "There was one more thing she said . . . oh! Here it is. At the end of your journey, you'll bring him home to meet your aunt—that would be me!—and take his vows."

I wondered if that was before or after we slayed the dragon. "What vows are those?"

She closed the notebook and beamed at me. "Wedding vows, of course. Didn't I say you're going to marry him?"

I looked at her. "You know this vision is asking me to do some things I never thought I'd do."

She patted my hand gently. "I know, dear, but you know what? Sometimes that's exactly what you should do. Whatever it is you thought you'd never do."

I was not convinced. "I'm too old for fairy tales."

She grinned at me and shook her head. "Baby girl, please! You are in your prime!"

3

F IRST-CLASS ACCOMMODATIONS on the Southern Crescent take all the sting out of overnight travel. Not only do you have your own tiny little bathroom, but a smiling brother in a blue sweater vest and sensible shoes comes to pull down your bed whenever you're ready to get in it. Aunt Abbie did me a good turn by getting this ticket. Traveling this way is peaceful. It slows you down instead of hyping you up like airports do, and that is just what I had in mind. I need time to think. Who knows what I'll be walking into once I get to Atlanta. The only thing I'd bet on is that it has nothing to do with what Beth Davis told me on the phone. *Legacy Project* my ass, but if she's willing to pay me thirty grand to do it, she can consider it done.

I couldn't believe she had the nerve to call me. I haven't even seen Beth since her son broke my heart two years ago on the most important date night in a hundred years. Dick Clark was counting down to the millennium and my fiancé was apologizing for not being able to stand up to his mother who was loudly accusing me of disloyalty above and beyond the call of duty.

In one awful instant, my love life and my dream job were both wiped out. Alone and unemployed was not where I had planned to be at thirty-two, so I packed up my car, drove back home to D.C., and discovered cocaine. My parents had passed, and I was alone in the world with no job to go to, a broken heart, and a nice inheritance to dip into. I was a coke dealer's dream, and the feeling was mutual.

When I was high, I didn't have to think about how scared I was. When I was high, I knew the answers to all the hard questions and would share them at the drop of a hat. Even better, when I was buying, I never had to be alone. That's how I almost lost the house. Buying company.

I did that from January of the millennium year until September 11 of the next one. On that morning, having sold everything I could sell and borrowed against the rest, I was on the phone trying to wheedle my longtime dealer into extending me some credit since I was down to crumbs and the week wasn't even half over.

The television had been on all night and the drone of the *Today* show was simply background noise like the traffic in the street outside. I had just decided to have sex with this guy in exchange for the drugs I wanted when I looked at the TV in time to see the second plane hit the World Trade Center. I dropped the phone, flushed the last of my pitiful stash, and started praying. I checked myself into rehab that same day.

I didn't know Son Davis had died there until I read it in the newspaper. It made me feel terrible, no matter what had happened between us at the end. He wasn't a bad guy. He was just weak. He didn't want to be. He just was. He lived his whole life being a creation of Beth's imagination, and it was a wonderful creation, but there was more to him than being the perfect son. A lot more.

We spent hours talking about what he was going to do once he went off on his own, but he never made a move. The closest he got was our trying to elope, and Beth snatched him back so hard it gave *me* whiplash. I think that's probably what attracted him to me in the first place, although I didn't know it at the time. He thought I was strong enough to pull him away from Beth, but nobody's that strong. Even now, she's still shaping his life to suit her purposes, whatever they are, which is what I'm still trying to figure out.

Beth Davis was born with the kind of charisma that changes people's lives. You might not see it if you pass her on the street. She looks like a million other short, round, just-missed-being-pretty brown-skinned women of *a certain age*. But wait until you see her in a roomful of mothers trying desperately to raise their hardheaded sons all by themselves. Wait until you hear her remind them they're allowed to have dreams. Wait until you hear her make the possibility of freedom sound so seductive you want to suck on it like a summer peach.

Beth's book, *Son Shine*, is the only self-published work ever to make the *Essence*, *USA Today*, and *New York Times* best-seller lists for the same six-month period. The book really isn't very well written, but it's so passionate and honest and hopeful about things that usually seem so hopeless, you can't put it down.

Son Shine tells the story of Beth's amazing journey from being the daughter of an unmarried, illiterate single mother who named her after Elizabeth Taylor, to being a single mother herself at sixteen, to becoming a best-selling author and one of the top motivational speakers in the country. The heart of the book is the birth of Beth's only child, Theo, who she always called Son. After the book came out, nobody ever called him anything else.

"I knew the first time I looked into my baby's little brown face that he was perfect," she writes in her introduction, "untouched by the madness of the world I had brought him into. That's when I knew whatever his daddy was or was not, could or could not do, I was going to raise him to be the kind of man I had hoped his father could be: *smart, strong, spiritual, sensual, and self-sufficient.* And if I did it right, when he was all grown up and some other mother's child opened her life's front door to my son, he wouldn't come up in there with a whole bunch of drama and confusion. He'd be bringing nothing but truth, good love, and *sunshine*."

My mother once said, after waxing rhapsodic about the 1967 March on the Pentagon, that the beauty of a successful demonstration is that it gives the protestors a chance to realize they're not alone. There's power in numbers, she said, but only if the powerless people making up those numbers are aware of their equally powerless comrades. First they have to recognize one another and say hello. Beth's work is about the business of making introductions.

The first time I heard her speak to a roomful of shouting, stomping, weeping, laughing black women, and me hollering as loud as anybody even though I didn't even have a kid, I quit my job the next morning and went to work for her full-time. I was speechwriter, special assistant, advance team, and travel agent. It was a twenty-four-hour-a-day job, and I was as good at my part as Beth was at hers. The first three years I worked for her were probably the most exciting, exhausting, fulfilling years of my life.

Everywhere we went, women were energized. They bought the books, memorized the tapes, signed up for workshops, and, when she started asking them, they registered to vote. Son quit his law practice and formed Son Shine Enterprises once things really took off. I was their first full-time employee, and they couldn't have found a more willing worker.

It was probably inevitable that Son and I would get together. Being on the road constantly like we were, he was surrounded by women who wanted to sleep with him because they loved his mother, but he said having sex with them would be taking unfair advantage, not to mention, as he put it, exhibiting behavior unworthy of a man with his own considerable charms and assets.

The only problem was, in those days we were moving around so much that he never had a chance to explore those charms and assets with anybody but me. Add to that the fact that we were regularly having those marathon late-night conversations that are as intimate as sex with none of the risks of being sorry in the morning. *Of course I called it love.*

I had been looking for someone like Son all my life. A collaborator. A comrade. Somebody who wanted to change the world as much as I did. I thought he was my soul mate, and I eagerly shared his dream of a life outside of Beth's orbit. Not that it wasn't exciting being with her. It was just that Beth, like a lot of charismatic people, is better appreciated at a distance.

But it wasn't just the charisma that drew me to Beth. She had a program. She was trying to change the world, one single mother at a time, and I wanted to help her do it. How could I resist? I was a child of the great movements who had never had one to call my own. My parents, college activists turned radical intellectuals, had raised me on stories of Martin Luther King and Malcolm X and their days as student demonstrators at Howard University. Those stories were one of the reasons I went to Howard, but by 1985, the only movement my classmates were interested in was hip-hop, which wasn't exactly what I had in mind. Music is music, but in a revolution, *land and resources are supposed to change hands.*

So I buried myself in the books, graduated in three years, and completed a master's in literature before I turned twenty-three. I accepted a teaching job at the University of the District of Columbia, thinking I could share my passion for *Poetic Language as a Tool for Liberation*—my master's topic—with black students eager to exchange ideas and insights with a bright new faculty member barely older than they were.

Two mind-deadening years later, I had yet to find any students who were as concerned about the poetry of Sonia Sanchez as they were about their upcoming tuitions, or their late periods, or whoever's new single was blasting on their car radios. In the course of one long weekend of self-examination when I attempted to answer the question of why was my life so totally messed up, I realized that I hated my job, had no romantic prospects and few friends, and the movement I was waiting for was still nowhere to be found. Sunday night, I let a friend talk me into going to one of Beth's speeches mainly because I was tired of bitching about my boring life. How could I have known everything was about to change?

And now it's about to change again. Beth didn't sound any different on the phone, a little nervous, but that's to be expected. She not only accused me of trying to ruin her business by stealing her son— she actually used the word *stealing* like he was a sweater from Saks— she called around to everybody I might have been able to ask for a job to say I couldn't be trusted and she just thought they ought to know.

Finding that out after months of mysterious rejections did nothing for my self-confidence or my cocaine consumption. In that sense, her needing my help is a vindication. She's desperate to get something done on time and done right. She needs the best, and she had to call *me.*

This Legacy Project she wants me to pull together is a tribute to Son's life and work. Since he died on a fund-raising trip for his alma mater, she's presenting Morehouse College with Son's personal papers for their archives. In return, they're naming the new communications center in his honor at a big *to-do* on May 5. The only problem is, it's already the middle of March, the planning committee doesn't know what they're doing, and things are such a mess that they wanted to postpone the whole thing until next year. This was totally unacceptable to Beth, who told them she was bringing in a consultant to take charge of things. That would be me.

It would be my job to pull the program together, write her a speech for the occasion, and produce a quickie biographical video on Son's life. I could tell it was going to be a lot of work, but nothing I couldn't handle, especially for the kind of money she was prepared to pay. Son Shine Enterprises must be thriving. The other big plus, aside from the money, is that the project is finite. After May 5, this job is over. At that time, it is my intention to pick up my last check, buy another first-class train ticket home, and tell the weasel to remove me from his database. All I have to do between now and then is keep my wits about me and remember that, this time, whatever goes on between Beth and me is *business*, not personal.

4

ONE OF THE PROBLEMS BLACK folks have is we're usually so busy making history that we don't take the time to record it. We keep forgetting that the one who shapes the story defines the hero and the hero defines the best of what a people can be. What's that African proverb about the hunter always being the good guy until the story is told by the lion? That's why Beth is donating Son's papers to Morehouse and why she's so frustrated at their seeming inability to put things in order.

The day of my arrival, Beth was scheduled to be in Macon, about an hour up the road, so we made plans to meet the next morning for breakfast. I scheduled a meeting with the Morehouse folks so I'd have an idea of what we're talking about without having to depend on Beth to give it to me straight.

Son was, in many ways, a perfect role model. He worked hard, graduated top of his class at Morehouse, and passed the bar only one year after graduating with honors from Emory Law School. It was Son who encouraged Beth to write her book and financed the whole operation so she could hold on to the rights and the profits. It was Son who started raising money for Morehouse scholarships and mentoring high school guys while Beth concentrated on the girls. It was Son who recognized the political potential of all those single mothers looking for a chance and told Beth they should have a voter registration table in the lobby wherever she spoke. It was also Son who wanted to start his own program for the brothers because he said it didn't make much sense to have a whole lot of enlightened women looking for love in the arms of a whole lot of unenlightened men.

There couldn't be a better place for Son's legacy to take shape than at the very institution where Martin Luther King Jr. first encountered the work of Mahatma Gandhi. It all sounded good on paper, but what I was encountering this afternoon was not Gandhi, but the reluctant admission that Son's Legacy Project was going nowhere fast.

"I can't believe there's been no progress at all," I said, following the Morehouse archivist down into the bowels of the old library building.

I'm sure my tone reflected both my incredulity and my displeasure, and Mr. Freeney, a dapper little man carrying a hundred or so extra pounds on his small frame, ducked a little like he thought I might revert to universal school-yard behavior and smack him right on the back of his round, brown head.

"The college agreed to handle this months ago," I said. "How can you tell me now you haven't even gotten started?"

"Budget cuts. There is no archival staff left," he said gently as we came to a halt in front of a door marked STORAGE. "There's just me. They let everybody else go. I don't know what's going to happen when I leave."

He reached into his jacket pocket and brought out a giant ring of keys of all sizes and began searching for the right one among the many unmarked others. He tried a key that didn't fit. Tried another. No luck.

"I'm sorry," he murmured. "I've been meaning to label these."

The next key he tried finally fit, and he turned it with visible relief, opened the door, and flipped on the light switch. There, haphazardly stacked in brown U-Haul boxes were all that was left of Son's thirty-five years on the planet. Inside each box, I knew, were speeches, articles, letters, trip journals, smiling photographs with beaming young mothers and their sons or equally delighted corporate donors handing over the checks that made Son the college's top fund-raiser five years in a row.

But none of this was in any kind of order. The boxes hadn't even been opened since Beth's staff packed everything up and sent it all over. At this rate, there was no way anything was going to be ready for the public by the first week in May.

"All right, Mr. Freeney," I said. I wasn't here to fuss. I was here to *fix it*. "I think we've got some work ahead of us. Do you have a suggestion for how we ought to proceed?"

The dusty air in the windowless room was oppressively still. The radiator hissed and rattled, and, even with the chill in the air outside, it had to be ninety-five degrees in that room.

"I do, I do," he said, ushering me back out into the hallway. "I think *you* should take over the processing of the Davis Collection."

He must have seen the surprised look on my face because he rushed on without stopping for breath like he wanted to get it all out before I said no.

"That would simply entail going through all the materials and producing an overview of what we've got. Then, later, we can separate the professional from the personal, arrange them chronologically, cross-reference for names, events, and public honors."

"I'm not an archivist," I protested. "I'm here to pull the program together. This is not my responsibility."

The idea of walking around in Son's life for the next six weeks did not appeal to me. People say that stuff about letting sleeping dogs lie for a reason: *it's true.*

"Mr. Freeney," I said, "I don't think that this is a workable solution to our problem."

He nodded slowly. "Of course I understand, but may I speak frankly?"

"Please."

"I knew Son Davis. I respected him and what he was trying to do. I went to one of his Brothers Only workshops and it changed my life."

Mr. Freeney took out a spotless white handkerchief and wiped his face from forehead to fat little chin.

"He believed in something, Ms. Burns. He stood for something. Now those papers in there don't tell the whole story—how could they?—but they're a beginning and who knows what young man might find something there to change his life just like Dr. King found something in Gandhi and became someone who could lead his people toward freedom."

Mr. Freeney reminded me of the movement people who were my parents' closest friends. They were still waiting for a leader to arise who would pick up where Martin and Malcolm and Medgar and all those unnamed martyrs left off. The possibility, however remote, kept them from becoming cynical, which is always the greatest threat to failed revolutionaries. Son seems to have done that for Mr. Freeney, just like Beth did it for me for a little while, and I know it's worth a lot. Cynicism is as deadly as cancer. It just takes longer to kill you.

He saw me wavering, and his voice was gentle. "I just think that his papers can be useful in a way that a big ceremony just can't. I think the legacy that truly honors Brother Davis is sitting right there in those boxes. *Waiting.*"

I didn't say anything to that, and we walked in silence back up the stairs to his office. I was mentally trying to calculate how many hours it would take me to go through all those boxes.

We reached Mr. Freeney's office and he pointed me toward a delicate antique rocker with a tapestry seat cushion. He eased himself into an equally delicate old swivel chair squeezed behind a classic rolltop desk. Overflowing bookcases lined the walls, and a fat calico cat was snoozing on the well-worn oriental rug. He was waiting for me to say yes or no to his proposition.

I closed my eyes, remembered the weasel, and resigned myself to the inevitable. "If it's my job to pull this collection together, then that's what I'll have to do."

Mr. Freeney sighed with relief. "Can we shake on it to seal the deal?"

"I'll need to move the papers once I get settled," I said.

"Move them?"

The idea made him nervous. Archivists like to keep things locked up so they can't wander off.

"I'll get Ms. Davis's permission."

He rewarded me with a smile. "Of course, of course. You can't very well work in the basement, can you?"

I shook his hand again, promising to let him know as soon as I finalized my living arrangements. We had settled the big questions. The rest of the details could wait until later. It was time for me to find a place to live.

5

I was looking for a place near the campus so I could walk to meetings. I had rented a car, but I like to walk. My own car had been traded away for dope a year ago, and I haven't had the money to buy another one. At first, it was horrible. I bitched and moaned every time I had to leave the house and walk the three blocks to the mass transit stop. I bummed rides and tried to borrow my friends' cars until they made me stop asking.

After a while, I had no choice, so I resigned myself to it, complaining mightily all the while. Then I started seeing the same people at the station every day and started speaking to them. Before I knew it, I was enjoying the chitchat we'd exchange until the train arrived.

After a few more weeks, I even started enjoying the walk. I'd take the long way instead of the shortcut, and, pretty soon, I even started recognizing my neighbors. After I got out of rehab, they all welcomed me back like I'd been away to war. The little old ladies around the corner actually baked me a pie and brought it over covered with a clean white dish towel like they were going to the county fair. That's the kind of community I like—a big-city neighborhood with a small-town sensibility—and it's just like the neighborhood that surrounds this campus.

A few years ago, the idea of taking an apartment around here by choice would have been problematic at best and foolhardy at worst. The Morehouse campus, like a lot of black colleges, was then a small oasis in the midst of an area plagued with crime, drugs, homelessness, and unemployment. I never lived in this neighborhood during my five years in Atlanta, but the stories that made the news about it did not inspire confidence.

But then things started to turn around. The crime went down, and the spirit went up. The mall reopened, and restaurants were always full of paying customers. Trash on the street disappeared, and community gardens dotted the landscape. Kids walked home from school in safety, and women moved around at night without looking over their shoulders.

Ebony and *Jet* had both done stories, and the *Washington Post* hailed the area as a model for African American urban communities. I remember being struck by how vague the articles all were when it came to answering the obvious questions: *How did this happen? What was the catalyst for this kind of dramatic change?*

More police? The city says no change in routine patrols. Better sanitary services? City trucks come every week, just like always, but nothing extra. None of the official explanations fit here. It was a mystery and one that had intrigued me since I first heard about the transformation. If somebody has figured out a way to get a neighborhood full of black folks to live together like they have some sense, I was more than a little interested in how they did it.

There was no denying the neighborhood had undergone a startling transformation. Gone were the boarded-up crack houses and overgrown vacant lots. The streets were clean of litter, homes and lawns were uniformly well tended, and garden plots, lying fallow until next month's spring planting cycle begins, were fenced off and identified with signs proclaiming their membership in the West End Growers Association. It really did have the feel of a small town, even though you could look over your shoulder and see the skyscrapers of downtown Atlanta less than ten minutes away.

I left the campus with no particular destination in mind and just walked around for a while. I wasn't nervous. I've been living in the black community all my life, and I'm very much attuned to its specific pleasures and equally specific dangers. One of the first things my mother taught me was how to tell the difference between *hostile* and *crazy*. This is an important distinction in all black environments since the insanity of American racism is too much for some black folks to handle, and we will *go off,* but in different ways and with different consequences for those who find themselves in close proximity at the moment of madness.

It is important to know, for example, that the guy who quotes Scripture at the top of his lungs is startling, but probably not dangerous like the steely-eyed shadow boxer who never says a word and squints at each person he passes as if deciding whether or not to throw a punch in his direction. The only ones who really scare me are the young hoodlums who claim as many corners as they can hold, sell as much as they can of whatever drugs we're buying, and make the streets a minefield not easily negotiated by the faint of heart.

Last time I drove through here four or five years ago after a late-night meeting on the campus, there were hard-eyed young predators on every corner, and I locked my doors for fear of being carjacked before I could get back on the freeway. This time it didn't feel dangerous at all. It just felt *alive.*

I stopped for the light before crossing onto Ralph D. Abernathy Boulevard and looked around. The rapid transit station nearby was receiving and disgorging passengers who seemed to be a mix of students, young mothers, and working people. The presence of dreadlocked T-shirt and incense vendors, all hawking their wares with great enthusiasm and equal charm, gave the street the feel of a busy third-world market. The absence of aggressive panhandlers or dope fiends asking for spare change was a pleasant surprise.

There were, in fact, no bug-eyed addicts or angry beggars at this busy intersection. Only three young brothers in dark suits and bow ties offering *Muhammad Speaks* or bean pies, depending on whether you were looking to feed your head or your face.

The mall across the street was a bustling beehive of activity with people moving in and out in a constant stream. The Krispy Kreme doughnut shop was flashing a sign for "Hot Doughnuts," and people in business suits, baggy blue jeans, and all manner of apparel in between were coming out with the long, flat box that meant they had just bought a dozen.

I turned down Abernathy, the area's main commercial strip, and kept walking. After the Krispy Kreme, I passed two men's clothing shops, a barbershop, an African import bazaar where you could also get your braids done, and a tiny Chinese take-out place. The West End News was nestled between a flower shop displaying a huge arrangement of birds-of-paradise that would have driven Aunt Abbie crazy, and a twenty-four-hour beauty salon that claimed expertise in touch-ups, blow-outs, wraps, perms, braids, waves, and weaves.

The windows of the newsstand were frosted so you couldn't see inside from the street, but next door I could see a few sisters in various stages of the hairdo process. One was under the dryer with her eyes closed and a peaceful look on her face. One was being combed out by her stylist, and two others were waiting patiently for their turns under those little heated caps that put the *hot* in hot-oil treatment.

I had never seen a twenty-four-hour beauty salon, and while it seemed like a moneymaking idea, I wondered if the women didn't get nervous leaving at four o'clock in the morning and walking to their cars all alone. On the other hand, if they felt safe enough to do that, maybe these days this neighborhood was the peaceful haven I had been led to believe it was.

Running off of Abernathy were a series of quiet, tree-lined streets, some with lovingly restored Victorian homes, some with multi-family dwellings, and a few small apartment clusters that housed the area's more transient populations without seeming to change the surprisingly serene atmosphere of the community as a whole.

I was strolling down one of those streets whose almost unearthly calm seemed a thousand miles from the bustling energy of the commercial strip. Not that there was no activity here. In fact, there seemed to be brothers in motion all over the place. Over there was a man working on his car. Two doors down was another man repairing a screen door. A little farther on, a man was raking leaves in the yard of a brightly painted cottage with a gaggle of pink plastic flamingos stationed along the driveway like sentinels.

Several of the men inclined their heads slightly to acknowledge my passing by, but otherwise they were all about whatever task lay before them. I realized how good it was to see men around visible and working. *And how rare.* When I heard the voice of Bob Marley coming from the open windows of a house at the end of the block, it seemed the perfect sound track for the serenity of the street.

> *"Don't worry about a thing,*
> *'Cause ev'ry little thing gonna be al-right . . ."*

I love that song. I played it so many times when I first got out of rehab that it's permanently etched on my brain. I stopped in front of the house where the music was playing and listened to it like they were playing it just for me.

The building was a four-unit gray stucco with a perfectly manicured lawn and a bright blue front door. The large lot beside it had a sign that identified it as one of the neighborhood's many community gardens and boasted three rows of the prettiest winter collard greens you ever saw. Too bad this building doesn't have a vacancy, I thought. This would be perfect.

That's when the blue front door opened and a man came out wearing a black cashmere overcoat, a black homburg, and sunglasses. He looked like Michael Corleone in *The Godfather* when the boy finally embraced his destiny and became a sho'nuff gangster.

He walked straight over to me, smiled pleasantly, and removed his glasses, rendering me temporarily speechless. "Can I help you?"

It was his eyes! This brother had the bluest eyes I've ever seen in my life. They were even more shocking—and that's what they were, *shocking*—because he was so perfectly dark. *Africa dark.* His skin was the kind of soft, velvety black you don't see over here much anymore now that we're all so mixed up and miscegenated like good citizens of the twenty-first century. As if in defiance of the Middle Passage, and despite the complicated racial mixtures that define the diaspora, this brother's skin was *original black.*

Did I say he was also fine as hell? He looked like a painting of an

African warrior king on one of those black history calendars, except for those eyes. Not baby blue, or gray-blue, or cornflower blue. His eyes were turquoise like the jewelry they make in the Southwest because that's the color of their sky at sunset. Turquoise like the water around the Caribbean islands where all you want to do is drink rum and make love.

I knew I was staring, but I couldn't look away. I took a breath and tried to collect myself. I don't rattle easily, but I hadn't expected Aunt Abbie's vision to kick in quite so fast.

"Do we know each other?" He was still smiling.

"I . . . I was just listening to the music," I finally stuttered. "Bob Marley."

"My painter is a big reggae fan," he said. "I hope it wasn't disturbing you."

"Oh, no. Not at all. I'm . . . I'm a reggae fan, too. Old school."

His eyes actually seemed to twinkle at me. "Are you new to the neighborhood?"

"I wish," I said, wondering when the big black Lincoln had pulled up soundlessly to the curb behind me. "There don't seem to be many vacancies around here."

He looked at me for a long moment, which was fine with me because it gave me an excuse to look back. I wondered if those eyes ran in his family. I could just picture them all sitting around the dining room table, twinkling at one another.

"This place has a vacancy," he said.

"It does?"

He took off his hat and extended his hand. "I'm Blue Hamilton. I own this building."

I didn't have to ask why they called him Blue. His hand was cool to the touch, but not rough.

"Regina Burns."

"It's the unit on the left, straight up the stairs. It's freshly painted, reasonably priced, and you'll be completely safe."

"How much is the rent?"

He smiled. "Why don't you take a look at it and, if you're interested, come by my office at the West End News. I'm sure we can work something out."

"All right," I said, remembering the newsstand with the frosted windows. Did he own that, too?

"Aretha can show you the place and answer any questions you have. If you like it, you can pick up the key this afternoon. How's that?"

"Wonderful," I said. "The truth is, I was standing here hoping there was a vacancy in this building just before you came outside, so your timing is perfect."

"That's my job," he said, as the man standing at the curb opened the rear passenger door. "I'm pleased I could be of assistance."

Then he bowed slightly, walked over to the car, and disappeared into its black leather interior. The man at the curb closed the door, got in behind the wheel, and eased the car on down the street before I could even say thank you.

I felt like I had fallen through the rabbit hole and come out into a peaceful place filled with thriving black businesses, industrious black men, a twenty-four-hour beauty shop, and a blue-eyed gangster with a house painter who likes Bob Marley.

There was only one thing for me to do. Go upstairs and introduce myself to Aretha.

6

THE BLUE DOOR LED ME THROUGH a small foyer with four silver mailboxes. The unit numbers were displayed, but no names. At the top of a short flight of stairs were two apartments. The door was open to the one on the left where the Bob Marley concert was still in progress. A woman with her back to me was touching up some detail work around the big front windows with a small paintbrush and singing loudly off-key in the way I do only when I'm sure there's no chance anybody will hear my croaking.

I hesitated in the doorway, reluctant to startle and embarrass her. I was thinking that whoever named her Aretha must not have heard her sing, when she turned and saw me standing there.

"Oh! Sorry!" she said, moving to turn down the volume on the boom box in the corner of the room. "I didn't hear you come up. Are you here to look at the place?"

"Yes," I said. "I met Mr. Hamilton downstairs. Are you Aretha?"

"One and the same," she said.

"I'm Regina," I said, enjoying the strength of her handshake.

Aretha looked to be in her mid-twenties, tall and pleasantly round with a bright, open face. She wore her hair in a close-cropped afro with three gold hoops of diminishing size in each ear and a tiny gold nose ring. Her small, well-shaped head, delicately balanced on her long neck, gave her the air of a wild swan, serenely confident of its own beauty without taking credit for it.

"I'm just doing spot finishing," she said. "I painted the whole place a week ago." She looked around with justifiable pride and grinned. "I'm a better painter than I am a singer."

She got that right. The spotless walls were a very pale gray, as were the rugs. There was a love seat covered in what appeared to be black suede, two chairs, and a small, round coffee table in the living room. Another small table and two chairs, at the far end of the room defined a dining area.

"I didn't realize it was furnished," I said, pleasantly surprised. My plan had been to head for the nearest Aaron Rents, but this place looked like an upscale hotel.

"Do you have your own furniture?" Aretha asked, opening the front blinds, exposing the large windows on the street side of the apartment. Light flooded the already airy room.

"No," I said. "I'm doing a project over at Morehouse, but I actually live in D.C., so this is perfect."

On one wall there were three large black-and-white photographs of smiling children. Shot close, printed oversize, and hung at eye level, they were such a cheerfully alive presence that I almost expected to hear a giggle.

"The light is one of the best things about this place," Aretha said. "I used to come up here and paint sometimes just because I was in love with the light."

"You're an artist?" I asked, sticking my head into the small kitchen. With its own window over the sink, it was as bright and cheery as the living room.

"I'm mostly a painter, but I'm doing more photography these days."

"Did you take these?" I indicated the smiling portraits.

"Yep. Those are my babies."

She didn't look old enough to have that many children. My surprise must have been more obvious then I intended.

"Not my biological babies," she said, laughing. "These are my friends' kids from home. Meet Diamante, Lil' Sonny, Daryl and Duane, they're brothers; Deena's twins, Kimmy and Karen; and this little pumpkin is my goddaughter, Mavis."

She pointed to each little happy face in turn and rattled off their names like a good teacher introducing her class to the new vice principal. Her affection for them was obvious, and it came shining through in the photographs she had taken of each one.

"They're beautiful," I said, meaning to praise her work.

She laughed again. "They look like angels, don't they? With their little bad asses!"

"Is there an alarm?" I asked, conscious of all those windows and a back door with no bars.

Aretha shook her head. "You won't need one. There aren't any break-ins around here."

"What?"

She smiled like she had heard this reaction before. "There are no break-ins around here. No rapes either."

I looked at her, and she returned my gaze as if to say, *Would you like me to repeat it?*

"No rapes in Atlanta?"

"Not Atlanta," she said, "just around here."

"What's *around here*?"

"Here in this neighborhood," she said. "In West End."

"No rapes in West End?" I knew I was repeating everything she said, but that was a pretty bold statement.

She looked pleased that I was catching her drift. "Exactly."

"Well, that's great, but—"

"Isn't it?" she said brightly. "Pretty amazing, huh?"

"How is that possible?"

"Mr. Hamilton doesn't let the men act a fool."

"Act a fool *how*?"

She looked disappointed. "See? That's what sisters always do. I tell you the men around here don't prey on us and you start asking for the particulars."

"I didn't mean to doubt you, it's just . . ." *What the hell?* Maybe it's true. "It's just wonderful."

"I didn't mean to snap at you like that," she said, smiling again. "I just know what Mr. Hamilton has done for this neighborhood and sometimes people don't get it."

"How is he as a landlord?" I said, nudging us back into more neutral ground.

She grinned. "The best."

Down the short hallway, the smaller of two bedrooms was also done in shades of gray and was refreshingly empty, almost like a monk's room might be. No clutter anywhere. There was a double bed in one corner, a small dresser, and one straight-back chair. The only homey touch was an antique quilt folded neatly at the foot of the bed.

"No pictures in here?"

She shook her head. "We keep this room plain. Mr. Hamilton says sometimes when you're away from home, it's good to have a place to sleep that doesn't impose itself on your dreams."

I liked the idea and the room immediately. Camping out here for a while would be a pleasure, not a sacrifice.

"Are you an artist?"

"No," I said. "Why?"

"Just curious. We've had some artists here before. Mostly musicians. Mr. Hamilton's friends, you know. We had a poet here once, but he decided he'd rather be a lawyer, which to my mind means he wasn't much of a poet to begin with." She tossed her head to dismiss the would-be poet from her mind. "Mr. Hamilton says being an artist is a young man's game, but I say, where would that have left Picasso?"

Where indeed.

She flipped on the light in the other room that was outfitted like a home office. It had a desk, a two-drawer file cabinet, a bookcase, and a huge worktable right in front of the windows. The desk chair looked expensive, like the ones that come from places like the Sharper Image and can be made to vibrate like the beds in a cheap motel without even putting a quarter in.

I walked over and looked out the window. Across the street, another one of the block's seemingly endless supply of industrious males was cleaning pine straw out of his gutters. A woman with a toddler by the hand and a bag of groceries on her hip was making her slow progress toward home. There was no traffic to speak of, and when cars did come along, they seemed to be doing the speed limit and not a mile more.

The young mother pointed out the man on the ladder to her child and the man, feeling their eyes on him, waved at the child, who waved back with his free hand and turned to smile at his mother for bringing to his attention such an amazing sight as a man on a step-ladder, cheerfully scooping debris from his gutters on a bright, almost spring morning. From where I watched, I could see his mother smile back and shift the groceries to a more comfortable position without breaking stride.

It begins with you, Beth always tells her audience. *A boy who is going to see himself standing on the world stage must first see the world through his mother's eyes. If that world is defined by bad drugs, bad men, and a complete absence of joy, that is what your son will think the world is made of because that is what he learned from you!*

I turned to find Aretha watching me. I had only one more question. "Why did you paint the door downstairs blue?"

She grinned. "I heard it's considered good luck in some North African countries to paint your front door that color. Sometimes, people put their kids' handprints in the design as additional protection against the evil eye, but Mr. Hamilton wasn't crazy about the hand thing, so I just left it plain."

"I think this place will do just fine," I said. "I think I'll take it."

Her smile lit up her whole face, and I was aware again of how unself-consciously beautiful she was. "Welcome to the building," she said, and shook my hand again as we headed toward the door.

"Do you live here, too?"

"Right downstairs."

It hadn't occurred to me, but that only increased the apartment's overall desirability. Another interesting woman on the premises is always a plus.

"Thanks for showing me the place."

"No problem."

As I started down the stairs, I glanced at the door across the hall from mine. "Who lives there?"

"That's Mr. Hamilton's place," Aretha said. "Didn't he tell you?"

7

THE WEST END NEWS MADE A great first impression. Well-stocked and well-lit, the place was browser friendly with comfortable chairs scattered around, making it easy to linger and enjoy the smell of fresh coffee in the air. Behind the small counter an old man in black pants, pressed so often they were shiny, and a big white apron was fiddling with a gleaming cappuccino machine. He nodded pleasantly in my direction as a young man reading the *South China Morning Post* waited patiently for his midmorning caffeine.

I started toward him to ask if Blue Hamilton was around when a tall, thickly built man came toward me.

"Ms. Burns?" His voice was a low rumble, but he smiled pleasantly.

"That's me," I said. "I'm looking for Mr. Hamilton."

"He's expecting you. Would you follow me, please?"

He sounded like an usher, but he sure didn't look like one. Though his wide shoulders were minimized by the careful cut of his expensive suit, he was a big guy. *Bodyguard big.* Maybe he was one of the ways my landlord kept the men from acting a fool. He looked like a pretty powerful deterrent to me.

My guide led me to the back of the store, through neat rows of magazine racks and newspapers that seemed to be arranged alphabetically by country of origin. Down a short hallway, he opened another door with a frosted-glass window, and the space suddenly opened out into what looked like an old-fashioned ice-cream parlor, without the Ben & Jerry's. There were three tables with four chairs apiece spaced a discreet distance apart, as if to allow for multiple confidential conversations.

Blue Hamilton was standing beside the one in the middle. He

was wearing a beautiful black silk suit, a blindingly white shirt, and a tastefully understated tie. He smiled and came forward to greet me as soon as I stepped into the room, and I found that having already experienced his amazing eyes earlier did not mean I was ready for them this time. In the movies, anybody with those eyes would have been either an alien, or possessed, or both. If he was trying to make sure I didn't miss him this lifetime around, he had sure taken care of that problem.

"Ms. Burns," he said, "welcome. Please have a seat."

He pulled out a chair for me with old-fashioned courtliness at the table where he had been drinking espresso and reading the *New York Times*. The tiny twist of lemon peel was still curled on the saucer under the dainty demitasse cup. The tall man stood waiting for further instructions.

"Can I offer you a cup of espresso?" Mr. Hamilton asked, his voice working those *s*'s. "Cappuccino?"

"Cappuccino would be great," I said, looking around a little.

The floor was covered in those little white octagonal tiles trimmed in black that are always cool to the touch, no matter how hot it gets outside. The walls were bare, except for six large framed photographs of smiling children. I recognized Aretha's work. The tops of the tables were pale pink marble. The tall man glided out the door and left us alone.

"I'd like to take the apartment," I said.

He nodded like he wasn't the least bit surprised, reached into his inside breast pocket, and pulled out two keys.

"Welcome to the neighborhood," he said, handing them across the table.

"Thank you," I said, but I didn't move to pick them up, a little flustered at how fast everything was moving. "But you haven't even told me what the rent is yet."

"A hundred dollars a month," he said casually. "No deposit, no advance."

"You can get a lot more than a hundred dollars a month for that apartment," I said, instantly wary. "Why are you willing to let me have it so cheap?"

"I'm not in it for the money."

"What are you in it for?"

Before he could answer, the tall man returned with a steaming cappuccino for me and another espresso for his boss. Mr. Hamilton waited until he glided back out before responding to my question.

"I'm a businessman, Ms. Burns. I own a lot of real estate, but the building you saw today is my home. It's the first place I bought when I came off the road for good, so it means a lot to me. I usually don't rent it out at all."

"Then why make an exception for me?" I pressed him a little. The universe said I can't be ungrateful. It didn't say I'm not supposed to be careful.

"Would you be more comfortable if I said a thousand dollars a month?"

A thousand dollars a month? That wouldn't leave me enough to pay the weasel! "I can't pay a thousand dollars a month!"

He grinned at me. "So have we agreed you're going to take the place and now we're just haggling about the rent?"

Why was I trying to talk him out of renting me the place I wanted? Whether or not he had been searching the winds of time for me like Aunt Abbie seemed to think, this was no time to look a gift horse in the mouth.

"You're right." I smiled. "The place is perfect for me. Can we start again?"

"Of course."

He extended his hand. "Ms. Burns, I'm Blue Hamilton. I understand you're interested in one of my properties over on Lawton Street. Is that right?"

He fell so easily into the charade that I couldn't help grinning.

"I'm not paying over three hundred," I said, pulling a figure out of the air, but knowing that a hundred dollars a month would make me feel beholden, and I didn't know him well enough yet to want to owe him.

"You're in luck," he said. "That unit rents for two fifty."

"You've got a deal."

"Do you want it in writing?"

"Your handshake's good enough for me," I said.

"I want to assure you," he said as we shook hands again, "that you will be completely safe coming and going at your convenience."

"You have that kind of control over crime in this neighborhood, do you?" I said, smiling pleasantly so he wouldn't take it the wrong way.

He smiled back. "I would never offer space to someone whose safety I couldn't guarantee."

This was truly a scene out of *The Godfather*. All this brother needed was a consigliere waiting outside the door with a list of people requesting an audience, I thought, as the tall man's shadow appeared in the window of the frosted-glass door. He knocked softly and stuck his head in. Mr. Hamilton nodded almost imperceptibly, and the man withdrew without speaking.

"Is tomorrow too soon to move in?" I asked, conscious of not keeping him from his duties, whatever they might be.

"Tomorrow is fine."

He didn't seem to be worried about time, but we had finished our business and our coffees. It was time for me to head back to my hotel. This had been a long day, and I was meeting Beth at her house for breakfast at seven-thirty in the morning. I stood up.

"I don't want to keep you," I said, getting up to go. "How hard is it to get a cab out front?"

Blue stood up immediately. "Not impossible, but I'm on my way downtown. Can I drop you somewhere?"

"I'm staying at Paschal's over on Northside Drive," I said.

Paschal's Motel is an Atlanta institution, legendary for their famous fried chicken and for their frequent feeding of broke civil rights workers during the sixties as a way to support the movement without ruffling anybody's feathers. They had recently moved to an expanded facility and I wondered suddenly if Paschal's was in the *no men acting a fool zone* that Aretha had been talking about.

"Paschal's is right on the way," he said, reaching for his coat on a hook near the door.

We climbed into the back of the black Lincoln for the ten-minute ride, and, in the dim confines of the car, his eyes glowed like sapphires. I wonder how long it takes to get used to having a friend with eyes like that. Not that we're friends, but if we were, could I sit beside him and not notice those eyes? I mean, don't Shaquille O'Neal's friends eventually get used to how tall he is?

"You're quite a negotiator," he said. "You're not a lawyer, are you?"

"I'm a journalist."

He raised his eyebrows slightly like he might want to reconsider renting me a place after all.

"I'm working as a consultant to a project at Morehouse," I said quickly. "They're naming a building after Son Davis, and they need some help pulling it all together."

"He deserves it."

"Did you know him?"

"I respected his work."

"That's nice to hear," I said. "We were friends."

"Then he's lucky."

"Why is that?"

"Because you can be sure they tell his story the way he'd want it to be told."

Spoken like a man who didn't know Beth Davis. The way *she* wants it to be told.

"That's my job," I said.

Paschal's was coming up on the right. I congratulated myself for not commenting on his eyes, or falling into them, during the brief ride.

"I do appreciate the lift, Mr. Hamilton," I said.

"My pleasure, and please call me Blue." He smiled.

I smiled back. *"Blue."*

The Lincoln glided to a stop in front of the hotel, and the driver stepped out to get the door.

"I'll be out of town on a fishing trip for the next couple of days," he said, "but Aretha always knows where to reach me. I hope you will feel free to contact me if I can be of any assistance."

"You're going fishing dressed like that?" I said, sliding toward the open door.

"Always," he said, with another slow smile. "Let's the fish know I mean business."

8

Beth's house was at the end of a leafy cul-de-sac in an Atlanta suburb whose distinguishing characteristic is the presence of Stone Mountain, a granite monolith bearing the carved images of four Confederate generals on horseback. They were presumably riding off in defense of slavery and Scarlett O'Hara, but they now preside over an integrated community of working people who want to be close to the city, but not too close.

The formerly all-white community had flexed enough to accommodate the initial incursions of black folks and several waves of immigrants and the place was certainly more diverse than it used to be. The only thing that hadn't changed was the economic status of the residents. Polls show middle-class people tend to want the same things regardless of race: safe streets, good schools, city services. Poor people want those things, too, but nobody ever asks them about it, since they rarely vote, and opinion polls tend to be tied to who's running for something other than the border.

Son and Beth bought this house with her first round of royalties from *Son Shine*. They ran the business out of a well-equipped home office and still had space for staff. I lived in this house for almost five years while I was working for them. Turning up into the driveway still made my stomach clench just a little. I took a deep breath and reminded myself that I wasn't going hat in hand. *She called me.*

Her new assistant, a young woman who identified herself as Jade, showed me in, offered coffee, which I declined, and said Beth would be down in just a minute. The room hadn't changed much. There was still the oil portrait of Son and Beth over the mantel. There were still the framed honorary degrees and overposed photographs of Beth with sponsors and celebrities. There were still Son's degrees and awards from first grade on, all neatly framed and arranged in a sort of mini-shrine. There were still the green velvet sofa and chairs where we used to sit and talk for hours, sometimes the three of us, sometimes in twos. It felt like home, except it wasn't. Not anymore.

From the beginning, Son had insisted that we hide our relationship from Beth, elope, and present our marriage as a fait accompli. I begged him to let me tell her, but he couldn't face her disapproval. I kept asking him why she would disapprove. I knew she liked me as an employee, so why not as a daughter-in-law? After I kept badgering him, one day he finally told me that when he had broached the subject with her, she had immediately dismissed the possibilities of a romantic connection between us by reminding him that I was "hired help" and not worthy of being his wife.

That hurt my feelings, but I never blamed Son, and we kept sneaking. Somehow she found out, and she went berserk. When she confronted him and he blurted out his plan to start up his own company based on developing a complementary male constituency, she accused me of planting the idea as a means to my own selfish ends, and him of being a cruel, ungrateful son who didn't seem to care that he was going to break his mother's heart and undo all the good work they'd done in the last ten years. Then she cried. He was no match for all that, so he apologized profusely and decided to break my heart instead.

Beth entered the room like she always does, walking fast like she's got somewhere more important to go as soon as she dispenses with you. As usual, she was simply dressed in full-cut pants and a dark tunic, her salt-and-pepper hair brushed smooth and twisted back severely in a style that served to focus your attention on her face. She was as striking as I remembered her, with those big dark eyes and that wide, surprisingly sensual mouth, but she seemed to have aged ten years in the last two. The loss of her son had clearly taken its toll, and I felt a pang of sympathy for her.

She must have seen it in my face because she relaxed a little and greeted me warmly.

"*Gina!*" She looked undecided about whether to hug me, so I stuck out my hand.

"Hello, Beth. It's been a long time."

"Too long." She looked at me like she really meant it.

"I'm sorry it took such a terrible thing to bring us together," I said.

Her bottom lip trembled slightly, and her eyes filled up with tears. "I am, too," she whispered, then cleared her throat as if to regain control of her emotions. "And thank you for coming. I know the circumstances might make these first few moments a little awkward, but for Son's sake, I hope that we can rise above all that."

"I hope we can, too," I said. *For thirty thousand dollars, I'm sure we can.*

This kinder, gentler Beth was not fooling me for a second. In the dictionary under *hidden agenda*, there should be her picture.

"I wanted to invite you to the memorial service at Morehouse in October," she said, "but I didn't get any answer at your house and I didn't have another number."

Of course, I was in rehab in October, but there was no reason to tell her that, just like there was no reason to believe she ever called me.

"That was thoughtful of you. Did you get the flowers I sent?"

I had sent a small bouquet, all I could afford at that point, to express my condolences. She offered me a sad, apologetic smile.

"There were so many flowers, but I know Son would have appreciated it."

Jade came in with coffee service for two on a silver tray, smiled at me apologetically as if to say, *You ain't got to drink it, but she told me to bring it,* and left without a word. Beth poured us both a cup.

"Do you still take it black?"

I nodded. We each took a sip, then she set down her cup, walked over to the mantel, and turned slowly back to me. Beth is so theatrical, even in a small setting like her living room, every scene is played for maximum drama.

"Shall we put our cards on the table, Gina?"

"And what cards would those be?"

"I know where you were in October."

I put down my cup. "Why doesn't that surprise me?"

"Is there any particular reason why you didn't mention it?"

Her tone was hovering somewhere between reproach and reprimand, and it pissed me off.

"I didn't mention it because it wasn't any of your business. You called me because you need my help. That's the only reason I'm here."

"I thought you were here because you're about to lose your mother's house."

Now *that* surprised me. Beth knew as much about the history of the house as the weasel did. When I considered her a friend as well as an employer, we talked a lot about growing up, and all my girlhood stories begin and end right in that house. How did she know I had almost lost it? Beth had an impressive network of professional and political contacts in Washington, especially since she had gradually intensified her flirtation with the Republican Party, to Son's chagrin, but I never expected this level of inside information.

"Have you been spying on me?"

Her smile was a study in insincerity. "Is it spying to be concerned about an old friend?"

"It isn't necessary," I said. "I'm not hiding anything. I had a cocaine problem and I made some really stupid choices. I've been to rehab and I'm in the process of rebuilding my life."

I sounded like a bad movie on the Lifetime channel, but I plowed on. "I'm doing this contract for the money and for Son. Anything else you'd like to know?"

"That about covers it," she said, gliding back to the couch with a much more genuine-looking smile.

I had the feeling I had just passed one of her tests. She wanted to see if I would lie. She could have saved herself the trouble. Lying is as toxic as cocaine. When I gave up one, I gave up the other one, too.

"Good," I said, "because now I have a question for you."

She raised her eyebrows slightly.

"When are you going to tell me what I'm really doing here so I can get going on it or tell you to find somebody else to do your dirty work?"

The eyebrows stayed elevated. "Why do you assume it's dirty work?"

That question didn't require an answer, so I didn't dignify it with one. Her face relaxed a little, but she was still watching me.

"When Son died," she said, "we were in the last stages of negotiations with a sponsor who was prepared to underwrite the kind of national tour we've always talked about. It was our dream, but when he was taken the way he was, I couldn't even think about touring, or anything else. . . ."

Her voice trailed off, and even I couldn't deny the pain on her face. She took a deep breath. "Then a few months ago, our sponsor reached out to me and said they were still very interested. When I suggested a national legacy tour, dedicated to Son's memory, they couldn't have been more enthusiastic."

"Who's the sponsor?"

Her eyes flickered away from mine and then back, but veiled. "I'm sorry. I can't say right now."

"No cigarettes or alcohol?" There are some things that can't be justified, even in dire economic straits.

She shook her head vehemently. "Of course not. I wouldn't cheapen Son's memory that way."

"Good. Go on."

"We're going to announce the tour in May when Morehouse dedicates the new communications center in Son's name, but . . ."

Again with the eye flickering. "But *what*?"

She stood up again, but this time out of nervousness, I think. "I can't afford to have anything go wrong."

Now we were getting somewhere. "What could go wrong?"

She didn't say anything, so I took another sip of my coffee and waited. When she finally spoke, she chose her words carefully.

"I've had some phone calls. A few letters."

"What kind of phone calls?"

"About Son."

"What about Son?"

"He went a little crazy after you left him, Gina. He wasn't always as discreet as a man in his position should be."

The idea that Son's equilibrium was thrown off by the way we parted was news to me. I was so surprised, I let her blatant misrepresentation of *who left whom* go unchallenged.

"He had a string of brief relationships with women he never would have considered his equals if he had been in his right mind—"

"And now they're calling you?" I said, cutting her off. The kinds of women Son might have had sex with on the rebound was of no interest to me.

She cringed at my directness. "Several of them have, yes."

"Blackmail?"

She nodded, her disappointment in this posthumous manifestation of her son's imperfection written across her face. "It's nerve-wracking, especially with the dedication and the tour coming up. Lord knows, black folks don't need another hero with feet of clay. Jesse Jackson ought to be the last!"

Under the circumstances, Beth's indignation didn't quite ring true. "Your sponsors probably wouldn't like it either."

Her eyes hardened along with her smile. "I'm sure they wouldn't."

It all made sense to me now. "So you want me to go through his papers and make sure Son didn't leave any incriminating evidence lying around to mess up your deal?"

I was being cruel, but I didn't care. She had been cruel to me, and now we were even.

"You're as sharp as you ever were," she said evenly. "I'm glad you haven't lost your edge."

"Why don't you do it yourself?"

Then her face seemed to crumple in on itself. The tears that had been a promise earlier now came splashing down across her cheeks. She made no move to wipe them away, and I had to resist the impulse to offer her a tissue.

"Because I can't bear it," she whispered. *"I just can't bear to touch his things."*

I felt sorry for her. However she had treated me, Son had been her life, and now he was gone. All of sudden, she was just one more grieving mother who had lost a son and wanted him remembered a little better than he actually was. That wasn't a crime. I swallowed hard and resisted the urge to embrace her. You have to understand that Beth was not only my employer for five years. She had been my mentor, my teacher, my friend, my shero. She was trying to shape and activate a constituency that had never felt or experienced its real power, and I had wanted so much to be a part of that.

I know, I know! Sue me! I told you I was the child of movement people. It's in my blood and Beth gave me a place to focus all that energy. I had loved it until she changed up on me and started selling herself to the highest bidder. When I saw her urge an auditorium full of first-time black female voters to cast their ballots for a good ol' boy who still called his secretary "sweetie face," I knew it was time to move on.

But by that time, I was in love with Son, so I stayed, and I stayed too long. The worst thing a true believer can do is to stick around once the bloom is off the rose, and by the time Beth accused me of disloyalty, she was right. I had stopped believing in her, but I was still on the payroll, so who was I to criticize? All things considered, we were probably about even.

"I'll take care of it," I said. "And the speech and the video, too, but first you have to promise me two things."

She took a small white handkerchief from her pocket and blew her nose delicately. "What's that?"

"No more spying," I said. "If you want to know something about me, ask me."

"Fair enough," she said, dabbing at the corners of her eyes. "What else?"

"Let's start from today," I said. "We can't change what happened, or what we think about it, but I did some of my best work with you. That's why you called me, and that's part of why I'm here. We both know I need the money, but I'd like to finish up the way I started, at the top of my game."

Beth just looked at me for a moment, then she reached into her jacket pocket and took out a check, discreetly folded in the middle, and handed it to me.

"Welcome back," she said with a thin smile. "Now, shall we have some breakfast?"

"No, thanks," I said, standing up and dropping the check in my purse without looking at the amount. "I rented a place near the campus yesterday and I want to get settled in this morning."

"Near the campus?"

She looked surprised, just like I knew she would.

"Are you sure you'll be safe over there? You know that neighborhood is pretty rough."

Rough? I thought about the people rushing in and out of the mall and waiting patiently in line at the Krispy Kreme. I remembered the ladies at the beauty shop and the young woman walking beside her tiny son and the people rushing toward the rapid rail station. I thought about Aretha with her Bob Marley music and that studious-looking young guy reading the *South China Morning Post* and waiting for his cappuccino at the West End News. None of them looked particularly *rough* to me. They just looked like people.

"I'll be fine," I said. "My landlord personally guaranteed my safety."

She snorted at that. "You must have some landlord. He ought to be chief of police."

"His name is Blue Hamilton," I said, walking with her toward the door. "Ever heard of him?"

"Blue Hamilton, the *singer*?"

Beth sounded surprised, but no more than I was. My *visionary adviser* was on the money again. "He's a singer?"

"Used to be. Dark skin, high cheekbones, blue eyes?"

"You know him?"

"Not personally," she said. "That's your landlord?"

"Handed me the keys himself."

"He still got those eyes?"

"Still got 'em," I said. "They're pretty amazing, actually. What kind of singer was he?"

"R and B. A crooner, I guess you'd call him. Sort of a cross be-tween Marvin Gaye and Al Green."

The idea of my ocean-eyed landlord singing like Al Green sent an involuntary tingle down my spine. "Was he any good?"

"He had one big hit when he was a kid, fifteen or sixteen, I guess. After that . . ." She shrugged. "Good thing he put his money in real estate. He was a real one-hit wonder."

Beth opened the door, and the softness of the air promised that spring was right around the corner.

"I'll call you tomorrow," I said, heading for my little rental car.

"Gina?"

Her tone stopped me as I was halfway into the car. "Yes?"

"I only ever wanted the best for Son," she said. "You know that, don't you?"

"Me, too," I said, and closed the car door behind me before she could prolong a moment that had no place to go but wrong.

We had agreed to let bygones be bygones. Beth and I don't have to agree on her role in Son's life, or where she was now leading her followers, or what my landlord was or is now. I *know* that Son would have been better off telling his mother the truth, and I know Beth's work suffers when her ego gets in the way, but most of all I know this: Blue Hamilton may be many things, but a one-hit wonder is not among them.

9

I TOOK MR. FREENEY UP ON HIS offer to help me move all that stuff from the campus to my apartment, and the next day, three well-built, but less-than-enthusiastic Morehouse students showed up at my door with a van full of boxes. I had the guys stack everything in the office, but there were so many cartons that I finally had to put some in the living room, too.

Once I tipped them each an unexpected twenty and made their collective day, the reality of what I was getting ready to do walked in and sat down beside me. Part archivist and part private detective, my job was going to require me to walk around, unannounced, in my ex-lover's life. In the abstract, I had considered mainly the time it would take to do it and the blessing of the money. Beth's first check was for ten grand. I kept two to live on and sent the rest overnight mail to the weasel, but sifting through Son's life meant sifting through parts of mine, too. I had to get ready for that so I wouldn't be taken by surprise when a photograph or a memo or a journal entry stirred up memories I had worked hard to put to rest.

I also had to be on the lookout for any information that Beth might consider damaging. I wasn't responsible for censoring anything. I was only charged with bringing to her attention anything that might not present Son in the most positive light. That didn't seem too difficult, but it was a level of snooping that made me a little uncomfortable. Son was my friend *first*, probably my best friend for almost three years before we segued into something else, and I respected him, imperfections and all.

It was a beautiful afternoon and the light Aretha had used as a selling point when she first showed me this place was pouring through the windows. What was I worrying about? *Nothing.* Everything was going great. I've been here only a week and I've already settled into a great apartment, made peace with Beth, gotten paid, and started working. If there ever was a time to take myself out for lunch to say, *Good job, Gina,* this was it.

I stepped out onto the small balcony to see whether I needed a coat or just a sweater. It was clear and almost balmy. There were few people out besides the mailman on his rounds, but a few doors down the street, some aspiring sax player was attempting the John Coltrane arrangement of "My Favorite Things" with disastrous results. If this had been a movie, the anonymous sax player would have had club-quality chops, and his impromptu performances would have drawn in listeners, just like hearing Marley had drawn me to this very house. But this *ain't* the movies, and this may very well be the worst saxophone player I have ever heard.

I stepped back inside, grabbed a light jacket, and headed out for the main drag. I had passed a couple of restaurants on my recent walking tour, and I'll bet one of them has a special that includes the macaroni and cheese I've been craving. As I locked my door, I couldn't help listening for any sound from across the hall. The fish must be biting *big time* because I hadn't seen any sign of Blue Hamilton since he dropped me off at Paschal's. Not that it was any of my business. Visions aside, the last thing I wanted to do was distract myself with a man. That's what got me in all this trouble in the first place.

When I stepped out of the bright blue front door (which still made me smile every time I looked at it) I could hear wanna-be Coltrane still plugging away. It was so bad I actually stopped to see if I could hear one note that belonged where it found itself.

"Pretty bad, huh?"

I turned to see a woman standing in the garden with her arms full of collard greens. She was about my age with her hair pulled back into two French braids and no makeup on her smooth, cocoa brown face. She was dressed like a farmer: bib overalls, denim jacket, yellow rubber boots that had seen better days. But it was her smile that caught my eye and held it. She had the deeply sweet smile of someone who is so plugged into the good in people that evil never occurs to her.

"The worst," I said, grinning at the accuracy of her musical assessment. "I hope he keeps his day job."

She laughed. "I think this is his day job!"

She picked her way out of the collards, shifted the harvested bundle to the crook of one arm, and held out her hand. She was wearing gardening gloves with the fingers cut off. "I'm Flora Lumumba. Downstairs, right."

"Regina Burns," I said. "I just moved in upstairs."

"Aretha told me. You get settled in okay?"

I nodded. "Are you responsible for these beautiful collard greens?"

"I don't know how beautiful they are this time of year," she said, smiling. "This is the last of the lot. But wait until July. Nobody can touch these gardens in the summer."

"I'd like to see that."

"You will," she said, still smiling.

My stomach growled to remind me I had been on my way to lunch. The idea of company suddenly appealed to me.

"I'm going to grab some lunch," I said. "Would you like to join me?"

"I'd love to," she said. "Come on in while I put these greens away. Have you been to Soul Vegetarian yet?"

"I haven't been anywhere yet."

"If you don't need meat, Soul Veg is great, and it's only a couple of blocks."

"Sounds great."

I followed her into her apartment, a cozy, colorful nest with lots of pillows, lots of books, and a couple of baskets of knitting sitting beside a comfortable chair in front of the TV. There were some very healthy house plants around, including one exotic flowering beauty that I couldn't identify. There were framed travel posters on the wall, featuring the kind of sparkling blue water and white sand beaches that make you leave home in the first place, looking for paradise three days and two nights at a time.

When we walked in, Erykah Badu was on the CD player telling her clueless boyfriend he better call Tyrone. Flora laughed and turned it down a little.

"That song cracks me up. 'But you can't use my phone,'" she sang along and laughed again, dropping the greens in the sink and spraying them lightly with cold water. "These young girls are fearless. When I listen to the music my daughter, Lu, listens to, I understand why they talk so much *stuff*!"

"How old is your daughter?"

"Eleven going on thirty," she said, rolling her eyes and reaching for a photograph on the front of the refrigerator. The picture showed a laughing young girl making rabbit ears behind the head of a man who was standing beside her wearing a father's indulgent grin. "She'd kill me for telling you this, but she started her period today."

"Congratulations," I said. "Or should I be saying that to her?"

She shook her head, grinning. "Who knows? This is a first for me. Other than my own, of course."

"Where is she?"

"At school! When she called to tell me, I asked her if she wanted me to come and get her and she said no. She got a pad from one of her girlfriends."

The girl in the photograph looked like a little kid to me, but now she was a little kid capable of having a kid. It struck me that men bond over contests where one dominates the other, directly or through the NFL surrogates. We bond over the things that define our lives as women: our periods, our pregnancies, our men, our children.

"So how does it feel to have a daughter who's almost grown?"

"A little intimidating," Flora said, shaking the greens and covering them with paper towels to absorb some of the moisture. "But you know who's not going to be ready for this at all?"

"Who?"

"Her dad. That's him in the picture with her. He thinks she's going to be his baby girl forever."

Lu's father was a tall, broad-shouldered man with a ruddy complexion and a large old-fashioned afro that framed his face in a perfect circle of sandy-colored hair. She had inherited her father's complexion and her mother's smile.

"Are you going to tell him?"

"Not me. She can tell him if she wants to, but unless she's ready for him to fly in with a chastity belt, I'd advise her to keep it to herself." She looked at me, patting the greens. "Did you tell your father?"

My father was an intensely shy man whose desire for human companionship began and ended with my mother.

I shook my head. "No way. I don't think I ever said the word *period* in front of him."

"I didn't have a chance to decide. My mother told my dad and then they both sat me down and had this excruciating conversation with me about how they trusted me to act like a lady and not bring any babies home for them to raise."

I groaned. "What did you say?"

"I said I wouldn't!" She laughed. "What do you think I said?"

Flora squeezed the greens into the refrigerator, and I handed her back the photograph.

"Hank's still in Detroit," she said, returning it to its place on the refrigerator. "That's where we live, but Hank got a big case where they really have a chance to send some crack dealers away for a long time, and it just got too dangerous. So Hank sent us down here to stay with Blue. He knew we'd be safe here."

I'll bet. "Your husband's a lawyer?"

"A prosecutor. One of the best." Love and pride shone through in her voice and her deep brown eyes. "They've been after these guys for years, but they're not going down easy. I could take the phone calls. After a while you get used to that, but when they threw a fire bomb in Lu's window in the middle of the night, I just freaked."

"They threw a fire bomb in your house?"

It sounded like a sixties story, but it wasn't. No white folks around this time. *Just us.*

"We weren't hurt, thank God, but we lost a ton of stuff. I was handling it pretty well, I think, but then I realized they had burned up our wedding pictures. That's when I really started bawling, but then Hank said don't even trip about some pictures because all he had to do was look in my face and he could see that whole day in his mind, just like it was a movie or something."

She touched the photograph lightly with her fingertips. "I know somebody has to stand up and say *there are still men here,* and I'm really proud of everything Hank's doing, but we've been here since October and it seems like *forever.*"

She stepped out of her gardening boots and into a pair of equally well worn clogs. "How long are you going to be here?"

"Not long," I said, feeling like I had moved into some kind of halfway house for women in need of safe haven. "I have to finish my project by May fifth and then I'll go back to Washington."

"Oh!"

She seemed surprised.

"What?"

"Nothing. I just thought Blue said you were going to be here longer than that."

"He must have misunderstood me."

She shook her head. "Blue doesn't misunderstand. He must have another plan in mind for you."

"What kind of plan?" How could he have a plan for me? He didn't even know me.

"Who knows? Blue is always plotting something. He never tells you until you walk up on it yourself, then he asks what took you so long." She smiled and picked up her keys. "Ready?"

10

THE SOUL VEGETARIAN RESTAURANT is nestled between a store selling traditional African clothing and a banquet hall whose price list for wedding receptions, graduation, anniversary, and Kwanzaa parties, and the occasional high school reunion was posted in the window. I told Flora I was doing a project at the school about the life and work of Son Davis, and she was pleased to hear it.

"He deserves that," she said. "I never met him, but the way his mother writes about him, and from all I've read, he seemed like a good man. He was always talking to the men as hard as his mama was talking to the women, which is the only way it makes sense to me."

When we stepped inside the restaurant, the spicy aromas and warm atmosphere appealed to me immediately. This was clearly my new favorite restaurant. The people who work here seemed to be part of some organization that has black entrepreneurship as part of its overall mission to *uplift the race*. They are soft-spoken, neatly dressed, and have the slightly self-congratulatory air that descends on some folks when they stop eating meat, even though they're still wearing leather shoes.

I ordered the eggplant casserole because I couldn't resist the thick layer of cheese on top and a ginger beer that was so spicy it brought tears to my eyes. Flora, who was clearly a regular, got the collard green quiche, apple-carrot juice, and a cup of jasmine tea. The booth near the window was open, and we took it. The food tasted even better than it looked, and for a minute we just enjoyed our choices. But my brain was still swirling around what she'd said back at her apartment, and I eased it back into the conversation.

"What did you mean about Mr. Hamilton having a plan for me?" I still felt forward calling him Blue.

"I didn't mean to make it sound sinister," she said, with a reassuring smile, "but I've known Blue for fifteen years. I know how his mind works. That's how he got me to take charge of the gardens."

She took a bite of her quiche and pointed her fork at the layer of collards in the custard. "These are my greens. My gardeners supply this place with all their vegetables in the summer. In the winter, all we can do are greens, but come summer? Our tomatoes are legendary!"

"Tell me about the gardens," I said, taking a tiny sip of my ginger beer, and hoping this would give me some idea about what kind of plan we were talking about.

"The gardens," she said. "How can I tell you about the gardens?"

"Start at the beginning," I said. It was cozy in here, and I was in no hurry to get back.

Flora wiped her mouth delicately with her napkin. "Okay. The first time I came here with Hank, there were still crack houses all over the place. Blue had just come off the road for good, and he had made plenty of money, so he started buying up property, including the place we're living in, but he was really focused on the crack houses. He had already burned down four or five of them."

Burned them down? My fork stopped midway to my mouth.

"He made sure nobody was inside," Flora said calmly.

"Where were the owners?"

Flora shrugged. "Absentee, I guess."

"Did anybody try to contact them?"

"Of course, but after a while, when things kept happening in the houses and the owners never even appeared in court—"

"Things like what?" I was trying hard to follow the line of reasoning that tells you it's okay to burn up somebody else's property if you don't like the way they chose to manage it. Last time I checked, the laws of the United States of America still applied in southwest Atlanta, and property rights were everything to the founding fathers. *They owned us, didn't they?*

Flora put down her fork and looked at me. "Have you ever lived near a crack house?"

"I don't think so."

"You'd remember if you had." Flora's voice was hard and tight. "Because it's a constant parade of the worst of what we've become. All crackheads care about is crack, and all crack dealers care about is money. It's a lethal combination, and you can't build a community around it."

She took a sip of her tea. "Blue tried all the good-citizen ways to deal with it. Calling the police, tracking down the owners, talking to the politicians, but nobody seemed to care enough to do anything. Then the crackheads killed a little kid for her lunch money right around the corner from here. Nine years old. She was waiting for the school bus, eight o'clock in the morning, and they dragged her into the crack house and strangled her." Flora's eyes were hard as granite. *"Then they raped her."*

There was nothing to say after that, so I didn't try. Flora didn't say anything for a few minutes either. I folded my napkin and set my plate to one side.

"That's the first house Blue burned," Flora said quietly. "And you know what? People were glad. They would have thanked him for it if they had known who did it."

That's always the thing that makes vigilantes so appealing, I thought. They take on the bad guys, *by whatever means necessary.* The problem is, who gets to decide who's a bad guy?

"Wasn't there an investigation?"

"Who's going to investigate a fire at a crack house with an absentee landlord?"

She was right about that. Abandoned and burned houses are a constant problem in too many of our communities, seemingly without solution.

"What happened to the men who killed the child?"

Flora shrugged impatiently. "What happens to crackheads? All I know is, once the house burned down, that was one less place for them to hide, and that's a good thing, right?" Her voice was full of fierce determination.

"Right," I said, knowing any other answer would be unacceptable. "Is that when he started planting gardens?"

That brought a smile back to her face, and the tension that had popped up between us evaporated. "That was *my* idea. He showed us these four or five burned-out houses he had finally been able to buy and was in the process of tearing down. He was so proud of what he was doing for the neighborhood, but he hadn't said what he was going to do with the lots once he got them cleared. So I asked him and he said, 'You want them?' "

"What did you say?"

"I just laughed. We were going back to Detroit in two days, but Blue was serious, so I finally said, 'Why don't you hold on to them for me, and when we come back at Christmas, I'll let you know.' He said okay, but I didn't really take him seriously. When we got back to Detroit, I forgot all about it, until we came back in December and Blue had leveled the houses and cleared the lots, plus three more. He drove me around to take a look, and as soon as I saw all that open land, I knew what to do. 'Gardens,' I told him. 'We've got to do community gardens!' "

Flora sounded as excited as she must have felt that day.

"So I made him a plan and we got some people who were interested in growing, mostly old people, and I'd come down every couple of months when Hank came down on business to make sure everything was on track, and it just kept getting bigger and bigger, until now the Growers Association has over fifty members. In the summer, they supply the produce for every restaurant around here."

She glanced at her watch and smiled apologetically. "In fact, I better get going. I'm meeting with the senior gardeners today, and they have absolutely no patience for late arrivals."

"I'll walk with you," I said, finishing the last of my ginger beer and still no closer to understanding what kind of plan Blue Hamilton could possibly have in mind for me.

Back outside, the air was a fine mist that promised a late afternoon rain. The folks at the banquet hall next door were keeping a watchful eye on a delivery of those delicate, horrendously uncomfortable chairs people use to torture their wedding guests; across the street, I could see shoppers browsing through the neatly organized racks at the Goodwill store.

When we passed the big, fenced-in hole in the ground where a building had been demolished but nothing had replaced it, Flora frowned and pointed an accusatory finger at the eyesore. "I told Blue he's got to get me permission to plant some corn and tomatoes in there this summer. That place is a disgrace. If they're not going to develop it, the least they can do is let me use it for the growers."

"Maybe he'll make them an offer they can't refuse."

I was just teasing, but Flora looked at me with an expression I couldn't read. I hoped I hadn't offended her.

"You know the other reason these gardens are so important?" she said as we started across the street.

"Why?" Thank goodness she didn't sound offended.

"Because in order to make this a livable space, a real neighborhood, Blue has to do a lot of things that play to his dark side."

I looked at her, but she just kept walking. *His dark side?* Have we now left *The Godfather* and gone off into *Star Wars?*

"I told him way back at the beginning, when he was just starting to burn the crack houses, that the problem he was going to have was finding enough ways to feed his positive life force to balance those other things."

Flora's eyes flickered over a man dozing on the front steps of St. Anthony's Catholic Church, but we were the last thing on his mind.

"The gardens are about *giving* life," Flora was saying. "They help Blue remember why he's doing all this."

Something in what she said reminded me of what my father told my mother once when she was fussing about the lack of any visible progress in some community group or another that was not organizing as efficiently as she thought they should have been.

"You're looking at it all wrong," my father said gently, at the end of my mother's tirade. "You can't work for black folks because you think *they're* going to be different. You have to do it because *you're* going to be different."

Flora was looking at me expectantly, and I realized she was waiting for a response.

"I understand," I said. *"Sort of."*

" 'Sort of' is good." She smiled and nodded her approval. "Blue takes a minute to get used to because he's one of a kind."

You got that right, I thought as she headed off to her growers meeting and I headed back to my boxes. Providing safe haven for the family of a righteous warrior like Hank. Burning crack houses and planting community gardens. A dark side that threatened to swallow the light. Blue Hamilton seems to be part Don Corleone, part Darth Vader, and part Johnny Appleseed. *I wonder which part lives across the hall from me.*

11

EVERYTHING WAS GOING SO WELL, I was afraid to admit it. I'm one of those people who believes that if you show too much pleasure when things are going your way, you run the risk of angering the gods and having them snatch it all away just to keep you humble. This is a deeply held blood memory, in spite of the fact that I don't consciously subscribe to any formal religion and would lean toward Buddhism if I had to pick one. My brain wants to meditate and embrace the middle path, but my heart wants to sacrifice small animals to a vengeful god who spends most of his time keeping track of sins and meting out punishments.

But if I could be sure the gods weren't listening, I would probably indulge myself in a teeny-tiny pat on the back. The weasel called to tell me he received the payment and was moving me from the "dead-beat never-gonna-dig-her-way-out" file over to the "so far, so good, maybe she'll make it after all" file.

Aunt Abbie's keeping an eye on everything at the house. She's also been spending a lot of time over at Howard talking to the women's studies students. They are very interested in the idea of post-menopausal visions, and she's a bona fide postmenopausal visionary, so it's a perfect match. When I told her about Blue, she wasn't as excited as I thought she ought to be, and I told her so.

"It's new for you, dear," she said gently. "I've already seen it all, remember?"

I couldn't argue with that, and I was in such a good mood, I didn't even want to. Three boxes of Son's papers had yielded a lot of good memories and nothing even remotely incriminating. When I told Beth that news, she was on her way to another speaking engagement in Albany and a week of workshops in Augusta. I could hear the relief in her voice so clearly that I wondered again exactly what she was so worried I might find, but I figured I'd know it when I saw it, whatever it was, so I told her to have a safe trip and promised to check in with her on the road in a few days.

Flora had come up yesterday to introduce her daughter, Lu, and to invite me to brunch on Sunday. I liked Flora, and I accepted with pleasure, mentally disregarding her telling me I didn't need to bring anything. Champagne is always a good neighborly offering, with a bottle of sparkling apple juice for Lu, whose direct gaze showed no sign of a spirit having been broken by her experiences with Detroit drug dealers. She was already as tall as her mother and wore her hair in the beaded braids that Venus Williams took back from the temporary popular-culture custody of Bo Derek. Aretha, whom I hadn't seen since move-in day, had been busy with a photography project, but Flora said she'd be there for brunch, too.

Renting this apartment might turn out to be the best part of this whole thing for me. It had been a long time since I had any friends who talked about something other than who had the good drugs or what they learned in rehab. Being here was making me remember the pleasure of real conversation. While I was growing up, my parents' house was always full of people stating and defending passionate positions about everything. My lunch conversation with Flora had felt as familiar as baked chicken on Sunday.

The only neighbor who remained elusive was Blue Hamilton, which was probably all to the good. I'm not sure I'm strong enough to deal with men just yet, especially men as intriguing as Blue Hamilton. The problem I've had all my dating life is that the guys who drive me crazy sexually never seem to care much about being a part of the righteous forward motion of all peoples of the world toward peace and freedom. This is part of my parents' revolutionary curse. I have to consider politics even in the midst of passion.

This is not a problem during the early stages of a youthful courtship when all you want to do is flirt and make love and flirt some more. The problem comes when it's time for the relationship to progress to real conversation, and the man who can whisper a litany of sexy promises guaranteed to get you where you want to go in bed becomes suddenly tongue-tied or, worse, *boring*.

On the other hand, my more politically advanced boyfriends were invariably lacking as lovers, mainly because they were always too busy bitching about the terrible state of mankind to focus effectively on the woman at hand. Son was the first man I ever loved who had a little bit of both, and you can see I almost lost my mind and my house behind it.

He was sexy as hell *and* seriously committed to changing the way black folks live our lives. It was absolutely intoxicating to be able to segue from an impassioned exchange about our latest voter registration efforts to a night of the kind of lovemaking I had only dreamed about.

After Son and I broke up and I became a dope fiend, my choice of male companionship was based on who had coke to share and who didn't. When I was high, I could tolerate a lot of bullshit from men simply to ensure my place at the table when the drugs came out. That was no longer an option, so I needed a new standard, a new criteria. But what were my choices? I had no idea what I wanted or what I was prepared to give to get it. Until I could figure it out, I thought celibacy made the most sense.

Which doesn't mean I wouldn't like some company sometimes. *Like now.* I had done a full week's work, and there was nobody around to witness my job well done. It was after midnight, so I couldn't very well pop downstairs and invite Flora in for tea. That wasn't exactly the kind of company I was talking about anyway.

See what happens? I started out being grateful for a productive and uneventful week and ended up whining about nobody to hold me. The only thing that pisses off that vengeful God I was talking about earlier, more than gloating is ingratitude, so this will never do. I stood up quickly, slipped a shawl around my shoulders, and stepped out onto my small balcony.

It was cool and clear and quiet as a farmhouse after everybody's gone to bed. Was I the only person awake in this whole neighborhood? Even my bad sax player had deserted me. But the sky was clear, and the fresh air felt good against my face. I closed my eyes, took a deep breath, stretched my arms high over my head, and exhaled in a long, satisfying *whoosh!*

"Working late?"

After I had jumped a foot in the air and come back down, I turned in the direction of the question. Blue Hamilton was standing on his own balcony across from mine. I hadn't even noticed him, but now, in the spill of the streetlight, I could see his outline and the glowing tip of the cigar he was smoking.

"Do you spy on all your tenants?" I said, "Or just me?"

He stepped forward into the light wearing a white shirt, open at the throat, and no jacket. He smiled pleasantly and blew a thin plume of smoke into the air.

"I can't be spying on anybody. I'm at home."

Even from here, I could see those blue eyes shining. I pulled my shawl around me a little tighter.

"You startled me."

"I apologize," he said. "I'm usually the only one out here this late."

I wondered how long he had been back from his fishing expedition.

"Would you like to come over for a drink?" he said casually, as if it wasn't almost one o'clock in the morning.

"It's kind of late. . . ."

I could still see his smile in the semidarkness.

"In Japan, it's already happy hour."

Still half-hidden in the shadows, I smiled back. Flirting is an art form if you do it right, and this brother was *on it*. "We're a long way from Japan."

"I've got some very good sake."

"I don't like sake."

"So does that mean you've accepted my invitation and now all we're doing is deciding on your drink?"

That's the same way he boxed me about the rent, but does it

really count as being *boxed* when all he did was ask me a question that allowed me to admit that a drink sounded wonderful and a little conversation sounded even better.

"I guess it does."

"Good. Then why don't you come on over and I'll see what I can do?"

12

B LUE HAMILTON'S APARTMENT looked exactly like I thought it would: *a men's den*. The walls were dark, almost navy blue, and so were the blinds. The black leather sectional sofa was huge, wrapped around an equally large glass coffee table. On one side of the room was a wet bar that was as well stocked as any restaurant I'd been to lately, and on the other side was an entertainment center housing one giant television screen, two smaller ones, a DVD player, two VCRs, a multidisc CD player, and what appeared to be an elaborate short-wave radio.

On the largest TV screen a black-and-white movie was in progress. A smiling woman was playing a guitar and singing in French while two men and a tow-headed child gazed at her adoringly.

"I know you don't like sake," Blue said. "So what can I get you?"

He acted like my stopping by was the most normal thing in the world, but it had been a long time since I had been in anybody's apartment at one A.M., and, I admit, I was a little nervous.

"I'll have cognac, please."

I'll never do cocaine again, but an occasional drink hasn't been a problem, and it won't be. Cognac is always a good choice when you want to be sociable, but it's important to keep your wits about you. You have to *sip* it, which already imposes a certain discipline on the proceedings.

"Cognac it is."

While he poured us each a splash in two giant snifters, I took a seat on one end of the couch and watched the woman on the screen kissing one man and going upstairs with the other. Their tender good nights were all in French, but there was no mistaking the longing in the eyes of the man left holding the sleeping child at the bottom of the steps.

"Do you speak French?" I said, accepting one of the snifters and inhaling the rich aroma.

He shook his head. "Not a word. I just like to watch foreign movies sometimes to see if I can figure out what's going on even though I have no idea what they're talking about."

"How many times are you right?"

"Almost always," he said, as I tried not to stare at his eyes, which seemed to be glowing in the room's low light. "But then again, how would I know?"

We shared another smile.

"I've actually seen this one," I said, recognizing *Jules et Jim*, François Truffaut's small masterpiece about two friends whose lives are shattered when they both fall madly in love with the fascinating but fickle Catherine. Over the course of the movie, she breaks both their hearts, leaves one a widower, and takes the other one with her to the grave. "Want to test your theory?"

"Sure," he said.

I could see immediately the idea appealed to him. We turned to the screen where Jules was sitting downstairs alone in his rocking chair while Jim makes helpless, miserable love to the faithless Catherine upstairs.

"Two men in love with the same woman," Blue said immediately. "A tragedy in the making."

"Always?"

"Always. Two men can't share a woman once they both fall in love with her."

"And she's married to one of them."

"That's even worse," he said, reaching for the remote to replace the movie with a CD of Nat King Cole at his ballad-crooning best, extolling the virtues of Route 66. He adjusted the volume for conversation and then turned toward me from the other end of the giant sofa.

I suddenly had a question, and this seemed the right moment to ask it. "Have you ever been married?"

He took a sip of his cognac. "Yes. Why do you ask?"

I liked that he answered without hedging. Some men seem to think inquiring about their marital status is no different than asking about the size of their penis. Blue didn't seem concerned.

I decided to tease him a little. "Well, you were smoking a cigar on the porch on a chilly evening rather than in the house. That's a married man's habit."

"None of my wives ever complained about the cigars." He smiled. "It's something I do for Lu. She's got asthma, and when she comes to visit, cigar smoke triggers it, so I don't smoke in the house."

"How many wives have you had?"

"Three."

"Three?"

"Is that too many or not enough?"

"That's a lot. Why so many?"

He shrugged gracefully. "I guess I'm a better friend than I am a husband."

I was in no position to confirm or deny on either count, so I tried a more neutral topic. "How was your fishing trip? You catch anything?"

He shook his head. "Not this time. My buddy lost his arms a couple of months ago, so he wasn't really ready to go out again."

"Lost his arms?" I tried unsuccessfully not to sound alarmed.

He grinned at me. "It's a fisherman's term. When you're deep-sea fishing, hooking the fish is just the beginning. Bringing him in is something else altogether. It can take hours for the big ones, and if you don't have the strength in your arms, you can't do it. Last time we went out, Peachy, that's my buddy, had to get somebody else to bring in this big marlin he'd been battling all day. Just about killed him to give it up."

His sleeves were rolled halfway up his arms, and I could see how muscular they were. Maybe he really had gone fishing.

"Couldn't he go after smaller fish?"

His blue eyes twinkled with amusement. They literally *twinkled*. "No. The point of deep-sea fishing is to conquer something."

"I thought the point of fishing was to relax."

"That's how men relax," he said, with another charming smile. "But we don't have to talk about fishing. How's everything with you?"

I let him slide on how men relax because I didn't really disagree. I just didn't appreciate his not being more apologetic about it.

"Everything's fine. I've met the other women in the building and found a couple of restaurants close by."

"Flora told me you two had lunch at Soul Veg last week."

"That's right. She told me all about the gardens."

"I'll bet she forgot to tell you about the party."

"She didn't mention a party."

He poured himself another splash of cognac. I demurred.

"Some of my associates and I are having a party next Saturday. We do it every year to raise money for one worthy cause or another, but mostly it's an excuse to get together and have a good time. I'm hosting, so I've got to be there early, but I'm sending a car for Flora at eight o'clock, and I'd like to invite you to come as my guest."

Was he asking me for a date? It didn't sound like a date. More like a *group* activity. Perfect. I hadn't been to a party in so long, I didn't even know what dances people were doing anymore. This could be my *coming-out* party.

"Thank you," I said. "I'd like that."

"Good."

"Who are you raising money for this time?" I sipped my drink slowly. The smell of cognac is the real pleasure. The burn of the liquid is just the price you pay.

"Precious Hargrove. She's running for governor next year."

"I'm an admirer of hers," I said. "Do you think she has a chance?"

He nodded. "If folks get behind her, I think she can win."

Somehow I hadn't thought Blue would be involved in politics.

There were more sides to him than I could count, and I knew I had barely scratched the surface.

"Brothers better get right," Blue said. "I keep trying to tell them. Sisters already got the mayor of Atlanta locked down. Now they got their eye on the state house, and they're taking no prisoners."

"Don't worry." I grinned. "It's just how women relax."

He laughed out loud at that and raised his glass. "Well, here's to relaxed black women. They get my vote every time!"

How could I not drink to that? I swallowed the last of my drink and set the glass down on the coffee table. Blue did the same. Either the cognac or the directness of his gaze sent a wave of warmth from the middle of my chest *down*.

"It's time for me to go," I said, standing up. "Thanks."

"I enjoyed it," he said, standing up with me. He was standing close enough for me to smell the faintest whiff of his cologne.

"You know when you said you were going fishing, I didn't believe you," I said, heading for the door.

"Why would I lie?"

"I don't know. You just didn't look much like a fisherman."

"I had a few stops to make first."

Uh-huh. "I see."

I stepped out into the hallway, and he did, too.

"If it'll make you feel better, next time I'll wear my fishing clothes."

"I feel just fine," I said, opening my door, which I hadn't bothered to lock. "Wear what you like."

He laughed again, and I allowed myself one final question.

"Are you going to sing at this party?"

He didn't look at all surprised by the question. "That's a young man's game."

"I heard you were pretty good."

"I had my moments," he said with a final twinkle. "Good night."

I'll bet you did, I thought. *I'll just bet you did.* "Good night."

13

THIS IS A GREAT NEIGHBORHOOD for walking. It's one of the few neighborhoods in Atlanta that actually has sidewalks. The absence of street predators and loitering groups of hopeless, hard-eyed men took away the feeling of running a gauntlet every time you step out the front door. Around here, even the liquor store had a clean parking lot and nobody outside looking crazy and trying to beg a beer.

The men I see walking through this neighborhood are invariably engaged in doing something constructive or walking like they got someplace to go and a certain time to get there. There're a lot of suits and ties and dark overcoats, too. There're a lot of homburgs and fedoras and highly polished shoes. When these guys pass you on the street, they touch their brims and say "Good morning." They don't actually say "ma'am," but it's clearly implied.

It took me a minute to get acclimated. I have a lot of protective armor to keep strange men at a distance, as any urban woman with any sense does, but none of it seemed to be necessary around here. After a while, when one of them would nod and say "Good morning," I'd nod and say "Good morning" back.

This afternoon, I went to the post office to return some papers to the weasel. He had included a note congratulating me for making my last payment early, which I thought was a nice touch. When human beings drop their insane, territorial bullshit, they can work out almost anything.

The line was moving slowly at the post office, and there were six people ahead of me, but I never fuss about long lines. Waiting gives me an opportunity for some uninterrupted people-watching. As folks pulled up to drop off their mail in the slot outside, I saw Aretha walk into the parking lot and head for the door. I was happy to see her and hoping she was still coming to Flora's brunch tomorrow.

"Hey!" she said, looking as pleased to see me as I was to see her. "I was just thinking I need to come up and see you!"

"You conjured me up."

"How's everything going? I haven't been playing the music too loud, have I?"

"I haven't even heard it," I said. "Everything's fine. What did you want to see me about?"

She was wearing a little cap pulled down low over her eyes and six individual earrings without a matching pair among them. "I told you I'm doing a lot of photographs now?"

I nodded. The smiling faces of the children on the walls of my apartment brighten the place up as much as the sunshine.

"Well, I'm working on a project now with some women who are working as strippers."

I liked the way she said that: "women who are working as strippers." Not "strippers." She made stripping what they did for a living, not who they were.

"A photography project?"

"I'm taking two shots of each one. First, they pose in what they wear to work. Hair, nails, makeup. *Everything*. Then they pose in something that reflects who they are offstage. It's really amazing to see what they pick for their real-self shots. They bring everything from church outfits, complete with hats, to jeans and a T-shirt with their kid's face on it."

I wondered how many of the women had children and if the men who wanted lap dances ever thought about the fact that they were grinding up on somebody's mama.

"That sounds interesting," I said. "How's it going?"

"Great. A lot of the women are referring their friends because they really like the pictures, but they don't always get the apartment number right. So if any of them come up to your place, just send them on downstairs. It doesn't matter how late. Sometimes they like to pose when they first get off work."

"No problem," I said. "I don't think I've ever met a strip . . . a woman making her living as a stripper."

"You probably have. You just didn't know it. When I was at Spelman, there were always a couple of girls earning their tuition at the strip clubs."

A quick mental scan of my classmates at Howard didn't turn up any likely candidates for secret strippers, but there's ten years between Aretha and me. In that one little decade, thanks to music videos, the character of the fantasy stripper, and her fantasy sister, the sexually rapacious, unapologetically materialistic ghetto goddess, with all the latest clothes and cars and no visible means of support, have emerged and become the dominant symbols of black women in the popular culture.

I don't think this is necessarily a positive development in the ongoing struggle for women's liberation, but it clearly impacts everything from clothing styles to the sexual expectations of adolescent boys who think there is actually a place where women are always perfectly coiffed, scantily clad, and ready for sex. Sometimes they even sing.

The line moved a few steps forward, and so did we.

"A woman came in the other day," Aretha said. "She was six months pregnant and getting ready to stop until her baby was born, so she wanted me to get a picture."

The idea of a pregnant stripper was new for me. "Isn't six months kind of late to be stripping?"

Aretha shook her head as we moved another few inches forward. An old woman at the middle window was slowly counting out the money she had been holding in her handkerchief for seven first-class stamps. The postal employee behind the counter was smiling indulgently like she had all the time in the world. Nobody in line seemed to mind, probably hoping she would grant us the same sweet smile when we finally got to the counter and greeted her face-to-face.

Postal workers have such a terrible reputation for being volatile and slow, but I never find them to be anything but calm, efficient, and patient to the point of sainthood, especially when we lose our minds and start demanding that our poorly wrapped packages reach our granny's house in time for Christmas morning, even if it is December 24 and we'd like to send it as cheaply as possible.

"Six months ain't nothing," Aretha said. "She told me there are private clubs where all the guys want to see are pregnant women, the bigger the better."

A friend of mine once told me that I would never really understand men because I had no clue about how low-down they are. Of course, I defended the brothers, by saying they can't be more low-down than I've seen them be, but then I hear this kind of stuff and I think maybe my friend is right. Pregnant strippers and prostituting children are both beyond the scope of my imagination.

"Is that where she was working?"

"No. That's why she's quitting. Six months is the most they'll go at the regular places before you have to take maternity leave."

"What did she wear for the reality pose?"

Aretha smiled. "She wore a pair of low-slung jeans and a little tiny T-shirt that said 'baby on board.'"

I was next in line. "Do you think she'll start again after the baby comes?"

Aretha shrugged. "Probably. She makes good money, and she doesn't know how to do anything else."

The postal worker who had accepted the handkerchief's worth of coins beckoned me over as the next in line.

"Your turn," Aretha said, but that was too abrupt an end to our conversation. "Want to walk back together?"

"Sure."

We each completed our business and headed back outside.

"I'm actually meeting Lu over at the school," Aretha said, "but we can walk that far together."

Brown Junior High School was right on the way, and Aretha and I fell in step easily together, me matching my shorter stride to her longer, loping one.

"I'm looking forward to brunch tomorrow," I said.

"Me, too. Flora is a serious cook. I think she's going to fry some catfish, and Lu promised to make me some biscuits. She's almost as good a cook as Flora. *Almost!*"

I tried to keep my voice casual as we strolled along. "Are you going to the party next Saturday night?"

"I wouldn't miss it," she said. "This will be my eighth year in a row."

"Eight years? That's a lot of parties!"

She nodded as we turned off Oglethorpe and headed down Peeples Street. "Ever since my freshman year at Spelman."

"You've been living here that long?"

"Since 1994. I grew up in a really tiny town in Michigan, and when I got accepted at Spelman, my aunt Ava was worried about me coming to the big city all alone, so she called Mr. Hamilton and asked him to look out for me. He gave me this apartment in exchange for picking up his mail when he's out of town and the occasional paint job." She grinned at me, recalling how we'd met. "I've been here ever since."

So I wasn't the first tenant to be given a break on the rent. My guess was that Flora and Lu weren't paying much either. I guess when Blue said he wasn't in it for the money, he wasn't kidding.

"He's kind of like my godfather," she said as we waited for the light at Abernathy. "That's why I'm not riding with you and Flora to the party."

"Why?"

She grinned at me again, two deep dimples reminding me of my mother's explanation when I asked her what dimples were.

"Angel's kisses," she had said, unwittingly plunging me into despair because I didn't have any. When I told her this years later, she laughed so hard she cried. I laughed, too, but I still harbored a grudge at the angels for not considering me worthy of their kisses.

"Mr. Hamilton scares the shit out of most of the guys around here already," she said. "If I arrive at the party in his car, I'll never get any play."

Before I could ask her what exactly they were afraid of, a stereo blasted into life down the street just ahead of us. Even from half a block away, we could hear the thumping bass pouring out of the car's open windows. It was a brand-new Lexus with so much gold detailing that it looked ridiculous. A tall young man who looked to be about twenty, in fashionably baggy clothes and a baseball cap, was leaning casually against the passenger door talking to two young girls, one of whom I recognized as Lu. Aretha saw her, too.

"What's he doing out here?" Aretha said, picking up her pace a little, like every second Lu spent in the presence of this guy was one second too many.

Lu and her friend were too busy giggling at something the man had said to see us coming, but he noticed our approach like the gold-toothed predator he appeared to be. His eyes swept over Aretha after dismissing me as somebody's mama, and he grinned a little wider to fully expose his mouth's full set of hardware.

"Well, now," he said. "We've got company."

Lu turned just as we reached them. "Hey, Aretha!"

"Hey, sweetie!" Aretha draped one long arm around Lu's shoulder, but her eyes locked on the man like she was memorizing his face for a police lineup. "Who're your friends?"

"You know ShaRonda," Lu said. "She's in my algebra class."

Aretha focused on the girl for the first time. Shorter than Lu by about six inches and skinny as a reed, this child's hormones hadn't moved her from girl to woman yet. Seemingly anxious to speed up the process, she was wearing a lot of makeup and an elaborate hair construction that seemed more suited to a nightclub than an algebra class.

"ShaRonda?"

The girl grinned sheepishly. "It's me."

Aretha laughed and reached out to hug her. "Girl, I didn't recognize you in all that makeup!"

"She look good, don't she?" said the gruff voice of the man leaning on the Lexus. The bass was still thumping, but I didn't recognize the female singer who was directing her lover on what to kiss and for how long.

Aretha turned to him with a look that would cut glass, and

ShaRonda spoke up quickly. "This is my uncle DooDoo. He just came to pick me up."

Uncle DooDoo grinned at Aretha. "The pleasure is all mine."

Aretha looked at him for a second the way you do a cockroach before you squash it. "Don't you work with King James Johnson?"

DooDoo looked surprised, then cunning. "Who's askin'?"

"I work for Blue Hamilton," she said quietly. "You're not supposed to be over here."

His increasing surprise and obvious confusion morphed into defiance. "I came to pick up my lil' niece." He reached out a muscular arm, and ShaRonda moved into the circle of it, her hair and makeup giving her show of familial support a strangely erotic flavor that I am sure was not lost on Aretha. "There's no law against that, is there?"

Aretha looked at him coldly, and then down at ShaRonda, who obviously wanted this moment to end before it got any worse. Aretha took a deep breath. "Nope. No law against that." She turned to Lu. "You ready?"

Lu nodded, turning to wave to her friend. "Bye, ShaRonda. See you tomorrow!"

"Okay," the girl said, hopping into the front seat beside her uncle, who cranked up the car and roared away before we even reached the crosswalk. There might not be a *law* against his presence around here, but he obviously got Aretha's point and wasn't prepared to push her.

Aretha turned a warm smile on Lu. "So how was your day, lil' bit?"

"Good," Lu said. "Are we still going to Greenbriar?"

"Yep."

They were catching the bus to the neighborhood's *other* mall. Medu Bookstore was having a reading, and Lu was interviewing the author, a historian, for her school project.

She turned to me. "You going with us?"

I shook my head. "Not this time."

This was a big sis/lil' sis outing. I knew better than to intrude. Lu rewarded my intuition with a smile of relief.

We crossed the street, and, as we fell into step together, Lu waved at several of her friends mugging in the windows of the bus.

"How long has ShaRonda's uncle been picking her up?" Aretha asked, her tone clearly communicating that he was not the guy you want to see making the junior high school a part of his regular rounds.

"Couple of weeks," Lu said. "Her mama had to go to rehab."

"I thought she just came out of rehab."

"She just came out, now she's back," Lu said patiently. "She's got a new boyfriend and he wants her to have a baby, but she doesn't want to do it while she's smoking crack. Why you asking about DooDoo?"

"He's not a good guy," Aretha said simply.

Lu shrugged. "He's okay. He buys a lot of stuff for ShaRonda."

"What kind of stuff?"

Lu looked at Aretha and frowned. "Clothes and makeup and stuff. CDs. He's her favorite uncle. She's even named after him."

"I thought her name was ShaRonda."

"It is. Her mama's name is Shaunice, and DooDoo is her mama's baby brother."

"So how does that translate into ShaRonda?"

"Shaunice and *Ronald*. His real name is Ronald."

"So why did she call him DooDoo?"

We passed a huge garden plot with an old woman and an even older man bent over checking something in the soil. Aretha waved, and they waved back.

"Everybody calls him DooDoo. ShaRonda said it's because when he was little, somebody said, 'That boy is always starting some . . .' can I curse?"

"Go ahead."

" 'Some shit,' and his grandmother said, 'Don't be cussin' in my house,' so the person who said it changed it to 'doodoo,' and it stuck."

I wondered briefly what it was like to go through life with a name like DooDoo. I guess ShaRonda lucked out when you think about it. She could have ended up ShaDooDoo.

"I don't think he's a good guy," Aretha said again.

"You already said that. What do you want me to do about it?"

Aretha looked at Lu, then smiled away her concern. "Nothing, lil' bit. You just be a friend to ShaRonda, and I'll keep an eye on DooDoo."

Lu giggled.

"What's so funny?"

"It sounds silly when *you* say it."

"It sounds silly when *anybody* says it! How you gonna be a grown man and call yourself DooDoo?"

"You should marry him. Then you'd be *Mrs. DooDoo.*"

Aretha crossed her eyes and stuck out her tongue, and Lu giggled helplessly.

"Mr. and Mrs. DooDoo!"

Now they were both giggling. I fell a few steps behind them to watch. There are moments that you want to remember exactly. Moments like this one. The three of us, walking home on a warm, almost spring afternoon, giggling away the danger that is always nipping at our heels.

14

W HEN I GOT HOME, SOMEONE had slipped an envelope under my door. I opened it up and inside was a plain white card
with black and white stripes around the border.

*"Mr. Blue Hamilton and the usual suspects request the honor of your
presence at their annual gathering. Come out. Drink up. Give back.
Eight o'clock until. Club Zebra."*

On the back of the card, he had written: *"I look forward to seeing
you on Saturday. No sake will be served. Blue."*

I held it in my hand for a minute, enjoying the weight and tex-
ture of the paper and wishing I was like one of those psychic creatures
on TV who can hold something and instantly know the whole history and intentions of the person who touched it last. Failing that, I
closed my eyes and tried to project myself into next Saturday so I
could check myself out at the party.

There I was, all right, walking through my own imagination like
it was a movie. Getting dressed in a beautiful blue dress that clung
where it was supposed to, and fluttered where it was supposed to, and
made me look really sexy. My hair was cut in one of those little feath-
ery numbers that Halle Berry works better than anybody, and I was
even wearing a new pair of shoes with pointed toes and amazingly
high heels.

I don't even wear high heels much anymore, but in this vision, I
was fearlessly working some pumps that looked like the ones on
those *Sex and the City* girls. Now there I was going downstairs to
meet Flora, who was wearing a peach-colored silk tunic and some
black silk palazzo pants. I saw us riding over in the limo, sipping
champagne like we did this every day. I saw us walk into Club Zebra
and then— That's where it stops. I can't actually get my mind past

the front door. I can't conjure up the moment when Blue Hamilton comes over to greet me in my beautiful dress and I look up into those amazing eyes and say— *See what I mean?*

Good thing I have a week to prepare, I thought, giving the invitation a place of honor on my refrigerator door, right next to the picture of me and my mom on the front porch of the house when I was about nine. She's got her arm around me, and I look really happy, just like Lu does in the picture she took with her dad. Every kid should have those moments. Those moments when you know beyond the shadow of a doubt that your mama adores you and your daddy thinks you hung the moon.

But that was a long time ago. The question on the table right now is, where am I going to find that dress by next Saturday night?

15

Sunday morning is one of my favorite times of the week. I'm also fond of Wednesday night and every other Thursday afternoon, but that's just me. Aunt Abbie and I had our weekly catch-up call as she headed out to whatever church she was visiting that week. She never joined one, but every Sunday she let the Spirit guide her to a place where she'd feel welcome. This morning, she was torn between the Catholic congregation around the corner from the house and the Baptist church a few blocks away.

As we signed off, I secured a promise that she would offer up a prayer for me wherever she landed, and she laughed.

"Why do you think I keep worshipping with these Negroes every Sunday in the first place?"

I laughed, too, but knowing that I had at least one person actively lobbying for my immortal soul made me feel good as I walked over to the West End News and picked up the Atlanta paper, the *New York Times*, and the *Washington Post*, then came back home and put on a pot of coffee. I enjoy newspapers a lot more since I started exercising more control over what I allow them to put into my brain. It started a couple of years ago during all the news stories about a guy who was eating people.

You remember that cannibal guy? Well, one morning I found myself at the breakfast table, drinking coffee and reading the most horrific details about how he was killing, cooking, and eating random young men in his apartment. When I got to the part about how he dismembered some of them and froze his favorite parts for later, I closed the paper, poured out the coffee, and left the news alone for a couple of days until I could figure out an approach that didn't leave me full of scary information I don't need about unfortunate people I don't know.

I decided to apply a simple test. Before reading any story purporting to be news, I ask myself one question: Is this story a personal tragedy or a community challenge?

For example, as a responsible citizen of the world, I need always to remember that babies are being killed *right now* in whatever wars the men are fighting. I need to keep that awareness uppermost in my mind so I'll take personal responsibility and be an active voice for peace. On the other hand, a front-page story about what human body parts are favored by an isolated madman whose insanity manifests itself as cannibalism is not required, or even particularly helpful. My mother always said a steady diet of scary bad news was just a right-wing plot to make people afraid to trust one another, and I used to laugh, but I think maybe she was right.

I wasn't going to read the whole paper right now anyway. A quick glance at the Arts and Leisure section of the *Times* while I drank a cup of coffee, and it would be time to go downstairs to Flora's. I had heard the sound of Al Green coming from her place earlier, so I figured Aretha was right. Al Green singing gospel music is the perfect background for a catfish Sunday brunch.

I had gotten a good bottle of champagne from Mr. Jackson's liquor store up the street, and happenstance had sent me an offering I was sure Lu would appreciate even more than the sparkling apple juice I had for her. Late last night, going through a box of photographs, some labeled, some with notes on the back in Son's famously illegible scrawl, I came across a photograph of him with his arm around a guy whose open face and reddish cloud of hair looked familiar.

Son was in his shirtsleeves, and the other guy had on a T-shirt that said BELIEVE. They were standing in a group of boys around eight or nine and they had the BELIEVE shirts on, too. Son and the guy were both grinning at the camera in a way that made me know the person taking the photograph was an attractive woman. They weren't flirting. She just caught them in the act of being two fine black men and they were as happy about it as she was.

I flipped the picture over to see if there was identification on the back and Son had written: *"Hank Lumumba. Good guy. Smart!*

Congressional material. Keep in touch." And at the bottom: *"July 2001, Detroit."*

It was Lu's dad, and he had made a big impression on Son. I thought she might like to see it and tell her dad what Son had had to say, so I tucked it in a folder to be carried downstairs with me at the appointed hour. I remember the first time I saw an old FBI photograph of my father making an impassioned speech from the steps of Frederick Douglass Hall in the middle of the Howard campus.

The students were getting ready to occupy the administration building, demanding black studies, and my father was firing them up for the confrontation that lay ahead. I remember being shocked at how young he looked and amazed that the FBI thought he was enough of a threat to start a file of his activities that continued for decades afterward, although he was never arrested or charged with a single crime.

It's exciting to bump up on somebody you love walking around in history. It makes you proud. Maybe I'll give this picture to Lu. Maybe she'll show it to her children, and her children's children, and say, This man is the reason your grandfather decided to run for Congress in the first place. Maybe she will teach them to say Son's name. I think he would have liked that. I think he would have liked it a lot.

16

Brunch at Flora's was an extended perfect moment. The food was sublime, starting with the fried catfish, cheese grits, and hot, homemade biscuits, proceeding through a bowl of the sweetest strawberries I've had in ages and some freshly whipped cream that literally melted in your mouth. The conversation was nonstop and convivial, with background music provided by the Right Reverend Al Green, who made loving Jesus sound so seductively secular that I was afraid the Lord would smack me down for the lust in my heart while I listened.

Lu was delighted with the picture of her dad and Son. She showed it to Flora with such excitement that Flora had to shoo her out of the kitchen where a frying pan of very hot grease and a four-hundred-degree oven made uninhibited displays of emotion less than practical. Lu couldn't wait to tell her dad.

It was Hank Lumumba's habit to call his daughter on Sunday afternoon for a good long chat. He spent the mornings, Lu told me, at a different church every Sunday to update one congregation or another on his progress against the dealers that had terrorized them for so long. He knew that the long trial process was mysterious to most of the people for whom the outcome would mean the difference between hearing birds or automatic weapons from their front-porch swing. So he asked each pastor for a few minutes of his or her time to say: "It's going our way. Don't worry. Don't be afraid. It's almost over. They can't win if we stick together!" Then he'd hang around afterward to talk to the old people who were the most scared and thank the pastor and make a small contribution to the building fund. Maybe Son's prediction was a prophecy.

He was still a prosecutor, but Hank was already keeping a politician's schedule.

It was almost one o'clock and we were nibbling at the last of the strawberries when Aretha casually asked Flora what she was wearing to the party next Saturday.

Flora groaned. "Don't start!"

Lu rolled her eyes. "She's threatening to wear her overalls!"

Aretha looked at Flora and wagged a disapproving finger. "There will be no overalls worn at this party. Just because Hank can't get here this year doesn't mean you're supposed to come looking like a bum!"

"She's exaggerating," Flora said. "All I said was if I don't find something soon, I'm going to be *forced* to wear my overalls."

Lu stood up and started clearing the dishes. "Ask her where she's been looking," Lu whispered to Aretha, sotto voce, as she headed for the kitchen with a load of plates expertly balanced on her arm.

Flora frowned after her daughter. "That is beside the point!"

"Ask her!" Lu's voice floated in on a laugh from the kitchen where we could hear her loading the dishwasher.

"Where have you been looking?" Aretha's voice was sweet as honey.

"At the Goodwill," Flora said, raising her chin defensively. "There is no reason to spend good money on a new dress I'll probably only wear once or twice."

"I told you," Lu said, coming back for some more dishes.

I wanted to tell Flora the outfit she had on in my imagination had looked good on her. Maybe she'd have more luck if she could narrow her search down to a peach-colored tunic and a pair of wide-legged pants.

Aretha turned to me like Flora wasn't sitting right next to her. "See, what we've got here is a woman who is well intentioned, but confused. She thinks she's being righteously frugal and a true woman of the people by picking through the few festive outfits the Goodwill has on hand, but, in fact, what she's doing is denying a woman who truly has no other resources the opportunity to take advantage of what would otherwise be available in her price range."

Lu was standing in the kitchen door, wiping her hands on a dish towel and grinning. So easy and natural was their teasing that they might have been three siblings.

Aretha turned back toward Flora. "Leave the Goodwill alone, Flo, and come shopping with me tomorrow. Two hours in Little Five Points and I guarantee we'll find something as comfortable as your favorite overalls, and much more flattering."

Flora looked hopeful but not convinced. "Two hours? And not a second more?"

"I promise."

"Okay. It's a deal."

Lu clapped her hands and gave her mother a quick kiss on the cheek. "Finally!"

Flora grinned at me and poured the last of the champagne into our glasses before we could decline. "With all my other fine qualities, you'd think these girls would forgive me a lack of serious interest in the world of high fashion."

"How fancy is this party anyway?" I said, wondering if I should ask to be included in the two-hour shopping spree.

Aretha shrugged. "Pretty fancy, I guess. After-five stuff, although some of the ladies go formal. Mr. Hamilton and his guys always wear tuxes. The other men wear tuxes or dark suits and," she smiled indulgently, "for the truly Afrocentric among us, a nicely embroidered ceremonial robe is always appropriate!"

"Remember that guy from Liberia who came last year?" Flora asked her. "He had those shoes that actually turned up at the end like a genie in a bottle."

"Too bad he won't be there this year," Lu said, grinning in Aretha's direction. "Maybe you could ask him to grant you three wishes."

"I don't need anybody to grant me three wishes, lil' bit," Aretha said, tossing her head so her long silver earrings danced and sparkled around her face. "I'm doing just fine, thank you!"

I wondered what she was wearing to the party. With her height and that lovely long neck, she could probably go as dramatic as she wanted to and not get lost in her look the way a smaller woman might. I'm only five three, so I have to be careful.

"Don't you want to make a wish about Kwame?" Lu was clearing up the last of the brunch feast without wasting this opportunity to tease Aretha.

"Who's Kwame?" I said.

"He's Precious Hargrove's son," Flora explained, "and a friend of Aretha's, so I hear, which is why my daughter is signifyin' so hard!"

"Ree and Kwame, sittin' in a tree, k-i-s-s-i-n-g!" Lu sang from the kitchen.

Flora grinned at Aretha, whose slight blush told me Lu wasn't far off the mark. "Any truth to these rumors?"

"We're *friends*, just like you said."

"Uh-huh."

"He's been away in graduate school for two years," Aretha said, looking at me and ignoring Flora and Lu, who were now openly in cahoots. "He's coming back to start working on his mother's campaign."

"Is that the only reason he's coming back?" Lu asked her mother. "What do you think, Mom?"

Before she could answer, Aretha cut in, cool as you please. "I guess you and ShaRonda found another place to watch the cable while we're at the party."

Lu immediately retreated. "No way! You said we could stay at your apartment until Mom got home."

The phone rang, and Lu checked the caller ID. Hank Lumumba was as good as his word. *Another perfect Sunday.*

"I'll take it in my room!"

"Saved by the bell!" Aretha called after her, laughing.

Lu closed her door behind her, and the three of us sat there for a minute, savoring what we all knew was the beginning of our friendship.

"There's some coffee left if anybody wants some."

"No thanks," I said, knowing I was as full as I could get without being uncomfortable. "Everything was wonderful."

"Thanks," Flora said, her eyes checking Lu's closed door and turning to Aretha. "Now what did you want to tell me?"

Aretha lowered her voice, and I leaned in to hear her clearly. "That DooDoo fool was up at the school on Friday when we went to pick up Lu."

"Who's we?" Flora's eyes went cold.

"Gina was with me. She saw him, too."

I nodded, glad we were alerting Flora to potential danger around her child.

"What was he doing?"

"He came to pick up ShaRonda."

"Lu's friend?"

"He's her uncle." Aretha's voice hissed out the word.

"Where's her mama?"

"Back in rehab. She wants to get clean so she can have another baby."

"She can't even take care of this one!"

"I know. That's why I figured we'd better pull ShaRonda in a little closer. He's already buying makeup for her."

Flora set her cup down harder than she meant to and shot another quick glance at Lu's door to be sure her daughter was still on the phone. "Do you think he wants to put her on the street? His own niece?"

"On the street?" I said. "As a prostitute? She's eleven years old!"

"They got eight-year-olds working over on Stewart Avenue," she said.

Aretha nodded in agreement. "ShaRonda's uncle works for King James Johnson. He's one of the worst of the pimps, and everybody knows it, but somehow he always gets off."

My head was spinning. What kind of man pimps a ten-year-old girl? What kind of john pays for one?

"They're getting bolder and bolder," Flora said. "Two more of the growers right over the line said some of his young hardheads have been trying to get them to plant reefer in the gardens."

"Anybody on this side of the line?"

Flora raised her eyebrows. "They're bold as hell, but they aren't crazy."

"What line?" I said.

"Mr. Hamilton doesn't cover any neighborhood outside of West End," Aretha explained quickly. "He doesn't have enough men to do more."

"The problem is, these growers are right on the border. They're technically not inside the area that Blue takes responsibility for, but these women have been with us since the very beginning, and they need to be protected. King James could grow weed anywhere. He doesn't need these old ladies to do it for him. He's just messin' with Blue, and Blue knows it."

"Which means he'll handle it," Aretha said. "In the meantime, let's keep an eye on ShaRonda in case she needs some help."

"She already needs some help," Flora said, reading my mind. I kept seeing the girl's slim, spandex-clad body leaning into the poisonous circle of her uncle DooDoo's embrace. "But let's change the subject before Lu comes back. I don't want her to start worrying about—"

Before her mother could complete the thought, Lu burst back into the room, grinning from ear to ear. "Daddy says call him back when your company's gone. He'll be home the rest of the day."

"How's he doing?" Flora would have her Sunday slice of Hank later.

"He's fine." Lu turned to me. "And he said thank you for sharing the picture and the note on the back. I read it to him. He wanted to know if maybe he could make a copy, if you don't mind."

"It's yours," I said, knowing it wasn't my place to be giving away the collection, but also knowing there couldn't be a better caretaker for this particular piece of Son's story.

Lu's eyes widened. "Thanks!"

"You're very welcome."

"What else did he say?" Aretha prompted.

"He said, next year, I'll be old enough to go to the party."

"He's wrong," Flora said calmly. "You have to be sixteen."

I could imagine Lu in a couple of more years. She'd be in full bloom. Ready for a perfect dress and a party where the men wore

tuxedos and called her "Miss Lumumba" to give her a taste of the social rituals that used to define interaction between grown-ups, but
seem hopelessly old-fashioned now.

"Daddy Blue said if you let me come next year, he'll sing for me."
Daddy Blue.

"Then we should let you come this year," Aretha said. "I'd be
willing to put up with you for a few hours in exchange for seeing
Mr. H on the stage again."

"Have you ever seen him sing?" I said. It hadn't occurred to me,
but she probably had. Flora almost certainly had.

Aretha nodded enthusiastically. *"Twice!"* she said, as if that placed
her among the luckiest women on the planet. "He's absolutely amazing. One of the best ever. He's . . . he's . . ."

I looked at Flora, who was grinning at Aretha's efforts to capture
in words Blue Hamilton's wonderfulness as a performer.

"Tell her, Flora!" Aretha threw up her hands in frustration. "You
saw him in his prime."

"What makes you think this isn't his prime?"

"Tell her!"

Flora looked at Lu. "Do you still have that picture he gave you?"

"The singing picture?"

"That's the one. Go get it for me, please."

Lu dashed back to her room, and Flora laughed softly. "I've seen
Blue perform a hundred times. He was still doing clubs when I met
him, and Hank was his lawyer, so we went down to the Royal Peacock to see his show."

The Royal Peacock was a legendary nightspot on Auburn Avenue, pre-integration Atlanta's main drag.

"I'm figuring, okay, this is my boyfriend's buddy. That's cool, but
he's definitely going to be local talent. I've never even heard of him,
right? But the place was packed and—what's that they always say
about the air feeling charged?"

"The air was *electric!*" Aretha said, like the kid who knows her favorite bedtime story by heart. "Go on!"

Before she could obey, Lu came dashing back with a color photograph of Blue on the stage and handed it to me. Aretha leaned over to look. Blue was wearing a white dinner jacket and holding the microphone in one hand while he reached out to a woman in the front row with the other one. The area around the front of the stage was crowded with young women in cocktail dresses and elaborate upswept hairdos. Some of them were reaching toward the stage. Some of them had been caught in midshriek by the photographer. Some seemed to be swaying in a private ecstasy with their eyes closed, even while their hands were still reaching, reaching, reaching. . . .

Blue looked just the same. His hair was a little longer, but he had the same mustache drooping around the corners of his mouth, and, oh yes, there were those eyes. He looked sexy as hell, and, based on the photograph, he hadn't even broken a sweat.

"That's how it was that night," Flora said. "That's how it always was. The minute he walked out there to sing, women would lose their minds. That first night I saw him, a girl actually *threw her panties on the stage!*"

Lu covered her ears. "Gross! You never told me that!"

"I figure if you're almost old enough to go to the party, you're old enough to know about the drawers," Flora said.

I was still looking at the photograph. He was so open, reaching for them as passionately as they were reaching back. This photograph left no doubt that a very intense exchange of energies was taking place. My question was, now that he doesn't do this anymore, *where does all that energy go?*

"See? You can't describe it either," Aretha crowed. "You're talking about what *they* did. You can't describe what *he's* doing. You just have to see it."

I handed the photograph back to Lu. I would have liked a chance to look at it longer, but in a less public setting.

"Why did he stop singing?"

Flora shrugged, taking the photo from Lu's hands and running her fingers over it lightly. "I don't really know for sure. You know men can never tell you *why* they do what they do."

"The first time I saw him sing at the party, he hadn't performed live in five years," Aretha said. "And believe me, it was worth the wait."

"You didn't throw anything on the stage, did you?" I had to tease her a little bit.

She laughed. "No, but it wasn't because—cover your ears, lil' bit!—it wasn't because I didn't want to."

"Gross!" Lu groaned.

"I warned you," Aretha said, still laughing.

"He sang at the party last year for Lillie, Peachy's wife, because everybody knew that would be her last one."

"That time didn't make me want to throw things. That time just made me cry," Aretha said. "He came right down to the table where Lillie and Peachy were sitting and sang right to her. She loved it. We all did."

"Maybe he'll sing something this year." Flora handed Lu back her picture. "Who knows?"

"He'll only sing if I ask him to," Lu said.

"And since when are you his agent?"

"Since I interviewed him for my school project. I know everything about Daddy Blue being a singer."

"I seriously doubt that," Flora laughed, "but if you've got any influence, use it. Regina deserves a chance to see your godfather in his element."

"Would you like to hear Daddy Blue sing?"

Would I ever! "I'd love to hear him sing."

"Then consider it done," Lu said, sounding just like Blue for the world.

Aretha laughed. "Good for you, lil' bit. Make yourself useful."

It was after two and time to pursue afternoon plans.

"I'm going to head back upstairs," I said. "Thanks for everything. It was lovely."

"My pleasure," Flora said. "I'm sure I'll see you before Saturday, but if I don't, why don't you just come on down at eight?"

"I won't be late."

Aretha and Lu were teasing each other again, and I knew Flora was getting ready to clear her voice of worry and call her husband for some sweet talk. My afternoon loomed lazily ahead with nothing but the still unread newspapers to claim my attention. I was about to open my door when Lu's head popped out and she took the steps up two at a time.

"You keep this," she said, thrusting the photo of Blue Hamilton into my hand.

Had she read my mind? "Why?"

"Now we're even," she grinned, and headed back downstairs before I could hand the picture back. I'm glad I didn't. The universe is going to get tired of sending me the stuff I ask for if I keep sending it back like the wrong lunch order.

So, I went inside, closed the door, and sat down to take a good long look at my neighbor *in his element*, but before I could even get started good, from across the hall came the faintest sound of someone singing.

17

JUSTIN'S RESTAURANT ON A BUSY afternoon is like a scene out of an urban romantic comedy. The people at the bar sipping peach martinis from perfectly frosted glasses were slender, stylish, and solvent. The dozen or so well-dressed people already seated at the linen-covered tables were examining their menus and conversing with waiters who wore identical well-pressed shirts and equally interchangeable smiles. The hostess was a tall, very thin young woman the color of bittersweet chocolate, beautiful in that angular way fashion models cultivate, and wearing the kind of little black dress that rarely leaves New York City.

She smiled a greeting and guided me to a table in the far corner of the room, where Beth and her assistant were already sipping their Perrier with lime. I had to smile. I had arrived ten minutes early and Beth had been here long enough to order drinks. She didn't get where she is by being careless. This woman was good.

"Gina," she said. "You remember Jade from the other day?"

"Of course," I said, taking the chair the hostess offered before she floated back to her station. We exchanged our greetings, and I asked the waiter for a Perrier of my own. We'd order lunch later.

"How was Albany?" I said.

Beth and Jade exchanged a look and then a smile.

"That good?"

"Better than that," Beth said. "It was *remarkable*."

Beth had only recently begun accepting speaking engagements again, and her followers were eager to see her, to support her in her loss and hear her new message, honed by tragedy but grounded, as always, in hope. She had booked a limited tour of the state over the next few weeks, and every appearance so far had been standing room only. The voter registration that Son had insisted on was going great guns, and, according to Beth, the lines to register were now as long as the lines to buy her tapes and get her to autograph her books.

Three years ago, when I was still on staff, Precious Hargrove told Son she intended to run for governor. He told her he intended to have registered twenty thousand black women to vote by that time and promised to talk to Beth about an endorsement. They shook hands on it, even though, at that time, I thought his estimate was unrealistic. From what Beth was saying, it was right on target.

"We've registered nearly—," Beth interrupted herself. "How many did we estimate, Jade?"

Jade flipped open a small notebook and scanned the page, flipped one more and found what she was looking for. "As of two nights ago, we estimated four thousand for the first two weeks."

"Four *thousand*? You're averaging . . ." I did the math quickly. Most of the venues where Beth spoke held a thousand people. She'd done eight gigs so far. ". . . five hundred a night?"

Jade said it with me. Beth was nodding with what can only be described as a hungry look on her face, and I don't mean for Justin's exotic menu offerings. This was a recognizing-the-next-level-of-your-own-power look, and, to tell the truth, it scared me just a little. Beth's ego was her blessing and her curse. When Flora said Blue had to deal with a struggle between his dark side and his better instincts, I understood immediately. Beth is involved in that battle, too, even though she would certainly deny it. Son was the one who had helped keep her on the high road. Looking at Jade, with her well-organized briefcase and her own hungry look, only slightly less predatory than Beth's, I didn't think she would be the one to provide the necessary balance.

"That's impressive," I said as the waiter deposited my Perrier near my elbow and disappeared.

"It's *remarkable*," Beth corrected me. "And these are all new voters. First-timers. They don't know the candidates. They don't know the process. They're *electoral virgins*!"

Jade scribbled the words in her notebook and, in parenthesis, she added EVs, and underlined it twice.

I had to admit, *remarkable* was the word for it. At this rate, by the time Beth wound up this tour at the ceremony in a few weeks, she would have the ear of almost twenty thousand EVs with new voter registration cards and no clue as to how to use them. Son's promise to Precious Hargrove was about to become a reality. He would have loved it.

"Precious Hargrove is going to love you," I said.

Jade opened her mouth to say something, but a fast look from Beth stopped her before she got out a single word. She looked quickly down at her notebook, as if she might have missed something crucial after she made a note of the phrase *electoral virgins* for posterity.

"Why is that?" Beth said, taking a small sip of her Perrier and dabbing her lips.

Jade avoided my eyes. *What were they up to?*

"Well, aside from your general *remarkability*, she stands to gain quite a bit from your endorsement. Twenty thousand votes and counting is nothing to sneeze at."

"Exactly," Jade agreed with an enthusiastic nod.

"That's why we've got to keep our options open," Beth said firmly.

She slid that *we* in like I couldn't notice, but I did. "What options are those?"

"It's too early to say," Beth said smoothly. "That's the whole point."

"You aren't thinking about endorsing someone other than Senator Hargrove, are you?"

Son would turn over in his grave if she threw her support to any of that motley crew of good ol' boys and party hacks who wanted to run. She shook her head and shared another little smile with Jade, which made me want to shake them both until their teeth rattled, as my mother used to say. Nonviolent to the core, my mother never actually shook me at all. I think she knew just the *idea* of rattling teeth would give me pause for thought and time to regain my senses.

"No, Gina," Beth said slowly. "Nothing like that."

"Thank goodness," I said. "You couldn't ask for a better candidate than Precious to motivate your troops."

"Well, that's not altogether true," she said. Jade was looking like the cat who swallowed the canary. "There's one person who might be even better."

"Who?" This game was getting on my nerves.

"Me," Beth said with a triumphant smile. "What about me?"

Now I was thoroughly confused. "What about you? You're not a politician."

She gave me a big smile. Jade did, too, with her little Mini-me ass. Was this her ridiculous idea, or did Beth come up with this on her own?

"That's probably a plus," Beth said. "People don't trust politicians anymore. You know that."

I turned to Jade. "Is this your idea?"

She shrank back a little, but she didn't take low. "There's a groundswell of support. Everywhere we go, people are asking her to run. They're practically begging her to just consider a draft."

"You've never even run for office," I said, incredulous. "Your work has always been outside of those channels, remember?"

"Times change," Beth said coolly.

"You can't have thought I'd think this was a good idea."

"I had hoped you could get behind it," she said. "It was always Son's dream."

That made me mad. "Son's dream was never for you to let your ego get you into a race for a position you're not qualified for even if you win."

"But you do concede that I could win?"

This is not why you came down here, I reminded myself. *Don't take the bait.*

"I don't concede anything," I said calmly. "This hasn't got anything to do with me."

"It does if we announce my candidacy at the dedication ceremony," Beth said, watching my face for a reaction.

She got one. *"What?"*

The waiter who was headed our way heard my shriek, reconsidered, and turned around.

"Calm down, Gina. Nothing is settled yet. I haven't committed anything to anybody."

That was probably true, but at this point I didn't care. This was only my problem if I let it be. *Take a breath,* I said to myself. *Let it go!*

"Well, keep me posted," I said. "You'll probably need a different kind of speech if you decide to do this."

I could have added "and a different kind of person to write it," but that speech was still part of my contract, money already promised to the weasel, so I focused on the reason I was here in the first place, conjured up a mental picture of his handing me a piece of paper that read PAID IN FULL, and waved at the waiter to let him know it was safe to return.

"Exactly," said Beth, nodding to her clone who nodded back. *"Exactly."*

18

EVERYTHING WENT GREAT AT Morehouse this morning. The dedication committee was so happy that I actually know what I'm doing, they're practically beside themselves. When I showed them the rough draft of the script for the video biography I'm putting together, Mr. Freeney looked like he couldn't decide whether to kiss me or run around the room three times fast. In fact, he was grinning like a Cheshire cat during the whole meeting. It wasn't until we were winding things up that he let the rest of us in on why.

"As most of you know," he said, still smiling broadly, "the president of the college recently extended an invitation to state senator Precious Hargrove to serve on our host committee. I am happy to report that she has accepted our invitation and agreed to serve as one of our cochairs."

He turned to me, practically beaming. "As you are aware, I'm sure, the senator and Mr. Davis worked together on many projects that positively impacted the neighborhood around the college, as well as the college itself."

The other members of the committee nodded as one head to affirm Freeney's assessment, and I nodded, too, but inwardly, what he said made me cringe. Precious Hargrove had no idea she had just agreed to serve on a committee to honor the son of a woman who was getting ready to stab her in the back.

"That's wonderful," I said. "I'm sure Beth will be pleased to hear it."

For the last few days, I couldn't seem to get away from the honorable Ms. Hargrove. She'd been topic A at lunch with me and Beth on Tuesday. Here she was on Thursday claiming her place on the committee. Plus, they were going to be raising money for her at the party on Saturday night. If anybody could match my landlord for proactive presence in the neighborhood, Precious Hargrove seems to be the one. I hope Beth's ego doesn't push her into a race against this woman. She might get more than she bargained for.

Mr. Freeney dismissed the meeting on that upbeat note. I stayed around long enough to answer a few questions about who was responsible for what between now and our next session and then headed home. I had made a dent in all those boxes, but there was a lot more still to do, and I had just started searching for the rest of the shots I'd need for the video.

So far, Beth's fears had been unfounded. If Son had a secret life, he also had enough sense to cover his tracks. Sometimes I almost wished I could find something scandalous. Something that would set Beth back on her heels for a minute. Something that would prove beyond the shadow of a doubt that she hadn't been in absolute control of her greatest creation. Something to indicate that he finally had found a woman strong enough to get him away from his mama. But so far, nothing.

My task for the afternoon was to start sorting a huge box that held a jumble of photographs, most of them unlabeled and undated. The people standing with Son and Beth are always smiling broadly. Son and Beth are usually smiling, too, but their expressions are always more controlled. Not unpleasant, but with none of the giddy pleasure that shows so clearly on the faces of their fans.

I liked looking at those photographs. They help me remember why I started working for Beth in the first place. These pictures remind me that her gift is making the possibility of female freedom, of female choices, of honor among women, seem as real and as vital as water. It's valuable and necessary work, but it won't help her get a health care bill through the Georgia state legislature or attach a child care amendment to a public education initiative. Those good ol' boys aren't impressed with *charisma*. They're impressed with *power*, and outside of the power to illuminate and motivate, Beth doesn't have any. An alliance with Precious Hargrove would be a step in the right direction, for both of them, but that can't happen if Beth insists on running herself.

The smell of Jamaican jerk chicken wafted out of the West Indian restaurant up ahead, but I wasn't tempted. It was too early in the morning for food that spicy. I know some people put Tabasco sauce on eggs, but I'm not one of them. I also resisted a sudden craving for Krispy Kreme, even though the hot doughnuts sign was flashing its ass off and the smell of all that icing will make you weak at the knees if you're not careful. Doughnuts I don't need. Not until after Saturday night, anyway. If it was going to be my coming-out party, I was going to come out looking good or what was the point?

When I turned down my street, the cars parked in front of the building reminded me that Flora had convened a meeting of the Growers Association executive committee at her place this morning. She was concerned about DooDoo and his boys harassing some of her gardeners. They needed a plan before the problem got out of hand. Flora had also invited Precious Hargrove as the state senator from this district, and she was pulling up just as I headed for my blue front door. Since I can't seem to get away from the woman, I decided I might as well reintroduce myself.

"Senator Hargrove?" I said, surprised to see her arrive alone.

"Yes?" She hit the auto lock on her gray Accord and came around the car toward me with the beginning of a smile that could adjust itself up or down depending on who I was or what I wanted. Precious Hargrove was a small woman whose political fearlessness and well-crafted campaign ads made her seem to be much taller. Even in chunky three-inch heels, she wasn't much taller than I was. She was carrying ten to fifteen extra pounds, probably the result of all those fried chicken dinners she was obliged to consume with her constituents, but with her smooth brown skin and intelligent eyes, she was a handsome woman who could have been pretty if she ever decided to lean into her looks.

At forty, she had been in politics for almost one-third of her life and she was either comfortable in, or resigned to, the dark, boxy suits and crisp white blouses that seemed to be her professional uniform. She allowed herself a pair of small pearl earrings, but otherwise her style was stripped of adornment. Senator Hargrove was all about business.

I stuck out my hand to show her I was, too. "I'm Regina Burns. I met you a few years ago with Son Davis."

Her mental memory bank did a quick scan and came up with what she needed.

"Of course," she said. "We were trying to get some people registered to vote, as I recall."

I was impressed. "That's right."

"Are you still working with Son Shine?"

"No. I live in Washington now, but I'm here pulling together the Son Davis Legacy Project over at Morehouse."

Her face clouded. "Son Davis was a great loss. He had a bigger vision than most people realize."

"Yes, he did. That's why I came back to do the project."

The cloud passed. "I've agreed to be one of the cochairs for the ceremony on . . ." She hesitated.

"May fifth."

She smiled. "So does this mean we'll be working together?"

"I guess it does." I smiled back.

"I'll look forward to it," she said, reaching into her pocket and handing me her card. "Here's my numbers. I'd love to talk with you about how the voter registration is going."

"Even better than Son expected," I said, wondering how much I could share with her without betraying Beth's confidence.

Before I could decide, I heard a sharp rapping on glass and turned to see two old women standing in Flora's front window. The taller of the two was gesturing at us to come inside. The growers were ready to greet their guest of honor, and I was holding up progress.

"I've got a meeting," she said, a phrase she had probably said as often as her own name. "Perhaps we can talk again soon."

"Actually," I said, "I live here. Flora invited me to the meeting you're on your way to."

She laughed, the small lines around her eyes testament to the fact that she did it often. "Well, we better get going before Bea Thomas comes out here to find out what's keeping us."

We started up the walk together, still under the watchful eyes of the two ladies in the window. I hadn't really intended to go, but I liked Precious Hargrove, and this would give me a chance to see her in action.

"Is this your first growers meeting?"

I nodded and held the blue door open for her. She grinned and stepped inside.

"Well, get ready. These folks do not play!"

19

FLORA'S APARTMENT WAS JAMMED. She spotted Precious and me immediately and waved us inside. In addition to her couch, the two living room chairs, and the four from around the dining table, she had set up six or eight folding chairs wherever she could squeeze them in.

"I thought you were gonna stand out there all morning," grumbled a tall, lean gray-haired woman who I recognized as the one who had been tapping on Flora's window.

"I'm sorry, Bea," Precious said, squeezing the woman's hand warmly.

"You not the only one with a schedule, you know."

"I know, I know!"

"She's here now, ain't she?" said one of the two men present. "You gonna waste your time fussin' or let the woman get in the door good?"

He shook Precious's hand. "Welcome back, Senator."

"Thanks, Mr. Charles," Precious said with a conspiratorial wink in his direction.

Bea gave up grudgingly. "I'm just sayin' . . ."

She was clearly the designated fusser. Every meeting seems to need one. Someone who cannot be pleased or pacified, who is a constant thorn in the side of anyone even vaguely resembling an authority figure. That was Bea.

Every chair was occupied, but Flora detached herself from a circle of three gray-haired women and one bald-headed man, all talking simultaneously, dashed into Lu's room, and came back with a three-legged stool and a small rocker. Precious waded right in, apologizing for being a few minutes late, asking after new grandbabies and ailing spouses with equal specificity. She was well known to the people in this room and, from their greetings, well liked.

I gave Flora a quick hug and claimed a space for the stool in the back so I could watch the West End Growers Association in action.

Flora got everybody settled and smiled a welcome to a roomful of her friends. There were about fifteen women ranging in age from fifty to eighty, and two men who looked to be somewhere in their mid-seventies. They all looked healthy; even the oldest ladies were surprisingly agile. If this was what gardening does for you, I ought to start working a plot of my own!

"Everybody got somewhere to sit?" Flora asked. These folks were in good shape, but none of them wanted to stand up for an hour. "Okay. We've got some serious business to discuss today, so let's dispense with reading the minutes and do that next time."

"So moved!" a little woman perched on the edge of Flora's wine-colored wing-back chair said quickly.

"All in favor?"

Every hand went up except mine since I wasn't really a member and didn't have voting privileges.

"All right," Flora said, moving right along. "Then let's have our minute of silence and get started."

The room was immediately quiet. Some of the people closed their eyes as Flora did, and simply sat still, breathing in and out in unison so that the whole room seemed to be sighing. The unexpected pause had what I imagined was the desired effect. We went from being a gaggle of excited individuals to being a group of thoughtful human beings. A moment of silence seems so much more civilized than banging a gavel.

Flora opened her eyes. "Good. Did I say welcome?"

"You too busy makin' us be quiet," said Bea.

Flora ignored her. "We have two guests with us today. The first one is my new neighbor upstairs, Regina Burns."

She pointed in my direction, and I raised my hand in a general wave.

"And the other one is an old friend of the Growers Association and of West End, Senator Precious Hargrove."

The assembled growers broke into enthusiastic applause as Precious joined Flora in front of the room.

"As you know, we've been having some problems just across Stewart Avenue. We want to report those as succinctly as we can to Senator Hargrove, in the hope that she can offer us some assistance. Miss Mattie, do you want to start?"

Miss Mattie looked to be about sixty. Her high cheekbones and straight black hair were testament to the Native Americans in her family tree. When she stood up to speak, she squared her shoulders like it was going to take more than some young hoodlums to scare her.

"I'm Mattie Jenkins," she said. "You all know me. I been part of this group since the beginning, longer than some of you, even, so I think I deserve some consideration."

"We all think so, Mattie," Flora said quickly. "That's why we're here."

Miss Mattie took a deep breath. She knew she was among friends, but she was still mad. "I know it. It's just that they been by my house three times in two weeks."

Precious frowned. "Three times?"

Mattie nodded. "They come and ring the bell just as bold as you please. Start asking me if I don't want to let them help me with my garden."

"Some help!" said another of the women.

"I know that's right!" Of course, that was Bea.

"I never let them in, of course," Mattie said, "but it's nerve-wracking to have them hanging around all the time. I told them I don't know nothin' about growing that wacky weed and to get the hell off my porch before I got my shotgun."

The woman next to me leaned over and whispered, "She would, too. Mattie always been wild!"

"Tell them what happened last week," a woman seated next to Mattie on the couch said.

"This is Jerry Tulane," Flora said for those who didn't know her. "She's down the street from Mattie."

Jerry waved a hand. "They been comin' to my house, too."

"Last week, we were outside in my backyard, just talking, and two of these guys opened the gate and walked in like they had a right to."

"Did they threaten you?" Precious was making notes in a small blue spiral notebook.

Mattie and Jerry shook their heads.

"Not yet," Jerry said, "but they'll be back. It's only a matter of time."

"We need some help over there," Mattie said. "The police keep sayin' they can't do anything unless they actually do something to us."

"It'll be too late then," Bea said loudly. "What good is it gonna do calling 911 after they already hit some poor woman in the head?"

The others began murmuring among themselves. Bea had put their fears on the table. Now what was Precious going to do to address them?

"I know you're concerned," Precious said. "You should be concerned. Some of our young brothers have gotten so desperate, they'll do things we never thought our children would be capable of doing."

" 'Scuse me for cutting you off," Miss Mattie broke in. "But these little hoodlums ain't nobody's brother, and they sure ain't nobody's child."

"You got that right!" Bea added her amen from the rear, and there was a little murmuring, a little shushing.

Precious waited for quiet. "That's where you're wrong. These little hoodlums are what our babies have become, but they are still our children. Even when they act a fool, even when they scare us, we can't deny their humanity. We can't—"

"I beg your pardon, Madam Senator," Mr. Charles said, holding up his hand, "but I don't think we got time to argue about whether or not they're human."

"Can we vote on it?" said a voice from the back, and a nervous titter rippled through the room.

Mr. Charles pressed on. "I think what we want to know is what can we do to keep them from trying to grow marijuana in our gardens."

Murmurs of assent. Precious took a deep breath. I felt sorry for her. The police were right. There was probably nothing to be done until the intimidation went one step further, and, as Bea pointed out, that would be too late.

"All right," Precious said. "Here's what I can do right away. I'll talk to the zone commander and ask him to increase the police presence on your block. I'll also ask him to talk to these guys and give them a warning about harassment. I'll also start the paperwork for issuing peace warrants that will require them to stay one hundred feet away from your houses. Do you know their names?"

Jerry and Mattie looked at each other and shook their heads.

"Who knows what their mamas called them, but they call each other . . ." Mattie looked so uncomfortable that Jerry picked up the slack.

"They call one DooDoo and the other one King James."

The assembled growers groaned. Precious didn't even bother to write the names down. I had the feeling these guys were both well known to her. So that's what ShaRonda's uncle spent his time doing when he wasn't baby-sitting. Harassing old ladies in their backyards.

"We know these two," Precious said. "We've picked them up before. We can pick them up again."

"But they don't keep 'em." Jerry's voice was almost a whine. These answers were not making her feel any better. "They let 'em right back out and then they even worse 'cause they mad, too."

"Hoodlums burned up a woman in Baltimore," the woman next to me whispered. "She kept callin' the cops on the dealers until they set her house on fire with gas. Burned up her kids and her husband, too." She shook her head. "What kind of person burns up a family just so they can sell crack on the corner?"

The question made me shiver because I didn't know the answer.

"Listen, I know it's hard," Precious was saying. "And I know they're scary sometimes, but we're going to work with you until we get these guys off the street. That much I can promise you."

Nobody said anything, so Flora stepped into the skeptical silence. "As you can see, Senator, we have strong feelings about the safety of our growers."

Precious nodded.

"We appreciate your coming, and we stand ready to work with you to get these guys off the street."

There was a smattering of applause. These were Precious's core constituents. They liked and respected her, and, at some level, they knew that what they were asking her to do was an impossible task, even for a smart, savvy, dedicated public servant. DooDoo and King James were just the most visible faces on a problem that runs so deeply to the heart of *what is wrong with us* that it takes more courage than most of us can muster to even consider it.

"Thank you," Precious said. "I know you wanted more immediate action, but I assure you this will be my top priority until we find a solution."

More spotty applause.

"And I want to thank you especially for calling on me and for not—" Precious chose her words carefully "—for not taking matters into your own hands."

You could have heard a pin drop. Even Bea didn't have anything to say to that. Precious picked up her purse.

"I'll call Flora as soon as I speak to the zone commander," she said, and Flora nodded. "And, as always, I appreciate your support and your positive presence in the neighborhood where I've spent the last twenty years of my life."

The growers allowed themselves to relax into her collective compliment.

"Stick with me now, okay?"

"You got it, Senator," Mr. Charles boomed, beginning a round of sincere applause this time that carried Precious out the door on the same wave of trust that carried her in. I wondered if I should slip out, too, but a plump little woman in a bright orange jacket closed the door behind Precious, like leaving was not an option, so I settled myself on my stool and waited for more adventures in participatory democracy.

I was reminded of my father's despair at the widespread inability of victorious revolutionaries to translate their passion for change into a willingness to submit to the unremitting tedium of actual governance. Flora and Precious's activism was the kind that required them not to propagate the latest theoretical approach to activating the masses, but to have actual exchanges with real people confronting real problems. They were the people who had to actually translate *the revolution* into Miss Mattie being able to grow her collard greens in peace.

The old man who hadn't spoken yet waved his hand at Flora.

"Mr. Eddie?"

Mr. Eddie stood up slowly. He was very tall and very thin and eighty years old if he was a day. Although most of the people were casually dressed, he was wearing a dark suit and tie.

"I don't mean to be speaking out of school," he said, "but now that the senator's gone, I'd like to know where Hamilton stands on this."

There was an immediate ripple among the growers.

"He's aware of the problem," Flora said, "but the block we're talking about is not within the West End community."

Mattie snorted. "Across the street! That's all! We're one street too far. Is that fair?"

"It's downright wrong if you ask me," Bea said. "Either we're safe or we're not. How can I be safe over here if I can't go see Jerry and be safe over there?"

"Any of us could be next!"

Flora waited patiently for things to settle back down. "You all know the problem. Mr. Hamilton has committed his assistance to the West End community. He has gone so far as to guarantee our safety within a certain well-defined area. We know what the boundaries are, and so does everybody else. If these guys stay on their side of Stewart Avenue—"

"Their side?" Jerry's voice was now an indignant wail. "So now I live on *their side*?"

Flora looked Jerry in the eye, but her voice was very gentle. "You have been offered comparable housing on this side. Both of you have."

"You know I can't move," Jerry said. "That was my grand-mother's house. Then my mama's. Now it's mine, and I intend to grow old in it with my memories to keep me company, and no little wild Negroes younger than my grandchildren are gonna run me off!"

I don't have to say that that really resonated with me. When is a house not a house? *When it's a history!*

There was scattered applause and lots of nods of encouragement.

"Let's vote," Bea said loudly, still agitating.

"Okay," Flora said calmly. "What exactly are we voting on?"

Silence. Flora let it sit there for a minute, and then Mr. Eddie stood up again. "I'd like to vote to ask Hamilton to extend himself far enough across Stewart Avenue to cover our two growers who need some help." He turned toward Mattie and Jerry and his voice was apologetic. "Because me and Charlie are too old to get it done, and somebody's gotta handle it."

"Speak for yourself, old dude!" said Mr. Charles immediately, and everybody laughed.

"All in favor?" asked Mr. Eddie.

Every hand went up. I watched Flora, but she just smiled. Her role seemed to be more facilitator than leader.

"That looks unanimous to me," Bea crowed.

"All right, Bea," Flora said. "I'm going to authorize you to convey that message to Mr. H at your earliest opportunity."

"Me?!" Bea's shocked surprise elicited another laugh from the group.

"That's one message he ain't got to worry about!" The woman next to me chuckled. "She ain't got the heart to talk stuff to that man. Trust me!"

Flora grinned and held up a hand for order. "Just checking, Bea. I thought for a minute you wanted my job."

Bea grinned back. "Not if it means I gotta look into Hamilton's cold blue eyes!"

She got the color right, but I don't remember any coldness.

"All right," Flora said. "I'll talk to him."

There was more enthusiastic nodding among the growers.

"Anything else?" She looked around to be sure she hadn't missed anybody. "Mr. Charles?"

"Don't y'all forget the party on Saturday night," he said. "I'm gonna have on my dancin' shoes and Eddie's threatening to do the electric slide again."

General laughter. I couldn't imagine the dapper Mr. Eddie doing the electric slide, but it was definitely a multigenerational dance open to old people with any sense of adventure, so who knows?

"Anybody who needs a ride, call me," Flora said, bringing things to a close. "Who's got the benediction?"

The tiny woman who had made the early motion to dispense with the reading of the minutes raised her small hand and stood up. The room quieted, and everybody reached for the hand of someone nearby. When we were all connected in our raggedy circle, the little woman smiled and her voice was soft as a child's in prayer.

"May the Lord watch between me and thee, while we are absent, one from another."

"Amen," we all said together and squeezed one another's hands gently. *"Amen."*

20

I THOUGHT AFTER ALL THE EXCITEMENT at the growers meeting yesterday this would be a fairly peaceful day just to balance things out. How wrong could I possibly be? Everything started out fine. I was making good progress on sorting a huge box of photographs. I had dragged it into the living room, where there was a lot of open floor space, so I could spread everything out and look at the photos as if they were scenes from a movie. I have only stills to work with, but I'm a big fan of those Ken Burns specials on PBS. I know if you have enough pictures and enough patience, you can hook it up so nobody even realizes nothing's really moving.

I had just sorted through a bunch of stuff from a trip to Chicago and reached for another folder when a single snapshot slipped out and floated to the floor. When I leaned over to pick it up, I knew immediately that the woman in the photograph was the one Beth had me looking for. It wasn't hard to figure it out. Looking at her smiling up into Son's face, it was clear that they were in love. Madly in love. My first thought was: Did he ever look at me like he's gazing at her? Did I ever look at him with such absolute adoration?

The woman was young, maybe mid-twenties, and strikingly lovely with a voluptuous body and a sweet face. She was wearing low-rise jeans and a tiny little T-shirt that said GODDESS across her breasts. Son was wearing a Hawaiian shirt, jeans, and the biggest grin I've ever seen on his face. They were seemingly unaware of the camera, sharing a private joke as they strolled along, his arm around her shoulders, her hand in his back pocket. In the dictionary under the word *lovers*, this picture would not be out of place.

I didn't realize I was crying over it until a tear splashed down and rolled slowly across Son's chest. I rubbed it away with my finger and sat down on the couch. What was I crying about? I looked at the picture again. Who was I kidding? I was crying because I *know* he never looked at me like that. And because I know I never looked at him like that either, and I was jealous. Not of this beautiful woman, but of her happiness with a man who loved her. *And how fucked up is that?*

"Pretty fucked up," I said out loud. "Pretty fucked up."

But I can do better. I can reach for my higher self like they always tell you in rehab and women's magazines. I can try to tap into the best of myself. I can try to think about this picture I'm holding in another way. *But what other way was that?* I closed my eyes and took a deep breath. What did Flora call it? *Having our moment of silence.* Maybe that's what I needed.

I tried to clear my mind and calm down. Two breaths, maybe three, and I could feel myself relax a little bit. Two more breaths and then two more and suddenly it hit me. This was what I had hoped for Son. My friend Son. This was what I had wanted to know immediately when I heard that he had died. Had he had a chance to love somebody the way I wanted him to love me? Had he been one of those who had a chance to make a call and tell his beloved to look for him in paradise? I wanted that kind of love for him, and this photograph was telling me he had found it. Was it fair for me to be mad just because he hadn't found it with me?

I opened my eyes and looked at the picture again. This time, I was able to share that smile. I was able to celebrate the sweetness of that moment and be glad for them. My better self congratulated me for listening to her, and I decided to reward myself with a cup of jasmine tea. For some reason, I carried the picture with me, and everybody knows there's only one place for photographs in the kitchen. I put it on the refrigerator door, right next to Blue Hamilton's performance snapshot, and considered the pair while I waited for the tea-kettle to boil.

I knew why those women in Blue's audience were reaching for

him with such shameless yearning. Because nobody in their own lives was reaching for them that way, and they didn't want to forget how it felt before they got too old to care.

And how old is that? said a little voice inside my head. *How old is that?* But before I could answer, someone knocked on my door. The answer to that question would have to wait.

21

I OPENED THE DOOR TO FIND Blue Hamilton standing there smiling apologetically. It was eleven o'clock on Friday morning, but he was dressed, as usual, in a dark suit and tie. I was dressed, as usual, in a pair of faded jeans and an oversize sweatshirt. Makeup and hair drama have never been my thing, but I found myself wishing that just once I could run into my landlord when I looked a little more pulled together.

"I'm sorry to disturb you," he said. "Is this a bad time?"

"Not at all," I said. "Would you like to come in?"

"Thank you."

He stepped inside, and his eyes took in the paper-strewn living room. Photographs covered the coffee table and most of the floor.

"Excuse the mess," I said quickly. "Sometimes it helps to lay everything out where I can see it."

"You looking for anything specific or you just looking?"

"Just trying to bring a little order to things."

He nodded, and I realized that was pretty much his job description, too. From the kitchen, the teakettle released a soft whistle.

"I'm making some tea. Would you like some?" I asked, enjoying the faint aroma of his cologne.

"Thanks," he said, stepping gracefully around the piles of paper lying in his path and taking a seat on the couch. He looked so comfortable, I found myself wondering if he had ever sat there before. The kettle's whistle was getting more strident by the minute.

"I'll get the tea," I said, heading for the kitchen. "Do you take honey?"

"I'll take it straight."

As I turned off the flame under the teakettle, my eye fell on his picture on the front of my refrigerator. *Oh, lord!* How embarrassing would that be if he saw it there. I snatched it off and stashed it quickly in the silverware drawer.

I set the two steaming mugs on the coffee table and took a chair. The sun was pouring in, and the smell of the tea and his aftershave made a spicy blend that any entrepreneurial aroma therapist would want to bottle for sale immediately.

"I haven't seen you around this week," I said. "Another fishing trip?"

He smiled and shook his head. "Not this time. I have a couple of other places in the city. I try to have a presence there, too."

"Kind of like a circuit rider?"

"Kind of."

I took a sip of my tea. "It sounds like what my grandmother used to say."

"What was that?"

"It's a sorry rat ain't got but one hole."

That made him laugh, and laughing made his eyes do that twinkling thing they do.

"My grandmother used to say that, too." He took a swallow of his tea. "But I think she was talking about something a little different."

"How different?" I tucked my feet up under me and wrapped both hands around my mug to feel the warmth. He had stopped by to tell me something, but he didn't seem to be in any hurry, so I decided not to be in one either.

He leaned back and laid one long arm across the back of the sofa. His jacket moved with him and rearranged itself in a graceful flutter. "Well, most people need a lot of different places to go, to live, to be, because *they* are a lot of different people. They act one way one place, one way another. Eventually, if they get enough places so they can let all their selves show, they can relax."

Aunt Abbie's voice was a tiny little echo in my ear. *He's not who he appears to be.* "So how many people are you?"

"My problem is a little different," he said. "My problem is that I'm only one person. It doesn't matter to me where I am. I don't change."

"Is that a problem?"

"Not for me, but it wears most people out."

"Flora and Aretha seem to be thriving," I said.

"They weren't the one I was worried about."

It dawned on me that he was talking about *me*. What was I supposed to say to that? Since I didn't have a clue, I took a swallow of my tea and waited.

Blue's grin was worth waiting for. "See what I mean?"

That made *me* laugh. I set down my mug. "I have no idea what you're talking about."

He nodded. "Good. That means it's working."

"What's working?"

"I wanted to give you enough time to figure out what you wanted to ask me before we had this conversation."

"Ask you about what?"

"About me."

The idea of having a chance to ask him all the questions I've had since the day we met when Aretha was playing that Bob Marley song was so unexpected I would have dropped my tea if I hadn't already set it down. He was giving me permission to go to the source, and he was right. I had a thousand questions! So, of course, I pretended I didn't have a single one.

"What makes you think I have any questions about you?"

"Flora and Aretha both suggested you might have a few things you wanted to clarify."

Busted. "Well, I did have one question," I said. "I was at the growers meeting yesterday."

He nodded, but his expression didn't give me any indication of whether or not he had talked to Flora yet about their request for his assistance.

"Some of the people, two women, are being harassed by some guys and when Precious Hargrove's solutions didn't satisfy them, they wanted to ask you to help."

"Flora told me."

"What kind of help are they talking about?"

"They want me to meet with the young brothers and encourage them to behave in a more sensible manner."

"Encourage them *how*?"

He put down his mug, and I thought for a sickening second I had gone too far, but his voice was calm. "Well, to really answer that question, I have to go back a ways."

"I've got time."

He looked at me steadily for a minute, as if he was trying to decide how to tell me something important. When he spoke again, his voice was quiet and hard. "Twenty years ago, I had a buddy whose sister got snatched two blocks from here. She was coming from the grocery store, and a man dragged her over by the railroad tracks and raped her and then cut her throat and left her lying there."

How many stories like that have we all heard? How fast do we learn to turn the pages of the newspaper, or put the FOR SALE sign up, or just thank the gods that it wasn't anybody we knew and loved who had met such a terrible, lonely, meaningless death?

"This cat, her brother, was on the road with me, played in my band, and this was his baby sister, so he was in a bad way when he got the news. When he came home for the funeral, I came with him. It was bad ... real bad. Then somebody told him that she wasn't the first one. Somebody had been snatching women around here for months, raping them, killing them, tossing their bodies into the Dumpster or leaving them in the street, and nobody was doing a damn thing about it."

Something in his voice made the hair on the back of my neck stand up, but I had asked him, so I had to listen.

"When we got back to the hotel, my buddy just kept drinking, and talking like you do when you're drinking, but something he said stayed in my mind. He kept asking how they could keep electing black folks to the mayor's office and putting in black police chiefs and still can't protect a woman coming home from the grocery store? 'That don't make no sense,' he kept saying. 'That don't make no damn sense.' And you know what?"

"What?"

"He was right. It didn't make sense. So I started trying to figure it out and one day I realized that the answer was obvious."

He looked at me expectantly, but it wasn't as obvious to me as it had been to him.

"And what was the answer?"

His voice was so quiet now, it was almost a whisper. "We had to get rid of the bad guys."

"The bad guys?"

He nodded.

"What bad guys?"

His eyes bored into mine. "I think you know."

Of course I knew. We all know. That's why we triple-lock our doors and run to our cars in the dark and don't walk in the parks alone and meet our daughters at the school bus. Rapists and robbers, wife beaters and woman haters, crack dealers and child abusers. *A bad guy is a bad guy is a bad guy. . . .*

"And did you?" I said. "Did you get rid of the bad guys?"

He sat back. "You tell me."

What had I noticed from the very first day? I could walk all over this neighborhood and never get nervous. The men spoke politely and always seemed to be about business. The absence of youthful predators and broken-down desperadoes was striking and wonderful. *I felt safe.*

"But how—?"

"I'm a reasonable person, so I always give a man the benefit of the doubt. If someone is acting a fool, I'll sit with him and try to figure out why."

"What if he didn't know what he was doing was wrong?"

He looked at me. "They always know."

That's why it's so scary. Did the guy who killed Blue's buddy's sister *know* what he was doing? And if he did, how could he do it anyway? And what are we supposed to do with him then?

"So what good does it do to talk to them?"

"Sometimes people need to be reminded of consequences. But I am only required to remind them once."

"And after that?"

"After that you have declared yourself on the side of chaos, and you will be treated accordingly."

On the side of chaos. That pretty well sums it up, I guess, and chaos is always bad for women and children, but I still had to know. I took a deep breath and went for it. "Have you ever killed anybody?"

He looked at me and his eyes softened a little, but his voice never did. "I'm a soldier, and we're at war."

He said it so calmly it didn't even seem strange. I knew there was a war going on between black men, but I had never heard one of them acknowledge it so directly and declare a side.

"Why doesn't that frighten me?" I said softly.

"I'm not at war with you."

"But how can you just decide to claim a part of a city and then—"

He interrupted me gently. "And then what? Make it safe for people to live in? Demand that the men act like men?"

"But is that your responsibility?"

"Absolutely."

"What gives you the right?"

He considered the question. "Well, it doesn't make much sense for me to be careful not to smoke a cigar around Lu and then send her out into the world and not make sure DooDoo and King James don't keep their distance."

All he had to do was say the names and I had an instant flash of Uncle DooDoo leering at Aretha while he draped a muscular arm possessively around his niece. Of course I wanted somebody to protect Lu from him. Of course I wanted somebody to make sure Mattie and Jerry could grow their collards in peace. Sure I liked being able to walk around after dark without looking over my shoulder and knowing there hasn't been a rape or a crack house in this neighborhood in five years. But what price was I prepared to pay for that safety? My head was spinning.

"You know what's funny about black women?" Blue asked gently.

"What's that?"

"They're the only women in the world that you have to talk into letting you protect them."

"Maybe we've just forgotten how."

"Exactly," he said. "And that's why I'm here."

"Why?"

"To help you remember."

The idea of protection is so central to everything that goes on between men and women, even when we don't admit it. Probably *especially* when we don't admit it. Blue's decision to take matters into his own hands and create a safe environment for people to live their normal, ordinary, everyday lives seemed so extraordinary in the face of the chaos we routinely accept as a community that I didn't quite know what to say. His unequivocal acceptance of the traditional male role appealed to me on a truly visceral level, but did that mean I had to become a more traditional female to balance things out?

My mind was already on overload, but I thought I understood something I hadn't before. Something personal.

"Is that why you stopped singing?"

He smiled. "I didn't stop singing. I stopped recording."

The distinction was, I'm sure, crucial to a singer the same way a writer will always separate the act of writing from the choice to publish.

"Is that why you stopped recording?"

"That's part of it."

"What's the other part?"

"The other part is a conversation for another day," he said, standing up and buttoning his coat. "I've taken up enough of your time."

"No problem," I said, walking him to the door. "But what did you come over here to tell me?"

"Whatever you wanted to know," he said, turning to face me.

The truth sounds funny sometimes when you just say it right out.

"I see."

"So how'd I do?"

I opened the door and looked right into his eyes. "So far, so good."

22

Beth was calling from Augusta. She had just registered six hundred voters and been waited upon by two black county commissioners and a committee of party regulars who were prepared to abandon their previous commitments and throw in with Beth as soon as she said the word. The fact that it was one o'clock in the morning seemed to make no difference to her at all.

My first impulse was to tell her to call me in the morning, but if I wanted to know what she was really doing, this would be the time she'd be most likely to slip and tell me. She was still high on the energy of all those women in the audience sending her their collective wave of love. This was that euphoric after-the-show moment when the ego, which cares nothing for pretense, is still in control.

"So what did you tell them?"

"I told them if they were really serious, they should send a delegation to Atlanta to see me where we could speak in a more relaxed atmosphere."

That meant she intended to invite them to her house so that she could be positioned under her portrait like a queen receiving her subjects.

"I'm sure they'll make a persuasive presentation," I said, determined to stay out of it. Beth had never paid the kind of dues Precious was paying at that growers meeting. People came to see Beth for inspiration. They came to see Precious for solutions to real-life problems.

"You should be at that meeting, don't you think?"

The idea could not have been further from my mind or of less interest. "It hadn't occurred to me."

There was a pause, and then Beth's voice reproached me. "We

talked about this, Gina. Unless you've reconsidered our agreement and you'd rather not do the speechwriting segment at all."

Suddenly I understood why Beth had wanted to break the project up into three discrete chunks. She knew exactly how much I needed to pay off the weasel, and she had offered it to me, to the penny, in three payments. If I abdicated on one-third of the work, she had a right to abdicate on one-third of the money, and if she did, how was I going to replace ten thousand dollars?

Beth had me between a rock and a hard place, and she knew it. The thing was, I couldn't even get mad. This was part of what I earned with my own bad behavior. This was just another way for the universe to reinforce all those rehab lessons about what it means to be a grown-up. Being indignant was beside the point.

"Of course not," I said calmly. "But these kinds of early sessions are rarely any help to a speechwriter. You haven't even made your final decision yet, have you?"

There was just enough air before she responded to let me know that the question was moot. She actually was going to throw her hat in the ring for governor. It was clearly a bad idea whose time had come.

"You'll be among the first to know," she said.

I had to smile. That was so like Beth. Not the first to know. But *among* the first.

"So how is everything coming along there?" she asked.

"Fine, except they've asked Precious Hargrove to be on the dedication committee, and she accepted."

Beth groaned. "How could you let that happen?"

"They didn't consult me. I don't think they were aware of a possible conflict of interest."

"This could be very awkward," Beth said, sounding annoyed.

"Very," I said.

"Have they printed up programs or invitations or anything yet?"

"No," I said. "Nothing's going to the printer until next week."

"Are you proofing everything first?"

"Of course."

"Good. That buys us some time."

"Some time for what?"

"To figure out how to get her off the list."

"She's one of the cochairs, Beth."

"Let me worry about that," she said quickly, moving on. "What about the papers? Are you making good progress there?"

"It's going very well," I said. "I've got about half the stuff pulled that I'll need for the video, so there won't be any problem there."

"You haven't come across any of the kind of material we discussed, have you?"

I hesitated, then lied, even though lying is another one of the things I'm working on. "No."

Of course, Beth heard the hesitation. "Are you sure?"

"I'm sure."

She let it slide, but I knew she didn't believe me. Too bad. I wasn't ready to surrender Son's private life to Beth's disapproving stare just yet.

"Good enough," Beth said, yawning loudly. "What time is it? Good lord, Gina! Why didn't you tell me? Did I wake you?"

"No problem," I said. "When will you be back here?"

"Tuesday. I'll call you when I get in. And Gina?"

"Yes?"

"It's good to have you back on the team."

23

I HAVE A LOVE/HATE RELATIONSHIP with malls, but I needed a dress for the party tonight, and Lenox Square offers a dizzying array of stores to choose from. Of course, many of the stores are aimed at the market segment that can still expose their midriffs without causing passersby to avert their eyes, but there are still lots of choices for people like me who aren't twenty-five anymore, but who aren't fifty yet either. That's one of the things I like.

The other thing I love about Lenox in a completely perverse way is the totally unapologetic excess. It's full of beautiful, totally unnecessary *stuff*. Even the food tends toward Starbucks coffee confections and the decadence of gold-boxed Godiva chocolates. The mall environment is meant to do one thing and one thing only: *make you spend your money.*

Everything here is in service of the shopping. The restaurants are either fast-food places where you can wolf down your lunch and get back to the business at hand or more leisurely establishments facing the mall where you can see people ducking into shops and emerging with bags. Faced with such temptation, you rush through the meal in order to be sure to catch the sale on more stuff you don't need.

Most of the time, I feel too guilty to enjoy the mall. My mother ruined it for me. She never went to the malls voluntarily and when I dragged her—only until I was old enough to drive myself!—she would ruin the whole trip by muttering continuously about the evils of American capitalism. When she went with me to buy a prom dress, she lectured me the whole time about consumer culture and how many poor people could use the money I was prepared to spend on whatever pastel creation I had set my heart on for prom night.

After I learned to drive, I'd go by myself, but my mother's voice stayed in my head, so I never could really relax the way guilt-free shoppers can. The personal being political takes a lot of the fun out of stuff if you're not careful. That's why Flora could spend only two hours in search of an outfit for the party. After that, she'd start feeling guilty and the fun was over.

But today, I was on a mission. I'd given myself until noon to find a dress that makes me feel the way I looked in my imagining of the party. When Aretha said the party attire was "after five," I knew I'd have to buy something. I can't even remember the last time I got dressed up to go out. "After five" seemed like a dress code from my parents' generation, but maybe that's why it appealed to me. "After five" had a sophisticated sound like "supper club" or "cocktails."

The dress I had in mind would match that nod to another generation's undeniable cool. It would have to have class and sass and be sexy enough to let my landlord know I was open to a friendship as long as it didn't include a celibacy requirement. I knew this was going to be a special night, and I needed a special dress. I also needed to wash my hair, get a manicure and a pedicure, and find shoes I could dance in, but one thing at a time. Once I had found the dress, everything else would fall into place.

But it was already eleven-fifteen. I'd been here since ten and *nothing*. I'd tried on a couple of things, but everything looked too young or too old or too fast or too slow or just not *special*. I took a break for a cup of overpriced coffee and watched people coming down the escalator, bags of perfect purchases slung over their arms, chatting and comparing notes. They had all found what they wanted and here I sat, sipping and sulking, when I remembered there was another option.

Aretha had guaranteed Flora that the dress of her dreams could be found in Little Five Points, a funky in-town neighborhood bravely resisting gentrification, and she was as good as her word. Flora's dress was a one-shouldered tangerine sheath that made her look amazing, and she had found it, tried it on, and paid for it all within forty-five minutes. Maybe my dress shared my mother's low opinion of the malls and wouldn't be caught dead in a store where Ashanti and J-Lo play on the in-store music system.

I left the mall, found a cab, and fifteen minutes later got out in front of Stefan's, a vintage clothing store whose window was already displaying my dress, an ice-blue satin number that hit midcalf and boasted a cinched waist and lightly padded shoulders. I loved it, and more important, I could see myself *working it*. I went inside, tried it on—it fit!—and told the smiling salesman to wrap it up. I headed out the door in less than half an hour.

I even had enough money left in my budget for an evening jacket. Of course, that was an extravagance, but it completed the outfit perfectly, and I figured if Blue Hamilton was going to send a limo for me, the least I could do is dress the part.

24

THE LIMO ARRIVED AT EIGHT on the nose, and Flora and I strolled out like we were used to traveling this way. Aretha wasn't coming over until later, so she stood in the blue doorway with Lu and ShaRonda, waving and issuing last-minute instructions on fashion and comportment.

"Don't forget to check your seams every once in a while." That from Aretha, who had talked me into a pair of stockings with seams to set off my forties-style dress.

"I won't."

"Don't forget to talk about something besides collard greens and compost."

That from Lu, who was concerned about her mother's ability to make appropriate chitchat without her dad's guidance.

"I won't."

ShaRonda, giggling and waving in jeans and an oversize T-shirt, looked eleven years old again. She didn't seem to have any advice, contenting herself with offering makeup suggestions that could all be summed up in one word: *more*. By the time we settled into the back of the black stretch that Blue had sent to fetch us, we had enough advice to last us.

Flora looked over at me as we pulled away from the curb, and we both burst out laughing. "You'd think we'd never gone to a party in our lives."

"Well, it's been a while for me," I said, "but I think it's like riding a bike."

"Or sex!" she whispered, although this car was so big, the driver's seat looked about a block away behind a glass partition.

Flora leaned forward and opened the small refrigerator where a bottle of that French champagne with the flowers on it was already chilling. "I knew Blue wouldn't forget about us," she said, draping a white linen napkin over the cork and twisting it out easily as I took two glasses from the tiny rack beside the fridge.

"Remember when we had to pretend we couldn't open champagne bottles without assistance?"

"When was that?"

"Before the women's movement." She laughed and poured us each a glass of the bubbling, golden liquid. "In the bad old days."

That made me smile. My mother was forever reminding me of the changes feminism had made in every corner of American women's lives. Whenever she would read one of those articles where some young, highly successful women say they're not feminists, it would make her crazy: "Who do they think made it possible for them to be sitting there behind that big desk, in that big job, acting like they got there by being smarter than every other woman in the world? They ought to read their history and bring their mamas breakfast in bed for a week just to say thank you!"

We raised our glasses.

"What shall we toast?" I said.

"Us," she said grinning. "Let's toast us in our brand-new dresses!"

We clinked our glasses and sipped our champagne as the limo glided through the dark streets bearing us toward the party. Club Zebra was located on the site of a legendary Afro-Atlanta institution, the Lincoln Country Club. In its pre-integration heyday, it boasted several hundred dues-paying members, a nine-hole golf course, and a clubhouse where they hosted parties that were always the hottest ticket in town.

When integration came, the membership dwindled, and, by the time the former members realized how much they missed it, it was closed. It stayed closed for about thirty years, and then ten years ago, some new people bought the land, redeveloped it, resodded the golf course, and opened a nightclub. Aretha had told me the history of the place and compared it to Harlem's famed Cotton Club, and Flora agreed.

"Here we are!" she said excitedly as the limo turned up a winding driveway with small lights leading the way.

The narrow road wound its way through a dense stand of Georgia's famous pine trees and opened out onto a scene right out of *The Great Gatsby*. Beautifully dressed women and tuxedo-clad men were alighting from cars polished high for the occasion. Even the old cars, of which there were many, *gleamed*. The pine trees ended at a rolling lawn and beyond the main building, ablaze with lights, you could see the dim contours of the golf course.

Valet parkers, young black men in blue uniforms, were busily keeping the traffic moving. Our driver pulled around the arriving crowd and eased in near a side entrance. As soon as we pulled up, the door opened and Blue stepped out wearing a beautiful tux and a smile of welcome. Immediately behind him were two other guys, also in tuxedos. One I recognized as the big man who led me to Blue's office the first day I went to the West End News. The other one, whom I didn't recognize, was wearing two-tone shoes and dreadlocks that hung below his waist.

The big man stepped up to open the door, and Blue leaned down to offer a hand.

"Ladies . . ."

"That would be us," said Flora, easing out daintily, kissing his cheek, and turning to embrace the guy in the two-tones. "Zeke! How much hair are you going to grow?"

Zeke laughed and embraced her as Blue extended his hand again to me. I took it and stepped out with the confidence you feel only when you look like yourself, *but better*. The dress hugged me in all the right places, but it suggested more than it gave away. I wondered briefly if my seams were straight, but it didn't matter. He wasn't looking at my stockings. He was looking at *me*.

"I'm glad you came," he said, taking in my outfit in one appreciative glance. "You look beautiful."

"So do you," I said.

He laughed, but beautiful was the word. He was beautiful like a piece of artwork or a reflection in a mountain lake. That kind of beauty isn't gender specific. It just *is*.

"This place is amazing," I said. "Is it real?"

"Meet the owner. You can ask him."

He put his arm around my waist lightly, and we stepped inside and into a small private sitting room that seemed a world away from the people gathering upstairs. The big guy whisked our coats away to some unseen closet, and the four of us stood there grinning at one another.

"Regina Burns, Zeke Burnett," Blue said. "The lady wants to know if your place is real."

Zeke shook my hand and smiled. "I'll take that as a compliment."

"Don't tell him how wonderful it is," Flora groaned. "Next thing you know, he'll move it all to Buckhead."

The city's thriving nightclub district was located north of downtown in an all-white neighborhood of million-dollar homes and pricey condos. The people there were still adjusting to the impact of the multiracial clubgoers who invade their neighborhood every weekend.

"Buckhead? Not a chance," Zeke said, shaking his dreadlocked head.

"And why is that?" Flora teased. "Because you *love* black folks too much?"

"Loving black folks ain't in it," he said. "They got too much crime out there!"

We all laughed, and I wondered what the Chamber of Commerce would think about a black businessman in all-black southwest Atlanta being nervous about crime in an all-white neighborhood that used to boast about its safe streets. I had that feeling again that I had fallen through the rabbit hole and come out in a world where everything was reversed. In this world, we stood in the safe oasis and clucked over the presence of crime somewhere *out there*.

"Welcome to Club Zebra," Zeke said. "I'm going to see if I can find a glass of champagne for my favorite gardener here." Flora slipped her arm through his. "May I leave you in the care of this Negro?"

I looked at Blue. "Can you vouch for him?"

"With my life," said Zeke.

"Mine, too," Flora added her two cents, still grinning.

"You can't ask for better references than that," I said. "I think I'll be fine."

Flora and Zeke exchanged a look like old friends who've been *signifyin' in sync* for years and closed the door behind them.

The silence in the small room was so sudden and complete that I heard music from upstairs for the first time. I recognized an old song whose tune was familiar but whose words I didn't know. Blue was watching me like whatever I did or said next would determine his next move. The fact that he was hosting a party upstairs seemed the furthest thing from his mind. I liked that.

These days, we have to compete with so much to get even a second of a man's undivided attention. From video games, to the NBA finals, to his work, to his boys, black men stay so busy you can't hardly get a bead on what they're feeling because they won't slow down long enough to show you. It was a real pleasure not to feel like half of Blue's mind was occupied elsewhere.

"I love this song," I said.

"Would you like to dance?"

"Here?"

He smiled slowly. "Don't worry. I know the owner."

I bought these shoes for dancing, so what was I waiting for? I moved into his arms and felt the closeness of our bodies like an electrical charge between us. He held me lightly, and we fell easily into a slow dance that felt like we'd danced it a thousand times before. I closed my eyes. We moved around the room a little, swaying together, but not too close. He seemed to share my belief that anticipation is still one of the most powerful *no-side-effect* aphrodisiacs around.

People underestimate the necessity for courtship rituals. I know we're both grown and there are no quivering virgins and fumbling first-timers in this room. But the things that moved us then, move us now. Maybe more, because now we understand that nothing is guaranteed. Maybe more, because by now we've all kissed somebody goodbye and not realized it was the last time until they were gone and it was too late to say all the stuff you didn't say. By now we know that everybody doesn't get to fall in love and live happily ever after.

It makes us skittish, knowing all this stuff and recognizing the transitory nature of things, which is why a soothing slow dance with the promise of more to come based on mutual comfort and consent is the perfect way to begin. He held me a little tighter, and I realized we were actually dancing cheek to cheek. It felt wonderful, like a movie scene, and my dress was perfect.

The song ended, and we stepped apart slowly. I felt like if we didn't go join the party before another song started, we never would. I guess Blue felt it, too, because he smiled and took my hand.

"Would you like to come upstairs and meet some of my friends?"

"I would love to." I slipped my arm through his. "What was the name of that song we were dancing to?"

" 'The Very Thought of You,' " he said. "It's one of my favorites."

"Mine, too."

"Maybe I'll sing it for you sometimes."

"How about tonight?" I asked, feeling bold.

"All right," he smiled. "You got it."

25

IT WAS LIKE STEPPING BACK IN TIME. An all-girl band was playing grown-folks music on a small bandstand. The vocalist, who
couldn't have been a day over twenty-two, was singing the Billie Holi-
day classic "Miss Brown to You" like somebody had written it just for
her. Their director, a sixtyish hipster with a kente kufi and a dark
suit wielded his baton like a proud paterfamilias. Aretha had told me
Club Zebra often showcased the talents of Spelman College music
students, and I took these very serious players in dark evening gowns
to be those young women.

Couples were seated at tables around the spacious dance floor
while white-jacketed waiters brought champagne without being asked.
The men, young and old, were all in dark suits or tuxes, and my outfit fit right in among the women's satin evening suits and silky "after
fives." People were still arriving in a steady stream, laughing and waving to their friends. All shades of the rainbow were well represented
under that big African American umbrella. From eighteen to eighty, all
gathering in one spot to enjoy themselves and one another. These
folks looked *good*, and they knew it.

Zeke was standing at the door greeting everybody by name so they
wouldn't forget this was still their neighborhood bar, except tonight
they had chosen to dress it, and themselves, up for the occasion. I stood
beside Blue for a minute and just took it all in. Flora materialized at my
elbow as Precious Hargrove arrived at the front door.

Blue turned toward me. "I've got to go greet the senator. I'll see
you later?"

"What about me?" Flora asked.

"You, too." Blue laughed and left us to resume his hosting duties.

I watched him moving through the crowd, greeting people, smiling, shaking hands, and remembered how it had felt dancing cheek to cheek.

"So what do you think so far?" Flora said, grinning at me.

"It's wonderful."

I was watching Blue greet Precious Hargrove and a tall, handsome young man with a fresh haircut and a suit that looked more Hugo Boss than hip-hop. Precious had on a bright red satin skirt and an ethnic-flavored embroidered jacket that flattered her roundness without emphasizing it inappropriately. She's running for governor, after all. She can't be too *foxy*.

Blue and the young man were laughing together, and Precious wore her motherly pride like a diamond brooch.

"Is that her son?" I asked Flora.

"Kwame," Flora said. "Smart, good-looking, and loves his mother. Precious did a good job with him."

"Where's his father?"

Flora shrugged. "Died when he was a kid. Want to grab a table?"

"Sure."

We were headed for some empty seats when a small tan man in a white dinner jacket intercepted us with a courtly bow.

"Ladies!"

"Peachy!" Flora said, giving him an enthusiastic hug.

When she stepped back, he looked at her, gave a low whistle, and turned to me. "Last time I saw this woman she was wearing hip boots and driving a pickup truck."

Flora laughed. "But I clean up nice, right?"

"You clean up very nice. I'm surprised that Hank let you out looking so fine."

"Stop flirting," she said, "and meet my friend Regina Burns. Gina, this is Lester Nolan. He's responsible for this gathering in the first place."

"Call me Peachy," he said, with another small bow. "Nobody calls me Lester unless they want to sell me something."

He was a very small man, with a full head of carefully brushed white hair, who looked to be in his early fifties. He was wearing the hell out of that dinner jacket, and he knew it.

"Peachy," I said as requested. "So nice to meet you."

"The pleasure is all mine. Where is your husband anyway?"

A small cloud passed over Flora's face, but she smiled brightly. "He's in Detroit fighting off the bad guys."

"Well, if bad guys are what you're looking for, Detroit's the place to be."

One of Flora's gardeners was waving her over from across the room, and she excused herself quickly to avoid more talk of Hank and left me alone with Peachy. That seemed to be fine with him. He turned to me and spoke as if we were the only two people in the room.

"You know why they call me Peachy?"

I knew he was going to tell me. "No, why?"

"Well, I grew up in a little town called Dublin, Georgia, on a plantation where all they grew was peaches. We had to pick peaches. We had to pack peaches. We had to can peaches. We had to make peach cobbler, spiced peaches, and peach pie. My father even made peach wine. Would you like to sit down?"

"Thanks."

The band had taken a short break, and I followed him to a table near the stage that had a small "reserved" card on it. A waiter appeared immediately and set down two glasses and a bottle of champagne in a silver ice bucket. Peachy nodded at the waiter to open it and continued his story.

"By the time I left Dublin, I was sick of peaches. The smell of them made me sick. The sight of them wasn't much better. So I decided to move to the big city and make my way as a musician."

The waiter poured us each a glass of champagne, left the bottle in the bucket, and disappeared. Peachy ignored it.

"So I saved up my money from pickin' and packin' all those damn peaches and I dreamed about coming to Atlanta. I prayed about coming to Atlanta, and I asked God to deliver me from those peaches. I told him if he could do me that one favor, I would never have anything to do with any kind of peaches for the rest of my days."

He was smiling broadly at his own tale since he had the advantage of knowing the punch line. I wondered what kind of musician he was, but he wasn't the kind of storyteller who left air for questions, so I just smiled back. You can't really drink champagne unless you toast first, so I ignored mine, too.

"One day, I figured, no time like the present, walked out to the freeway, and hitched a ride headed for the big city. The guy who picked me up was a horn player who had a buddy who was trying to put together a band. So I told him I could play guitar from hanging around the juke joints, and he took me to the audition with him. That's where I met *him* for the first time."

I was getting confused. "Met who?"

He raised his glass. "Our host, Mr. Blue Hamilton."

He tapped my glass lightly in what I guessed was a toast to Blue, but the story didn't stop there.

"So I played for him on somebody else's guitar, and he hired me on the spot. He sent everybody else home except me and my buddy, and we just started working on some arrangements immediately. Blue liked the old songs and I did, too, so we hit it off right away. When it was time to split, I told him we had just got into town and asked him which way was the YMCA."

The memory made him chuckle, and he took another small sip of his champagne.

"He said, 'aw, nigga, you ain't gotta be stayin' at the Y. Good as you play, you can come stay with me 'til you find a place.' So I said 'Cool,' and promised not to wear out my welcome. He said not to worry about it, and everything was everything until we pulled up in front of his apartment and the sign said 'Peachtree Street'!"

He rolled his eyes in such comic distress that I giggled.

"So I had to tell him thanks, but no thanks. I'd go on to the Y until I could find a place."

"Because of the street name?"

"That's just what Blue said that night, but I told him like I'm telling you, a deal's a deal. No more peaches. No way, no how!"

"So what did you do?"

I spotted Blue over Peachy's shoulder scanning the room, and I knew he was looking for me. I resisted the impulse to wave.

"I carried my no-peaches ass to the YMCA and slept on a lumpy mattress for three dollars and fifty cents a night until I could pay for a place."

Blue walked up in time for the punch line.

"Because I had *integrity*."

"Is this Negro bending your ear with the story of his life?"

I smiled up at him. "He was telling me how he got his nickname."

"I gave it to him."

"He didn't tell me that."

Blue grinned at his friend. "I figured if peaches were the driving force in his life to the extent that he'd live at the Y for a month—"

"It wasn't a month!"

"—that ought to be his name just to remind me that even though he's my ace, when it comes to peaches, his judgment is just a little left of center."

"A deal's a deal," Peachy said. "The man upstairs knows why I did it."

Aretha appeared in the doorway wearing a flowing pair of pale purple evening pajamas with a tight mandarin collar that set off her lovely neck to perfection. Long silver earrings swung in her ears while she chatted with Kwame Hargrove, whose mother was probably circulating and shaking hands. They were both smiling as they headed for a corner table. I thought about Lu's teasing: *Aretha and Kwame, sittin' in a tree, k-i-s-s-i-n-g.*

"You doing all right?" Blue said, taking a seat at our table and squeezing my hand.

"I'm fine," I said, taking another small sip of champagne. The line between social drinking and silly drinking is too easy to blur if you aren't paying attention.

The band was returning to the stage, and the tables were filling up with couples and foursomes who were chatting, laughing, greeting old friends. Behind us a young couple waved at their friends on the bandstand, who acknowledged them with an unflappable cool that identified them as jazz musicians even more clearly than their ability to play their instruments.

Peachy chuckled. "These young sisters are something else, aren't they?"

I nodded, glad Blue was still holding my hand. Our table was right at the edge of the tiny stage and as I watched the women launch into the version of "My Favorite Things" that my less gifted neighbor has been trying for, I wished my mother could have seen them. Sure, it would have touched off a long discourse about what her generation sacrificed to get us this far down the road, but looking at these girls at their keyboards and drum sets, I figure she had some braggin' rights coming.

Zeke escorted Precious Hargrove through the crowded room, deposited her at a table near the other side of the stage, and headed straight for Blue, who squeezed my hand again and stood up.

"We're going to make a few presentations," he said. "You've got the best seat in the house."

"Show time," said Peachy, polishing off his champagne and winking at me as he stood up and straightened his dinner jacket. "How do I look?"

"Fabulous!" I said, and he did.

"Gentlemen?" Zeke appeared at the table. "The hour is upon us. I'll welcome everybody and call this Negro up." He inclined his head toward Peachy, and his dreadlocks shifted and swung the way they might have in a Jamaican breeze. "He can present the check to the senator, and then Blue can give us a few words of wisdom."

"A very few," Peachy said.

"Well, Brother Blue is always a man of few words, so I don't think there's any problem there."

Zeke waited for the girls to finish their number and took to the stage as the audience applauded warmly. Peachy and Blue stood near the steps, waiting for their cue.

"Thank you to the Club Zebra House Band," Zeke said, and the girls grinned at one another, fully aware that their college would probably be surprised at the name he had given their collective alter ego. "And welcome. This is a special night and one we look forward to every year."

The audience, which now included people standing at the rear of the room and in the doorway, applauded again. Flora threaded her way between the tables and sat down next to me, still clapping.

"I didn't mean to abandon you," she whispered. "Peachy didn't need to remind me that Hank wasn't around tonight."

"No problem," I whispered back. "Do you know why they call him Peachy?"

She rolled her eyes. "Peach pie, peach cobbler, peach wine . . ."

We giggled, and I saw Blue glance in our direction and grin. I grinned back.

"We want to give a special thanks to the ladies who worked so hard on this year's committee," Zeke was saying from the stage. "And when I say *ladies*, I mean real ladies—the members of the Sensuous Ladies Social Club. Miss Green, are you here?"

A pretty brown-skinned woman in a tight green dress that celebrated her curves instead of trying to camouflage them waved from another table and blew him a kiss. "Thank you, baby!"

"Watch out, now! You know my wife doesn't like anybody calling me *baby* but her!" Zeke said as the crowd laughed. "I could introduce some more of y'all, but if I start that, we'll be here all night, so let's get to the most important reason for this gathering, which is to give away your money."

More laughter. "You the best at that!" a voice shouted from the rear of the room.

Zeke laughed, too. "About to get better, so get out your checkbooks and give a big Club Zebra welcome to the man who started it all. Peachy Nolan, come on up here and relieve these well-dressed folks of their cash."

Zeke surrendered the mike to Peachy and left the stage as people rose to their feet in a heartfelt greeting. Peachy, clearly pleased, waved them back into their seats.

"All right, all right," he said, "what do the young people say? I'm *feelin' you*, but we got business."

I saw Zeke go over to Precious Hargrove's table and escort her to the steps on the other side of the stage.

"When me and Blue started hosting this party fifteen years go, it was just something we did at his house or my house to honor the memory of my baby sister, Miss Janet Cassandra Nolan, and raise some money for anybody who was trying to do something good around here. We started with a couple hundred bucks for the soup kitchen over on Lee Street. Then we bought some band instruments for Washington High School and some athletic equipment for the program at the Boys and Girls Club."

I hadn't realized until that moment that it was Peachy's sister's murder that had changed the course of Blue's life. The party was only a symbol of what was a much greater offering from one friend to another.

"And as y'all started makin' more money, we were able to do more and we gonna keep doin' more because if we don't, *who the hell will?*"

More applause.

"Talk to 'em, Peachy!" Miss Green called. "Talk to 'em!"

Peachy waited for quiet before continuing. "So this year, we're doing something different. We're going to give some money to a political candidate, something we've never done before, but that's because we never had a candidate like this one before."

There was a smattering of applause as people began to realize who he was talking about. Standing next to Zeke, waiting for her cue, I saw Precious smile her acknowledgment. Sitting beside Kwame, Aretha clapped enthusiastically.

Peachy motioned for quiet. "Now I could take an hour or so of your time and tell you what this sister has done for the people of her district, including this neighborhood right here, but we ain't got that kind of time, so I'm just going to say her name reflects how we feel about her, and we are more than happy to give this contribution to support her efforts to make history. Ladies and gents, and the rest of y'all who snuck in the side door, put your hands together for state senator Precious Hargrove, the next governor of Georgia!"

The room erupted into sustained applause, accompanied by whistling, whooping, and the general mayhem that accompanies the presentation of popular politicos to the people whose dreams they carry. Zeke walked Precious to the mike where Peachy was waiting.

"It is an honor to present you with checks totaling ten thousand dollars to support your candidacy."

The applause was now full of pride not only for Precious, but for their own impressive fund-raising efforts. I looked at Blue, standing alone, watching the presentation with a small smile of satisfaction.

Precious accepted the checks and a hug from Peachy, and stepped up to the mike. "I am honored to accept this contribution from my good friend Peachy Nolan on behalf of so many of you. It is my intention to use these funds to help me run the best-organized, most participatory campaign this state has ever seen. It is time for our voices to be heard, and believe me, when I am elected governor, they will be heard!"

Applause, applause.

"I'm not going to make a speech, since that would be a true example of preaching to the choir, and because Peachy told me not to!"

Laughter. Peachy loved it, wagging a finger in her direction like a disapproving teacher.

"So I'll just say thanks and you can rest assured, I will never, ever let you down."

It was probably the shortest speech I've ever heard from a campaigning politician, but she read the crowd exactly right. They were already supporting her. A speech they didn't need. Applause followed her back to her table as Peachy reclaimed the microphone.

"Sock it to 'em, Senator!" Peachy said. "Sock it to 'em!" He glanced in Blue's direction as if to be sure his friend hadn't eased back into the crowd. "And now I'd like to bring to the stage the man who makes it all happen around here. The man who took it upon himself to reclaim this neighborhood for hardworking people trying to raise their children in peace. The man who gave up the bright lights and the big cash to come on home and be a part of this community. The man who isn't afraid to do what has to be done, *whatever it is*." He grinned at the audience. "And did I say he can sing his ass off?"

"You got that right!" a woman shouted.

"But I'm wasting your time telling you what you already know, so let's bring him on up here. The man I'm proud to call my friend and my brother. Mr. Blue Hamilton."

The audience literally went wild. Peachy came back to sit beside me and left Blue alone on the stage. He said something to the band-leader, who nodded and took up his position in front of the girls who were watching him expectantly.

"Sing, Blue!" another woman's excited voice called out.

More wild applause greeting the suggestion. Blue waited for silence and then spoke so quietly we all leaned forward so we wouldn't miss anything he said.

"It was my intention to come up here and thank you for your support and for your money, and sit down."

Immediate groans of disappointment, but he had said it *was* his intention. Was there still a chance that he might sing?

"But a friend of mine has a song she wants to hear, so I thought if I can get the band to help me out," he nodded at the director, who raised his eyebrows and hit a downbeat that the girls responded to perfectly, "and if you all don't mind—"

He looked around as if to entertain any objections.

"*Sing, Blue!*" the woman cried out again.

Blue laughed and pointed a slender finger in my direction. "All right then, this one's for Gina."

I blushed, realizing that people were craning their necks to see who I was and why their hero would be dedicating a song to me. Flora was grinning and hunching me like we were in high school, but I tried to be cool.

"You go, girl!" somebody yelled, giving me a shout of encouragement that was immediately shushed as Blue stepped up to the mike
and began to sing.

"The very thought of you, and I forget to do, the little ordinary
things that everyone ought to do."

You could have heard a pin drop. He had a wonderful voice, a
smooth, smoky baritone as rich as dark chocolate and filled with the
sound of a life fully lived. He rolled the words around in his mouth
like candy, and the young women on the stage were watching him
with as much admiration as the audience. He was looking straight at
me, and I couldn't look away.

"I'm living in a kind of daydream," he sang. "I'm happy as a
king."

But it wasn't the words. It was the *feeling* he was sending through
the words. Whatever the words said, he was offering them like a gift,
an apology to every woman in the room for every time somebody
had broken her heart or not been the man she hoped he could be.
Something in his voice was apologizing for all the betrayals from the
moment the slave ships pulled up on the shores of West Africa until
now. He was confessing to every crime, real and imagined, that black
men have ever committed against black women, and, more than that,
he was trying to make it right.

What he was doing with his voice had nothing to do with the
lyrics of the song I had requested. What he was singing was *an ancient song* and one we all recognized so clearly that, when he reached
out a hand, we had to reach back, the way you have to stand up at
the stadium when the wave rolls over you, no matter how much you
thought you wouldn't.

By the end of the second verse, I had fallen so deep into what I
heard in his voice and saw in his eyes that I couldn't have climbed out
if I wanted to, which I didn't. I didn't know if this was a gangster
movie or a revolutionary romance or a sci-fi thriller where the hero
has X-ray eyes or a corny old-school musical where the heroine ar-
rives on the scene wounded, but on a mission, and the hero sweeps
her off her feet with new definitions of manhood and then takes her

to an old-fashioned speakeasy in the middle of an unexpected urban oasis where people still laugh together and talk together and your landlord may also be able to stand on the stage and make magic.

It felt like a fairy tale, and, if it was, then this would be the moment where I stop trying to figure out *why* and start wondering *when*. This is the moment where I don't try to reason it out. I just try to lean in. The moment when I realize that maybe I'm falling in love. Maybe for the first time. Maybe for the last one. But it feels just the way I thought it would, hoped it would, prayed it would, and if this were a movie, this would be the moment where everything around the lovers fades away and they recognize in each other the promise of something sweet, and then even sweeter. If this were a movie, this would be the moment where the heroine considers the possibility of a happy ending and the hero just keeps singing his blue-eyed ass off like he couldn't stop if he wanted to. . . .

But it wasn't a movie, and the song finally came to an end. There was a moment of absolute silence as the last notes faded away, and then the crowd erupted into delighted applause. The youthful band members looked at one another in amazement, having experienced their first taste of the magical possibilities of the life they'd chosen, and there I was, applauding as loud as anybody, grinning at Blue, and resisting the impulse to toss my brand-new silk undies on the stage like those long-ago Royal Peacock audiences. After all, it ain't that kind of movie.

26

THE NEXT TWO HOURS WENT BY in a blur. Aretha came over to introduce me to Kwame, who was so clearly smitten that he could hardly take his eyes off of her long enough to say hello. Flora introduced me to a steady stream of her gardeners and neighborhood folks. Peachy made sure I met all the old-timers, and Precious Hargrove found time to come over to say hello, but I could hardly hear a word they said. I just kept thinking about Aunt Abbie's vision. *He will sing an ancient song.* Add that to those big blue eyes, and you've got two out of three. That's all my brain kept saying: *Two out of three. Two out of three.*

After a while, Flora looked at me strangely. "You okay?"

I nodded and tried to play it off. "I never heard anybody sing like that before."

"And you never will," she said. "It's like there's something in his voice that says everything you want a man to say and mean it."

"Exactly!" I said. "How can he do that?"

Flora shrugged. "I don't know, but women always respond to it the same way. We go crazy!" She laughed. "I don't know what I'd do if he ever sang right to me the way he did you tonight. We've been friends for fifteen years, but I might not be able to trust myself!"

"I'm not feeling all that trustworthy either," I said, and I wasn't kidding.

"Don't worry," she said, waving and moving in the direction of yet another gardener. "I'll make sure you get home okay."

"And then what?"

"Then you're on your own!" She laughed over her shoulder.

Across the room, I saw Blue in a circle of admiring women, all smiling and touching his arm, his hand, his shoulder. They were still in the warm glow of that ancient song just like I was, but they were free to enjoy it without hearing another voice inside their heads that seems only to know the words: *Two out of three. Two out of three.*

Blue looked up from the swirl of his admirers, caught my eye, and held it; there was something so familiar about that look that I couldn't help but smile. He smiled back, inclined his head slightly in my direction, and turned back to a woman at his elbow who wanted an autograph, another at his side who wanted to take a picture. And what did I want, watching him from across the room? *I wanted some answers.* Visions are fine, and two out of three ain't bad, but if you're going to change your whole life, a perfect score would be nice.

27

FLORA WAS AS GOOD AS HER WORD. At two A.M., Blue walked us to the same limo that brought us, and I wished for nerve enough to invite him to stop by for a drink after he had bid farewell to the last of the night owls, but all I could manage was a thank-you for a lovely evening. I needed some advice. Some clarification. Some guidance, but Flora was already grinning at me like she knew a secret I hadn't walked up on yet, so I wasn't able to enlist her help to sort things out. I needed an objective voice. Someone older and wiser. I needed to talk to my visionary adviser.

I hugged Flora good night at her door and hurried upstairs to kick off my shoes and dial the one person who would understand what the hell I was talking about and not think I was totally crazy.

"Aunt Abbie? Did I wake you?"

"When's the last time you knew me to be up at two in the morning? What's wrong?"

"Nothing's wrong. I'm sorry. I should have waited until—"

She interrupted me impatiently. "Then what's right?"

"Nothing. I mean, everything is fine."

"Listen, girl, I know you didn't wake me out of a sound sleep to tell me nothing's wrong and nothing's right. That news could have waited until a decent hour to be conveyed."

I took a deep breath. "He can sing."

"Who can sing?"

"My landlord, the one with the blue eyes? He can really sing."

I could hear her chuckling. "Is this the moment when I get to say 'I told you so'?"

"This is the moment when you get to tell me what I'm supposed to do now."

"Keep doin' what you're doin'."

"But what if he really is . . ."

"Is what?"

"I don't know! The *one*! The one you said was looking for me across time and stuff."

"Seems pretty obvious to me. Two out of three is almost a done deal."

I could hear her yawning. Here I was trying to get some advice about the rest of my life, and she was only half awake.

"I'm sorry if I'm boring you," I said, trying to be sarcastic.

"Oh, don't get snippy," she said calmly. "You're working yourself up for no reason."

"This kind of stuff doesn't happen! Not in real life!"

"Then go to bed and don't worry about it."

"But what if it *is* happening?" I was whining like a four-year-old.

"Then you are a very lucky woman who will have wonderful tales to tell your grandchildren." She yawned again.

"You're a big help."

"I'm sorry, sweetie, but I had the vision, didn't I? What do you want from me?"

She was right. Everything was happening just the way she said it would, and here I was waking her up to fuss. I took another deep breath.

"You're right," I said. "It's just kind of scary, you know?"

"Have you told him about the vision yet?"

"God, no!" I said, wondering how you tell a person your crazy aunt said he was your man in a past life.

"Maybe you should."

"Why?"

"You're not going to be able to figure out what he is until you know for sure what he isn't."

"What does *that* mean?"

"Who knows? You'll have to figure it out. Good night, sweetie!"

She hung up without waiting for me to respond. I clicked off the phone more frustrated than I was before, and walked over to the window just in time to see Blue's Lincoln pull up out front. I hadn't turned on the light, so I didn't think he'd see me standing there, but he got out, turned his face up, and raised his hand in greeting like I was standing in a spotlight. Two out of three might be enough for Aunt Abbie, but it wasn't good enough for me. Blue Hamilton had some explaining to do, and there was no time like the present.

I waited for him at the top of the stairs, and he greeted me with a smile of real pleasure.

"I must be living right," he said.

"How's that?" I smiled back at him.

He stopped two steps shy of the landing, so I was looking down into his face. "You're waiting for me, right?"

"Absolutely."

He stepped up so we were looking eye to eye. "How much more proof do I need?"

"I need to ask you something."

"All right," he said, opening his door. "You don't have to ask me out here in the hall, do you?"

I hesitated for just a second, but he saw it.

"Of course, if you're more comfortable out here, that's fine, too," he said, still smiling.

"I'm sorry. Of course we don't have to talk out here."

"Perhaps I can offer you a drink," he said as I followed him inside. "And then you can tell me what's on your mind."

"Thanks," I said as he hung up his coat. "To tell you the truth, I'm not even sure if I want to ask you something or tell you something."

We were both still dressed for the party, and in the mirror behind the bar we looked relaxed and elegant. He poured us both some cognac and came to sit beside me on the couch. He picked up a remote and Miles Davis came pouring out of the speakers seductively. His music is so beautiful it can make you cry, but he treated women so badly, it's hard for me to listen to him without getting mad.

Blue looked at me and clicked the music off immediately. "Not a big Miles fan, huh?"

I shook my head.

"Serves him right, *mean motherfucker*."

I laughed. Sade replaced Miles as the background music to my confessions.

"Better?"

I nodded. "Much better."

He picked up his glass and leaned back. "I'm all ears."

I took a deep breath. How could I ease into this without making him think I was completely insane?

"Do blue eyes run in your family?" I blurted. *Oh, great! Now he'll just think I'm rude.*

But he didn't look at all surprised or offended. People had probably been asking him about his eyes all his life.

"No," he said, "I'm the only one."

"Did you ever think it was . . . *odd*?"

"I thought it would make me easy to find if anybody was ever looking for me."

"Has anybody been looking for you?" I asked softly.

"Other than you?"

I swallowed my cognac in one long gulp. He looked at me with an expression I couldn't read, and when he spoke, his voice was very gentle.

"It is you, isn't it?"

"What do you mean?" I whispered.

He set down his glass and slid over closer to me. He took my hands in both of his, and I looked into his eyes like I might find the answers there without having to ask the questions.

"Tell me what you know," he said. "Tell me exactly what you know."

Well, crazy or not, here I go! "My aunt had a vision. . . ."

"What kind of vision?"

"A voice told her a man . . . a man in Atlanta had been looking for me."

"Why was he looking for you?"

"I don't know," I said, glad his hands gave me something to hold on to. "But she said I would recognize him because . . ." *I couldn't say it. This sounded so crazy!*

"Tell me."

"Because he would have blue eyes."

He squeezed my hands suddenly and let out a sound somewhere between a gasp and a moan. "*I knew it! It is you! Thank God! It is you!* I had almost given up hope, and then I saw you that day listening to the Marley and you haven't changed a bit. Still that serious little face." He touched my cheek lightly. "Still those beautiful brown eyes."

"Who are you?" I asked, moving away from him just a little.

"Don't you know me?"

I shook my head. I would have remembered those eyes, but there was something else so familiar about him. "No."

He stood up and walked over to the window. "We've been apart for too long." He turned back to me slowly. "What else did your aunt tell you?"

"She told me you were not who you appear to be."

That made him smile. "And who do I appear to be?"

"That's what I came over here to ask you," I said, relieved to have come back around to my original question.

He came back to sit beside me, and his face was suddenly serious. "Do you trust me?"

"Yes."

"Good, because what I'm going to tell you might sound strange at first."

"At this point, nothing sounds strange to me."

"Then I need you to do something for me."

"What?"

"Look into my eyes."

"Is this a line?"

He laughed softly. "No, Gina. I don't have to work this hard to get women to look in my eyes."

That was probably an understatement. "Then why?"

"I want to answer any question you want to ask me, but first you have to be able to look at me. You have to be able to look into my eyes and see the truth is there; otherwise, you might not know what to believe and what to chalk up to playacting and bullshit."

He was right. The questions I wanted to ask required me to trust him to tell the truth, and required him to trust me to know what to do with it. How could I do that if I couldn't even look him in the eye? We were close together now. I turned to face him, knee to knee, tried to make my heart stop pounding so hard, and looked deeply into his eyes.

It was like looking at sunset and sunrise and the full moon over the ocean. This close, his eyes were not one uniform shade, but an ever-changing kaleidoscope of turquoise and robin's egg and aquamarine with tiny flecks of gold. The black of his pupils stood out like a bull's-eye in all that blue, and his lashes, which I had never been close enough before to notice, were straight and thick and almost invisible against the soft black of his skin.

But the color was just the beginning. His eyes were full of stories and sorrows and strengths and something else I couldn't name. Not yet anyway. And in the depths of his eyes, there was no meanness or manipulation or lying. Looking into those eyes, I felt like I could trust him with my life.

"All right," I said softly, so I wouldn't break the spell. "Now tell me who you really are."

28

H E SPOKE SLOWLY, AS IF THE RIGHT choice of words was all that would keep me from covering my ears and dashing back across the hall to the safety of my own apartment.

"I've been here before," he said, and stopped.

"In Atlanta?" I prompted him gently.

His voice was very quiet. "I've had other lives."

"What?"

He sounded sane, but most people don't talk about past lives so casually unless they're psychics or Buddhists or bohemian movie stars or visionary postmenopausal aunts.

"Last time I was here, things were different. I wasn't part of a group of people still trying to get over the effects of slavery," Blue said. "I was a free black man leading a nation of free black men."

My mind was whirling. I walked over to the window and looked out to be sure this was still southwest Atlanta. *It was.*

"Go on."

"We created a great civilization. Our libraries were the envy of the world. Our armies were invincible. Our culture was a rich melting pot of all those who found their way to our shores, and our healing powers guaranteed each citizen a long and fruitful life."

I felt like I was listening to a utopian fairy tale. "Your nation sounds like paradise."

His smile was sad. "It was as close as men have ever gotten, but that was the problem."

"Problems in paradise?" I smiled, but he didn't.

"We brought them on ourselves," he said. "And we ignored them until we were beaten by an enemy who should never have been able to bring us to our knees. And do you know why they were able to defeat us?"

Something stirred deep inside me and I heard a voice that sounded like mine say softly, "Because you wouldn't listen!" But I just shook my head. "Why?"

"We were defeated by an enemy that was able to infiltrate and finally overwhelm us because they had a powerful internal ally we had never considered. And do you know who that ally was?"

"Who?"

"Our women. The women we called our wives, our mothers, our girlfriends, our sisters," he said sadly. "The women we said we loved, but never paid attention to. The women we protected from everybody but one another. The women who had our children and never saw us again. The women we ignored and abused and neglected and underestimated even when they tried to warn us about the inevitable consequences of our foolishness."

This all sounded so familiar I wasn't sure if he was talking about past lives or present ones. The conversation felt surreal, but not *weird*, and that's a pretty fine line in a conversation like this one when you're talking about past lives and such.

"And did they try to warn you?"

He looked at me strangely. "*You* tried to warn me. It was *you* trying to tell me what was coming if we didn't change our ways, but I didn't believe you."

"Why not?"

"How could I? *I was the emperor.*"

In men's stories, they're always the emperor or the king or the president. In women's stories, we're always beautiful and smart and loved, not necessarily in that order.

"I told you that what you were suggesting would destabilize the entire nation."

Somehow I didn't think the person he was describing would find destabilization a bad thing. "What did I say to that?"

He smiled a little at the memory. "You said destabilization was nothing compared to what was going to happen if we didn't get right."

I liked my past self. She sounded like my kind of woman! "So why didn't you do it?"

He shook his head. "Because, like most men, I was an arrogant fool."

Good answer, I thought. "So what happened to me?"

He took a deep breath. "After a series of rapes and child murders, you left the palace and became a leader of the women's revolt against us. When you saw I could not be convinced, you left a letter saying you would never return until women were safe on the streets and in their houses and in the arms of the men they loved, and then you disappeared into the mountains with a small band of warrior women and I never saw you again."

His eyes were sparkling with regret or tears, I couldn't be sure. I didn't know what to say. *A rebel leader of angry women? Is that what drew me to Beth? The promise of access to women warriors?*

"I've been searching for you ever since," Blue said.

"So you could apologize?"

He took my hands again. "So I could make it right. The war that sent you into the mountains is still raging, *but not here. Not in this house. Not on this block. Not in this neighborhood.* In this neighborhood, women will walk in peace and safety and freedom so you'll learn to trust me."

"And then what?"

"And then if I am very patient and very lucky, you will fall in love with me again and we can continue our journey through time together the way we're supposed to."

I stood up suddenly before I knew I was going to. *Was this the plan Flora had been talking about?* I didn't know, but I have my own journey to complete. I have my own house to secure from the weasel. I wasn't here to fall in love with an exiled emperor, I don't care how blue his eyes are and how ancient his song.

"I've got to go home now," I said, heading for the door before he could say another word. I had asked for it, but I was on overload.

He stood up immediately, his face full of concern. "I didn't mean to frighten you. I know it's a lot to absorb."

"You didn't frighten me," I said, smiling. "Maybe that's what's scaring me."

That made him smile, too. He opened the door and took my hand. "I hope we can talk about this again."

"Yes," I said. "We will."

"Good night then."

"Good night."

I closed my door behind me and then leaned against it until I heard Blue's door click. My mind couldn't even begin to process all that he had told me, so I didn't try. There was plenty of time for that tomorrow. Right now what I needed was some sleep. I hung up my new dress, fell into bed, and pulled the covers up to my chin.

It wasn't until that brief moment just before you fall asleep that I realized Aunt Abbie had been right again. He was *none* of the people he appeared to be. *Or was he?*

29

I DIDN'T GET MUCH SLEEP. My brain was going a mile a minute trying to make sense of my evening. When I did doze off, my dreams were so vividly real that I'd wake up thinking I was back there with Blue in that past life, a female freedom fighter, prepared to die for the struggle. That's what I couldn't get out of my mind. I admired that woman. I wondered why I didn't remember *being* her. Or maybe she had just made herself known in ways I hadn't known how to read.

Blue said I was part of a band of women warriors who were demanding change. That's exactly why I'd signed on with Beth in the first place. Because she had crafted a movement for change where women were in charge instead of somewhere behind the scenes, servicing whatever charismatic man was up front, reading the speeches we wrote like he had thought them up himself. Beth's movement was female in its heart and soul, and my response to it was so strong and immediate it shocked everybody but me. Is that because Beth was truly wonderful or because I had been looking for those warrior women from my past life and this was as close as I could get? Was I just like Blue, wandering through the twenty-first century looking for fallen comrades and lost lovers and leaders who died before they had a chance to change and grow and grow wiser?

The idea that any of this could be true appealed to me and made me feel foolish in equal measure. If I opened myself up to the possibilities, my imagination ran wild. I saw myself sitting around the campfire—once you take to the hills, there's always a campfire—talking to my sisters. Planning. Strategizing. I saw myself trying to lobby the emperor for our interests and failing.

The emperor's scenes are always in a palace, not around the campfire. You know the kind of palace I'm talking about. The one with the marble steps and the flowing fountains and the handmaidens (how's that for a job title?). The palace in Hollywood's vision of *Cleopatra* and *Ben Hur* and *The Ten Commandments*. That's where I'd be lobbying the emperor. I'd be wearing some kind of flowing blue biblical robe number and Blue would be there wearing the tux he'd worn last night, but it didn't matter. I couldn't convince him to help us, and neither my arguments nor our long friendship could help us navigate the moment in a way that didn't end in disaster. So, I took to the hills, *and then what?*

On the other hand, even if I completely dismiss the possibility of past lives and Amazonian insurgents hiding in the mountains, I still had Aunt Abbie's vision to contend with. I had taken a journey I wanted to avoid, and met a man with blue eyes who sang an ancient song and was not who he appeared to be. All of that was undeniable and fit right into what Blue had told me last night, *but what did it all mean?* And what about that dragon and the damsel in distress? When were they going to show up?

The next morning, I walked into the West End News so deep in my consideration of possible past lives that I didn't notice Uncle DooDoo walking in right behind me. I was headed for the cappuccino counter when I heard his voice, too loud. Too mean.

"Where the fuck is that blue-eyed nigga who think he the godfather?" he shouted.

All conversations and motion among the six or seven patrons already there stopped, except for the big man in a dark suit who headed straight for DooDoo, who was still standing in the doorway, poised for flight. He had come to bluster, not to really fight anybody.

"King James say tell him keep his ass on this side of Stewart Avenue or take the consequences."

The man in the suit reached the door as DooDoo leapt into a waiting SUV and squealed off down the street. Nobody moved. The cappuccino-maker was hissing gently, but the old man who served it remained motionless. Then the man at the door turned to all of us apologetically.

"Please accept my apologies for this disturbance," he said calmly.

"Brother Richard, give these good people what they're drinking on the house."

I was already standing at the counter, so I ordered my cappuccino and stepped aside as we all breathed a sigh of relief that a meaningless burst of bravado hadn't escalated into something more deadly. Doo-Doo was bad news. Every sighting or report was worse than the last one. I wondered what had happened across Stewart Avenue that brought DooDoo across the line with a message from King James.

But I guess it's only fitting, I thought, heading home with my cappuccino to go and the Sunday *New York Times* tucked under my arm. Who other than a king would have the temerity to challenge an emperor?

30

IDIDN'T BOTHER TRYING TO GET to Beth's Monday-morning meeting on time. There was no need. The players at this kind of session never change. There's always a contingent of hacks for hire who go with the prevailing wind, offering their expertise to the highest bidder. There are always the bright-eyed professional women in those red power suits with American-flag pins that have replaced the gold-toned American eagles they favored under Hillary Clinton's reign. And, of course, there will be the young would-be movers and shakers in designer suits and IBM top-salesman smiles, hoping for a place in the inner circle based primarily on style, charm, and the vague promise of corporate contributions if cards are played correctly.

I had been in these meetings with Son many times. People whose job it is to notice such things had long been aware of Beth's political potential, but Son always cut them off at the pass. Beth was about as well suited to the down and dirty of Georgia state politics as I was, and Son knew it. But Son was gone now, and Beth was making decisions on her own.

By the time I pulled in behind all those sleek new BMWs and Cadillacs and even a Lexus or two, coffee had been served and those assembled were busily kissing Beth's ass.

"You have no idea what a groundswell of support there is out there," said one alarmingly slender woman in her forties, whose variation on the red power suit was a burgundy version, and whose lapel boasted an AIDS awareness ribbon cast in gold and decorated with rubies. "We were frankly overwhelmed when we floated your name at the coalition and the response was so completely positive. No one had a negative word to say."

Jade scribbled in her ever-present notebook and tilted it for my information: *"She's from the Coalition of Conscious Women Voters."* I nodded my appreciation. Unasked, by me anyway, she was providing a simultaneous translation and a list of speakers as the hyper-cheery group took turns giving Beth reasons to think she could win the governor's race. There were representatives from what politicians like to call "a broad coalition" of groups. In addition to the Conscious woman, there were two state senators, a minister from one of those mega churches with ten thousand tithing members, a councilwoman from Albany, a banker from Macon, and assorted pseudo activists whose party affiliations change like the weather but who are always accorded a spot at these meetings because of the unseen hordes of "community people" whose interests they claim to represent.

I recognized a few Atlanta businessmen who had never been big Son Shine supporters before, and a county commissioner whose one and only claim to fame was that he was black *and* Republican in a state where the GOP has, until very recently, been referred to derisively as "the party of Lincoln." There were even two young white women who, like Jade, seemed to be staffers, not full participants. I wondered which of the black people present had achieved this peculiar new status symbol: a white woman with a notebook to keep track of who had been promised what in exchange for what else.

"I know it seems a little early to jump out there," one of the smoothies in a thousand-dollar suit was saying to Beth with a dazzling display of perfect teeth, "but the fact is, we'll be playing catchup even if we start today. We have to hit the ground running if we're going to mount a credible campaign."

" 'Credible'?" Beth said, raising her eyebrows. "If I thought 'credible' was the best we could do, I'd thank you for your time and send you on your way."

She smiled when she said it, but her tone conveyed exactly who had the power in the room and who did not. As if anybody needed reminding. She was, as usual, seated with her back to the portrait of her and Son in a big wing-back chair that had probably spent its last life in somebody's throne room. Beth's tone froze the smoothie in midbeg, and he smiled his apology for a poor choice of words.

"I'm certainly in no position to pressure you, Ms. Davis. None of us is." He spread his arms to include his fellow supplicants, who nodded their agreement. *We're not worthy!* "It's just that the possibility of having you on the Republican ticket is such an exciting one that it's hard to wait."

Republican ticket? Beth was going to run as a *Republican?* In a state where those guys are on the wrong side of everything she stands for, *or used to,* how could she consider such a thing? Was the GOP the sponsor she had been talking about? *Oh, hell no!*

There was a murmuring and a nodding of heads. Beth smiled indulgently and put down her cup. Those assembled leaned forward in unison as if someone had cued them so as not to miss a word.

"I am humbled by your visit here today," she said. "Some of you have driven several hours to get here, and even those who came from across town had to brave the rush-hour traffic, so that was no picnic either."

They laughed softly, grateful for the acknowledgment of their efforts.

"Your enthusiasm for the possibility of my entering the political arena is highly contagious, and I don't mind confessing that I'm tempted to give you my response right now."

They actually held their collective breath, but there was no way she was going to let them off that easy. Their desire to hit the ground running would in no way impact her own impeccable sense of timing. Beth could not be rushed by anyone.

"But how could I make such an important decision without taking the time to deliberate? To consider what I can bring to this race and to this state at this critical juncture in our history. How could I possibly justify your faith in me if I act on impulse rather than intuition, intention, and intellect? And, yes, I say 'intuition' right up front because my woman's intuition will continue to be something I will call on during this process just like I always have."

They murmured their approval, the women a little louder than the men.

"And right now my woman's intuition is telling me it's time for us all to get back to work, but I promise you this: You'll have your answer in the next two weeks."

More murmuring and nodding, then the mega minister smiled unctuously and spoke for the group. "Sister Davis, you have been more than gracious with your time. If you will keep us in your thoughts, we will keep you in our prayers."

"Amen," said the county commissioner.

Beth stood up as they began gathering their things, shaking hands, offering her cheek for a fast, impersonal kiss, and promising them her decision soon, very soon. As she made her way to the door and stood there for her farewells, Jade stood discreetly beside her, scribbling notes and reminders so that each thank-you was specific, each pledge of support was recorded, and no promise could be forgotten in the swirl of the days ahead.

I've been that person. The invisible staffer, making sure no detail is overlooked. Public life, elected or otherwise, is built on the details. Jade was smart, focused, and committed. Watching her, she reminded me so much of *me*, I almost felt protective. *Almost.*

When Beth closed the big front door behind the last of her visitors, she was smiling like the cat who swallowed the canary. "I think that went well, don't you?"

"Very well," Jade said, and they both looked at me.

"Since when are you a Republican?" I said, cutting to the chase. "You hate everything these guys stand for, remember?"

"I never said I was a Republican." Beth's tone was conciliatory, but underneath there was ice. That tone used to intimidate me. Now all it did was fully activate my instinct for self-preservation.

"Don't play that game with me," I said. "Are you?"

"I'm just keeping my options open. You might be smart to do the same."

"What does that mean?"

Beth turned to her assistant, still hovering nearby. "I'll talk with Gina alone for a few minutes. I'll call you if I need anything."

"Of course," Jade said, heading downstairs without a backward glance.

Had Beth talked to me in those same curt commands? She probably had, at least toward the end of our association. That's when I noticed it, anyway. In the beginning, I was just happy she spoke to me at all. Shero worship is a powerful thing, and I was fully in its grip during the first five years. Looking at Beth now, it's hard to remember those days, until she smiles, like she's smiling now. That's when it all comes flooding back, and I have to remember to keep my wits about me.

"I know this is a lot to absorb," Beth said gently, unconsciously echoing Blue's words, "and I know on the surface it might seem that there are a few contradictions in what I'm doing."

"A *few*?"

She sighed like she was trying not to get annoyed. "Listen to me, Gina. These are perilous times. White folks got more on their minds these days than some raggedy black women in Georgia dragging their kids around asking for a handout."

I was shocked to hear her categorize her work and her followers that way. "Is that how they look to you?"

"That's how we look to *them*, and that's what important. The days of guilt money are gone, and they are not coming back."

"So where does that leave us? Blood money or bust?"

Her smile only managed to curl the edges of her lips before becoming a sneer. "Always so quick to judge, aren't you?"

This was getting us no place fast. "Listen, Beth, we don't have to do this at all."

"Yes, we do. Let's put everything on the table, shall we? I'm getting ready to take things to the next level, and I want you to be a part of it. You're the best, and I want nothing less."

I looked at her. "No, thanks."

"Hear me out before you say no so fast."

"Go on."

Beth's voice was urgent. She wanted to convince me, and she was prepared to work hard to do it. "Yes, they're Republicans, okay? But does that mean we can't do business with them? Does that mean we can't make the best deal for the women I represent?"

"You mean those raggedy black women asking for a handout?"

Her eyes hardened. "Yes, those same raggedy women who are inspired by my message because it's a message of hope. It's a message of self-determination steeped in sacrifice—"

"You don't have to convince me. I wrote that speech, remember?" I said, cutting her off.

"It was one of your best," she said. "And it's still true."

"So how can you sell them out to people who you know spend inordinate amounts of time trying to blame them for everything from higher taxes to moral decay?"

"I haven't sold anybody out to anything," she snapped. "No decisions have been made yet."

"Still trying to get the best deal?"

"Isn't that what politics is all about?"

"I thought politics was supposed to be the art of the possible."

Beth sighed deeply and sat back in her chair. The exchange had escalated into unpleasantness faster than either one of us had anticipated. This was as good a time as any to change the subject. I reached into my purse and withdrew the snapshot of Son and the mystery woman.

"Shall we agree to disagree for a moment? I've got something I need to show you."

"All right," Beth said, looking relieved. She had achieved her goal. All cards were on the table. She could try to lean on me later, but right now she needed to see what I had in my hand. "What is it?"

"I found this with Son's things." I handed her the photograph and waited.

She turned it over to see if there was a name on the back. Of course there wasn't. "Who is she?"

"I thought you might be able to tell me," I said. "Do you know her?"

Beth shook her head. "Not this one."

"This one what?"

She looked at me, and there was pain in her face. "I told you we've gotten some anonymous calls. Some blackmail attempts. Women

172

claiming Son had promised them this or that. Con artists looking for some money in exchange for not telling lies on my son when he's not around to defend himself." She shook her head as if to banish unpleasant memories. "None of them hold water. Once we put somebody on it, the stories always evaporate."

"Have there been any other pictures?"

"No."

Something in her voice made me know she was lying. "Well, so far this is the only one I've come across. I'll keep you posted."

She was still looking at the picture intently. "How could he be so foolish? Photographs always come back to haunt you. The last thing I need at this point is another stripper claiming to have been my son's lover."

"Who said she was a stripper?"

She looked up from the picture then, suddenly wary. "You did."

"No, I didn't."

Did she know the woman? I could see her casting around for a lie to cover her slip of the tongue.

"I probably just assumed that's what she was because that's what the others were," she said, thinking fast.

"Right," I said, getting ready to go. There was no reason to press her. It was none of my business. She was paying me to screen for scandal. I was just doing my job. "I've got a meeting over at Morehouse. Is there anything else we need to discuss?"

"I don't think so." She stood up with me and tucked the photograph into the pocket of her tunic. "I'll give this to my investigator and let him handle it."

"Fine. If I come across any others, I'll pass them on."

"I know you will," she said at the door. "And Gina?"

"Yes?"

"Let's just try to keep our options open as far as the politics go, okay?"

I wanted to say that my options, open or otherwise, did not include helping her mess over a righteous black politician like Precious Hargrove, but I didn't. The weasel was expecting another payment at just about the time Beth had promised an answer to her new admirers. If part of my job was to let her think I could be convinced to help her if her answer to them was yes, I would just have to string her along until my contract was over and I was a debt-free woman again.

It seemed a small price to pay, so I just smiled. "Fair enough."

She rewarded me with a big Beth smile and an air kiss in the general vicinity of my right cheek.

"Does that mean I still have time to talk you out of it?" I asked as I stepped outside into the warm spring day.

She laughed. "It means you still have time to try!"

31

BLUE HADN'T BEEN AROUND SINCE Saturday night, but a few hours ago, I *felt* his presence so strongly, I opened my door and listened carefully to see if I could hear him across the hall. *Silence.* His car wasn't out front, either, but I *felt* him headed this way as surely as if we had made a midafternoon appointment. Maybe it's a kind of telepathy because of the past-lives thing. *Who knows?*

I tried to go back to work on a draft of Beth's speech. I wasn't ready to admit that she was going to run for office yet, so I was still writing it as if she wasn't. I've written lots of speeches for Beth, and I know the cadences of her voice so well it didn't take me any time to fall back into those rhythms again. But once I had felt Blue headed this way, I couldn't surrender to Beth's voice again, and there's no point in trying to write *her* speech in *my* voice, so I decided to knock off for the day, take a shower, and treat myself to dinner.

I had just stepped into a pair of black pants and pulled on my favorite black sweater when I heard a knock on the door. His timing couldn't have been better. A neighborly invitation to join me for dinner would be totally appropriate. Even emperors in exile have to eat.

When I opened the door, he apologized immediately. "I'm sorry for disturbing you. Is this a bad time?"

"Not at all," I said. "Come on in."

He was wearing, as usual, a dark suit and a lightweight black overcoat. I tried to imagine him in more casual clothes, but I really couldn't. Maybe it was an imperial holdover. In this life, he couldn't wear velvet robes and carry a scepter, but a beautiful suit and a cashmere coat were not out of the question.

"Thank you," he said, following me inside. "How have you been?"

"Fine, thanks. You?" *Where* he had been was none of my business, but his overall well-being was perfectly polite conversation.

"Fine," he said. "Except I received a report about the disturbance at the newsstand and I understand you were there at the time."

"It wasn't much," I said. "A lot of bluster. When your man stepped in, the guy ran out and drove off."

Blue nodded. "Good. I'm sorry it happened, and especially sorry that it happened in my place."

"That guy's bad news," I said. "Aretha and I saw him up at Lu's school the other day."

"She told me. He's operating in a gray area there because he's picking up his niece, but this has nothing to do with that."

"He said you had crossed Stewart and somebody named King James didn't appreciate it."

Blue looked at me. "I had to talk to some of his people this weekend. They tried to push their way into Mattie Jenkins's house. She slammed the door, but they tore the screen and scared her."

I remembered Miss Mattie's righteous indignation at the meeting. "Is she okay?"

He nodded. "She's fine, but King James's boys crossed the line."

"What do you mean?"

"Remember when I told you I always give a man the benefit of the doubt and let him know when his behavior is unacceptable?"

"And you're only required to do it once?"

He was pleased that I'd remembered. He didn't have to worry about that. I remembered every word.

"This was my second meeting with those young fools."

It dawned on me that this hadn't been a meeting where discussion was on the agenda. That was why DooDoo had been so angry. I felt myself shiver. If he hadn't gone to talk to them, what had he gone to do?

"Oh," I said. "Did you—?" *How do you ask somebody if they've killed anybody since the last time you saw them?*

He didn't make me figure it out. "Verbal harassment and a torn screen don't make a capital crime."

I relaxed a little. "Now you sound like a lawyer."

He smiled slowly. "I'm not a lawyer, but I have to be clear about what I'm doing around here. It's too easy to get confused and start thinking the power is mine to do with as I please. If you're not careful in my position, you start using your power to take people out just because they're stupid or sorry or lazy or they got a smart mouth or a mean streak or they exercise bad judgment or they just can't stop lying."

He looked at me and slowed down the rush of his words. "But that would be wrong. Those are just things that some people do, and everybody has to deal with it the best they can. I have to be sure I only step in when some brother is acting a fool and can't be reasoned with."

"Then you reason with him?"

"Then I do what needs to be done."

I took a deep breath. That's what Peachy had said at the party the other night. *He does what needs to be done.* "And what needed to be done this weekend?"

He looked at me hard then, and his eyes were like a kaleidoscope, shifting colors until they finally stilled. "There is no question you can ask me that I won't answer, but the details of what I do aren't really worth discussing. I have accepted responsibility for the safety of a very small space, and as long as the people who live here want me to continue in that role, I will."

"What happens if they want to go back to depending on . . . more traditional methods."

"Like what?" he asked gently.

"Elected officials, the police. You know what I mean."

"You were at the growers meeting when Precious spoke?"

I remembering feeling sorry for her powerlessness. In essence, all she could do was tell them to be careful and call the police if anybody got assaulted. "Yes. I was there."

"And what protection could she offer? None. She's the best there is at what she does, and I respect her, but there's not a damn thing she can do by herself. Even with all the cops and all the programs and all the speeches, she needs some help from the men who live around here. She needs to know we got her back."

"Does she approve of that arrangement?"

He grinned at me. "She didn't seem concerned about it the other night at the club, did she?"

He was right about that. She was running for governor, and she had accepted a large contribution under the auspices of Blue Hamilton. Their mutual respect had been obvious, and more important than any public acknowledgment was the fact that Precious made her home in West End. She had raised Kwame as a single mother in the same small house she still lived in a few blocks from here. She had chosen to live under Blue's informal protection.

"No, she didn't seem concerned at all," I admitted.

"And the answer to your question is, if they asked me to stop doing what I'm doing, I would stop. And then do you know what would happen?"

Of course I knew. The predators would return. The crack houses would reopen. The war against women and children would pick up where it left off. West End would become just another black neighborhood under siege. King James and Uncle DooDoo would be in charge. I shuddered at the thought.

Blue saw me shiver and knew he had his answer. "I'm not going to let that happen," he said quietly.

"Because you used to be an emperor?"

"Because I'm still a man."

The simple directness of that statement was both its strength and its challenge. The signs the demonstrators carried in Memphis right before Martin Luther King was killed said only I AM A MAN. We all knew what that meant, and we embraced it, endorsed it, longed for it. But something happened between then and now. The definition of what a man *is* and what a man *does* has been so corrupted and compromised by a pop culture that will tell you *anything* to sell you *everything* that now we have manhood defined by cars and clothes and random sex and money made *by any means necessary.* Blue's clear, unequivocal declaration was a throwback to a time when manhood was still tied to family and community by ribbons of love and protection and responsibility and caring. I felt myself relax again.

"Good answer," I said, smiling.

"Was it a test?" He smiled back.

I laughed. "Probably."

"Well, I'm glad I passed."

His eyes were doing their trademark twinkling, and even though taking that long look the other night had made me less likely to stare, it didn't completely eliminate the problem.

"I was just going to get some dinner," I said, reaching for my coat and my keys. "I'd love to have some company if you're free."

"It would be my pleasure."

"I was going over to Youngblood's. That okay with you?"

Youngblood's R&B Cafe was owned by a popular Atlanta DJ whose radio career was built on oldies and whose restaurant featured photographs of the greats, assorted R&B memorabilia, and a menu featuring items like Aretha Franklin fried catfish and Al Green grouper. It was a traditional black restaurant where the sometimes slow service was forgotten as soon as the fabulous food appeared.

"Do they still have the Gene Chandler T-bone steak?"

"They sure do," I laughed, heading out the door and taking the arm he offered.

The evening was clear, but Youngblood's was too far to walk and Blue's Lincoln was sitting out front. I couldn't imagine him sitting in the passenger seat of my little car.

"Shall I drive?" He obviously couldn't imagine it either.

"Sure," I said, glad he had given his driver the evening off and it was going to be just the two of us. Youngblood's had good food and good music, and the night was young. This wasn't really a date, but it wasn't two buddies going out for a beer either. What it was remained to be seen, but there was no rush. Once you start entertaining the idea of past lives, *real* time becomes a lot less significant. We had all the time in the world.

32

WALKING INTO YOUNGBLOOD'S with Blue was like taking Denzel Washington to the prom. To use one of my father's least genteel expressions, the other patrons didn't know "whether to shit or go blind." The hostess greeted Blue like visiting royalty and showed us to a corner booth by the window. The young waitress who came to take our drink order was so nervous she dropped the menus on the floor.

I ordered lemonade, and Blue ordered sweet tea. The flustered waitress disappeared to get the drinks while we glanced at the menu. The Gene Chandler T-bone steak was in its usual place of honor among the entrees, and I knew I was sticking with my favorite, the Mary Wells fillet of salmon, so we didn't need much time. The black-and-white photograph above our table showed Al Green at the Atlanta Civic Center, sweating and smiling and singing like his life depended on it instead of just his livelihood. At the edge of the stage women were reaching and swooning, and Al was reaching right back. I decided to come clean.

"I've seen a picture like that of you," I said.

He smiled, but I could tell he was surprised.

"Lu showed it to me. Actually, she gave it to me."

His smile got a little wider. "Why would she do that?"

"I found a picture of her father with Son Davis, and when I gave it to her, she gave me one back. Sort of like an even exchange."

The waitress returned with our drinks, her eyes still bugged out with amazement at who was sitting at her station, and, being *so-o-o-o* careful not to spill a drop. She took our orders and disappeared again.

"So what did you do with it?" Blue said, sipping his tea.

Why hadn't I anticipated the question and prepared a feasible answer? My mind was a complete blank. I had no choice but to tell him the truth. "I . . . I put it on my refrigerator."

He smiled at me in a way that made me feel like I'd been caught with an autograph book in my purse. "Oh?"

"I kept trying to square the guy in the picture with the guy who lives across the hall from me."

"Not possible," he said with a low chuckle.

"It has to be possible," I said. "You are both of those guys. I saw you at Club Zebra, remember, or was that your evil twin?"

"No twin," he said, laughing. "But that guy is a creation of my imagination who stimulates the imaginations of a lot of women at the same time. Some of it is stuff I practiced so I'd get good at it, but a lot of it is just something I was born with, like these eyes."

"Do you think of yourself as charismatic?"

"Sure. Don't you think I am?"

I really blushed then, and he had his answer. "Yes, I do," I said, trying to sound casual and failing. "That's what made me want to look at that picture Lu gave me enough to put it on the fridge."

"A place of honor . . ."

"Always," I said. "And then after I saw you the other night . . ."

What was I trying to tell him? That I don't trust the power that charismatic people wield as their birthright? That I don't fault them for it—*Shaq didn't ask to be tall*—but Beth taught me a valuable lesson and I didn't want to forget it. What you see when you look at people who are, like Blue said, just born with something special, is not always what you get.

I took another deep breath and nodded toward Al Green. "What does it feel like to have that kind of effect on people?"

Blue considered the question. "It feels great," he said finally. "When it all goes right, it's an amazing exchange. Good sex is the only thing that even comes close, but that's the problem."

"Good sex is the problem?" I've heard it described as many things, but *a problem* is not on the short list.

He chuckled again at my shocked expression. "Not exactly. More like the lack of it. I realized that what I was doing with the music was making women feel trusting, vulnerable, open to persuasion."

He was right about that. A male friend of mine at Howard always said he liked to take women to see the crooners in concert because by the end of the show they were so filled with romantic fantasies and sexual longings that he was practically guaranteed a night of wonderful lovemaking. "Brian McKnight can't take home but one lady," is how he put it. "All the rest are available." Blue was talking about the "McKnight effect."

"Why is that a problem?" I asked, after our waitress brought our orders and refilled our glasses without being asked. Didn't Blue know that those fantasies are part of why we go to concerts in the first place?

"Because too many women were going home to men who used that vulnerability against them. Who didn't build on those good feelings once the show was over. Who didn't understand that there's always supposed to be an exchange going on. That's the beauty of it. *The exchange.*"

His face clouded, and his food was untouched. The waitress hovered, but she left us alone when neither one of us gestured in her direction.

"But too many brothers don't get it. They're still trying to trick women into loving them instead of understanding that if you make a woman feel comfortable whatever idea she comes up with is going to please you, too."

That sounded promising. I nodded and took a sip of my lemonade.

"I knew the women who came to see me sing had a lot to give and nobody around to give it to who would appreciate the gift. That's not going to be a fair exchange."

He sounded like he had been listening to the endless conversations I've had with my girlfriends about this very problem.

"It seemed to me that there were some basic things we needed to get straight among the brothers before we'd even be worthy of all black women were prepared to give us for almost nothing in return."

"Things like what?" I said, taking a bite of my Mary Wells and trying to stay calm. The idea of a fine, strong, smart, talented man trying to figure out how to be *worthy* of some black woman's affections made me practically giddy.

"Like the way we talk to you. Like all the hitting and terrorizing of you all that we do. Like the lying and the bullshit. Like the way we treat our kids."

He was ticking off every woman's secret list of things we'd like to fix in the men we'd like to love. "Is that the other reason you came off the road?"

He nodded slowly, and his eyes looked sad. "It just didn't seem fair. If I was making a promise my brothers weren't prepared to keep, I was as bad as they were."

The waitress couldn't stand it anymore. She eased back over with a look of concern on her face, her eyes flickering over Blue's untouched plate.

"Is everything okay?"

"Everything's fine," he said. "Thanks."

She hesitated, then took a deep breath and went for it. "Mr. Hamilton?"

"Yes?"

"My aunt said you are her favorite singer of all time. She's always talking about how you're the reason she married my uncle."

He smiled up at her. "And how did I do that?"

"They went to see you at the Royal Peacock, and when he proposed afterward, she said she didn't know if she was saying yes to him or to you!"

Blue laughed. "Is he good to her?"

The waitress nodded vigorously. "They been married twelve years and the way he always sending flowers and kissing on her, you'd think they was still in high school."

"Well, you tell your aunt I said thanks," Blue said. "And tell your uncle I said keep doing what he's doing. If it ain't broke, don't fix it."

She giggled. "I'll tell him. And . . . could you sign a menu for me to give her?" She thrust one in his direction. "It would mean a lot to her."

"Sure," Blue said, accepting her pen and smiling apologetically at me across the table as I munched on my baked potato. "Excuse me."

"No problem," I said, smiling at the waitress so she wouldn't think I had an attitude. I was loving it.

"What's your aunt's name?"

"Sweetie."

He looked at the young woman, the pen poised above the paper. "Her real name is *Sweetie*?"

The girl looked embarrassed. "No, but that's what everybody calls her and she'll kill me if I let you sign it to Theola Mae."

Blue chuckled. "All right, *Sweetie* it is."

In the empty corner near the desserts, he wrote: *"To Sweetie, my number one fan. Yours truly, Blue Hamilton."*

He handed it back to the waitress, who beamed. "She gonna love this, Mr. Blue. . . . I mean, Mr. Hamilton. Now all I gotta do is sneak this menu out so Youngblood won't try to keep it!"

Blue reached in his pocket and handed the girl a hundred-dollar bill. "Tell him I paid for it."

She blinked her eyes in amazement. "How much you think a menu cost anyway?" she whispered.

"About a buck and half, tops," Blue said calmly. "Why don't you keep the change?"

"Oh, my God! Thank you, sir! Thank you for the autograph and for the tip. Thank you, thank you. . . ." She backed away, still beaming.

Blue grinned at me.

"Sweetie lucked out," I said. "Does that make you feel any better?"

"I'll tell you what would make me feel even better."

"What's that?"

"If you would ride down to the beach with me this weekend."

For somebody like me, who has always wanted to live within walking distance of the ocean, this was like saying, Want to ride down to paradise for the weekend?

I tried to play it cool. "What beach?"

"Tybee Island," he said. "It's right outside of Savannah. About four hours from here. Peachy's wife's birthday is this Saturday, and I don't want him to spend it by himself. This is the first one since she passed."

"I'd love to," I said. "I had a good time with him at the party."

"He told me."

"I have to be back for a meeting at the college first thing Monday morning. Is that okay?"

"No problem," he said, looking pleased that I had accepted his invitation. "We can go up early Saturday morning and be back by Sunday night if you want. I've got a house down there and there's plenty of room for guests."

"You've got a beach house?"

He nodded. "It's got four bedrooms, although Lu has got a pretty strong claim on one of the ones downstairs."

That way, he let me know Flora and Lu had already been his overnight guests. Their past presence certified the place as a woman safe zone. I appreciated his sensitivity.

"I won't take Lu's room," I said.

He smiled. "I think I've eaten my fill. Shall we get our strawberry shortcake to go?"

I laughed. "Our waitress will probably offer to carry it out to the car."

He raised his hand at the young waitress, who hurried over to see what else he might need. Sweetie's decades of devotion were about to be repaid not only with an autograph, but a story she and her niece would tell forever. It would begin with, He walked in just like anybody else would, and end with, And he handed me a hundred-dollar bill like it was no more than a five and told me if it ain't broke don't fix it.

The thing about Blue was that the flip side of that also held true. He was about the mammoth task of trying to fix what was *broke*; of trying to rebuild the trust and rekindle the love, one woman at a time, starting with *me*. Not bad for a slow Tuesday night at Youngblood's.

33

WHEN PRECIOUS HARGROVE CALLED and said she needed to see me, I agreed immediately. She said she had something to show me and it couldn't wait. Of course, I knew it was about Beth. There was no other urgent business possible between me and the senator. What had Beth done now in her quest for open options and deals with the devil?

We agreed to meet at Soul Veg for a cup of late afternoon tea. When I walked in at just after three, Precious was the only person there. She waved, and I grabbed a cup of peppermint tea and joined her at a booth near the big front windows. It seemed appropriate that we could watch our neighbors going by as we talked. All you can see from Beth's house is trees.

"Thanks for coming," Precious said as I slid in across from her. Her expression was hard for me to read, but she was unhappy about something. That much was clear.

"I'm glad you called me," I said. "What's wrong?"

There was no point in a bunch of meaningless chitchat. We were here to do business. What *kind* of business would emerge, but it had nothing to do with commenting on the sudden cold snap or her son's blossoming affair with my downstairs neighbor.

Precious sighed and withdrew a white business envelope from her purse. She slid it across the table toward me. It had been sent to her home with no return address. On the lower front corner, I would see that someone had written the classic plea for postal mercy: PHOTOS! PLEASE DO NOT BEND!

"This arrived two days ago," she said. "I've been trying to reach Beth ever since, but I haven't gotten any response."

I picked up the envelope and pulled out a folded note and a

snapshot. It was the woman in the photo with Son that I had given to Beth, except Son wasn't in this picture. In this picture, the woman was wearing a demure pale green dress and holding a little boy on her lap who looked so much like Son that the conclusion was inescapable: *This was his child.*

I looked at Precious.

"Read the note."

I opened up the single piece of plain white paper. Someone had typed: *"I wonder if Beth Davis is going to include her grandson on her campaign brochures,"* and then an address.

There was no signature. No blackmail demand. Nothing but a question for which neither of us had the answer.

"Who sent it?" I said, refolding the note carefully, but unable to take my eyes off the picture. The woman looked radiantly happy, and the small boy was smiling at the camera like one of those commercial-world babies who coo their unending approval of Pampers or Huggies or Gerber's so sweetly that we buy the product just to please them.

Precious shook her head, frowning. "I have no idea."

"How hard is it to get your home address?"

The question elicited a small smile. Her political career was based on accessibility. "I'm in the phone book."

"Any ideas at all?"

"Well, I have no idea *who*, but I think I know why."

I was still trying to absorb the idea of Son having a child. Was that what Beth was trying to get me to find at the bottom of that great big pile of bullshit she'd been feeding me?

"I think whoever sent this is pretty sure Beth is going to be a candidate for governor and pretty sure I'd like to keep her out of the race if I can," Precious said. "They'd be right on both counts."

Her tone was devoid of emotion. She was making sure we both understood what was being discussed. I kept quiet.

"There are a couple of problems here," she said. "The first one is that her candidacy would effectively split the black female vote and nullify all the work I've done building a record and all the work she's done registering new voters."

"She hasn't said she's going to run."

Precious looked at me. "I know that she's considering a draft. There has already been a committee formed, and she's promised them an answer in two weeks."

I was impressed. Precious had a network that reached into Beth's living room, and Beth didn't even know it.

Precious clasped her hands on the table and leaned forward. "Let me be very clear about this. I don't care if there is a child or not. Son Davis was a good man who did a lot of good things for this community, and if he had lived, I'm sure he would have done a lot more. I always felt that his perspective, in addition to Beth's, was crucial to the whole mission of Son Shine."

"It was."

She nodded. "But this message comes from somebody who wants her out of the race pretty badly and is prepared to play dirty to make that happen."

She picked up the envelope like it pained her to have to touch it and looked at me. "I think her candidacy will be the worst thing she could do for the women who trust her. It will make my job immeasurably harder, but this is the life I've chosen, and I'm not prepared to use blackmail to pressure her to withdraw."

She slid the envelope back toward me with the tip of her index finger. "Give this to her and she can do with it what she will."

I picked up the envelope and stashed it in my purse quickly. "I don't think she has any idea that she has a grandson."

Precious sat back and took a sip of her tea. "I think," she said putting her cup down gently, "that it's been a very long time since anything surprised Beth Davis."

We both sipped our tea for a minute. I felt bad. Precious and I were on the same side, but I was working for Beth. There was only so much I could do, but I was prepared to do all of that.

"If it means anything, I've been trying to tell her what a bad idea I think this is."

Precious shook her head. "It's worse than that. She's being used. Once black folks split between me and her, a strong white candidate will be able to slide right in without owing any of us anything."

"Have they got a strong white candidate?"

"They always have a candidate," she said. "We're the only ones who go at this hit and miss."

That tone was as familiar to me as a lullaby. My parents and their friends spoke it to one another when they had been outvoted or out-financed or outadvertised by a lesser white opponent whose victory came by default because, as my father said, Negroes failed to rise. This was the voice of the true believer, forced to confront the disorga-nization that Marcus Garvey said was the race's most indomitable foe. I knew the pain and disappointment in that tone, but I also knew that within the deepest disillusionment, there were the seeds of the next campaign, the next confrontation, the next chance to pull it all together and *win*.

"The sad thing is," Precious said, "that the two of us make one perfect candidate. Beth can move a crowd better than any-one I've ever seen, but she couldn't get a bill out of committee if her life depended on it. I can remember everybody's name, where they live, where their grandbaby goes to school. I know how to make alliances with people who never thought they'd be doing business with a black woman and not give up who I am in the process. I can take a bill from an idea to a reality, and I've run five campaigns without ever incurring a penny of debt, financial or moral."

She was ticking off her credentials, and I knew she wasn't brag-ging. When I told Beth that Precious was an ideal candidate, I wasn't kidding.

Precious smiled and shook her head. "But there's one problem. As a speaker, I'm just not very exciting. Well informed, overprepared, sincere, but just no . . . pizzazz."

She was absolutely right. Her performance at the growers meeting was a prime example. What she needed was a good speechwriter. Someone who could take the raw material and shape it into something that sings. Writing for Beth was always a pleasure because she's already so charismatic. It's like having Mary J. Blige record your song. If you are any good at all, she's going to make you sound *great*. Writing a speech for Precious would be a different kind of challenge, but she already had the big three: *passion, program,* and *purpose.* All she needed was number four: *polish.*

"The governor isn't required to have pizzazz," I said.

"But the *candidate* for governor had better."

She was right again. We smiled at each other. No point in denying the obvious.

"So, I'll work on my pizzazz, and you give Sister Davis that envelope. I assume she'll take it from there."

"I'm sorry," I said, and I was. These women should be able to make an alliance. Their united front could change the face of Georgia politics overnight. Pitted against each other, they were easy to neutralize.

"I'm sorry, too," Precious said, and her voice had softened around the edges. She smiled at me across the table. "Beth was one of my sheroes, you know. She's the reason I went into politics in the first place."

"Really?"

She nodded. "It's a great story. I'll tell it to you one day, but right now, I've got a meeting."

"I'll hold you to that," I said.

She stood up and gathered her things. "I appreciate the delicacy of your position," she said. "But you might give her a message from me."

"That's why I'm here, isn't it?"

Precious smiled. "Tell her I intend to stay in this race, tell her I intend to win, and one more thing."

"Yes?"

"Tell her I'm not getting off the Legacy Committee. Son Davis was a friend of mine and a friend of this community. If she's planning to announce anything at the ceremony, she'll have to have enough nerve to do it to my face."

"I'll tell her."

34

IT WAS A BEAUTIFUL DAY. I walked home the long way, realizing I was beginning to recognize some of my neighbors. They'd wave and I'd wave. It was only a matter of time before I knew their names and they knew mine, but I wasn't thinking about the beauty of neighborhood comradery at the moment. I was thinking of Son's secret life. That sounds melodramatic, but having a kid your mother doesn't know about by a woman she's never met qualifies as pretty secretive, I think.

What did Precious say when I said I didn't think Beth knew about any grandchild? *It's been a long time since anything surprised Beth Davis.* There was so much going on at our short meeting, I didn't have time to ask her to explain. Maybe I should ask Beth instead. She was in Augusta with Jade doing a series of workshops and a dinner speech tomorrow night. I looked at my watch. If I hurried, I could catch her at the hotel before she went out for the evening.

I turned down my block and hurried toward home. Wanna-be Coltrane was playing his heart out, but I didn't recognize the tune. If I were his teacher, he'd definitely get an A for effort, but beyond that, there was a lot of work ahead of that child!

Flora and Aretha were in the garden, and I could hear their laughter as I came up the walk. Flora was standing among the last of the winter greens with a bunch of them held in the crook of her arm like she'd just been elected Miss Black America and this was her soulful bouquet. Aretha was moving around, snapping pictures and laughing encouragement.

"Hold that! Hold that! Stop laughing! You're supposed to be dignified!"

Flora really laughed at that as she spotted me. "Would you tell this child any woman who carries a bunch of collard greens at her coronation has already put dignity behind her?"

"Way behind her," I said.

"Aretha's recording the last of this crop for posterity," Flora said, still laughing.

"Queen of the collard greens!" Aretha said, still snapping away. "Go get in the picture," she said, waving me over.

I went obediently to stand beside Flora. "Your majesty," I said, giving her a little curtsy.

Flora grinned. "I prefer 'your highness.' "

"You see," I said to Aretha, "she's only been a queen for a few minutes and already she's a diva!"

"That's the end of the roll," Aretha said. "We just caught the good light."

"Now I see why those supermodels get paid so much to do this stuff," Flora said, heading inside. "Anybody want tea?"

I shook my head. "I've got to make some phone calls. Thanks."

Aretha came in behind us, her camera slung around her neck the way somebody else would have worn a gold chain. "Not me," she said. "I've got a dinner date."

Flora and I gave this the required double take and rolled our eyes at each other.

"That's three nights in a row," Flora whispered loudly, like Aretha wasn't standing right there.

Aretha laughed. "And it's going to be four, five, and six if I have anything to say about it!"

"Listen to this girl!"

Aretha's eyes were shining. "Tease me all you want. He's my *soul mate*."

"That serious, huh?"

"Exactly that serious," Aretha said, disappearing into her apartment with a suddenly shy smile.

"I know you have to go," Flora said, "but mark next Friday on your calendar."

"Consider it marked," I said. "What's the occasion?"

"Lu's turning twelve, so I'm having everybody over for cake and ice cream."

"I wouldn't miss it."

"Good."

She turned to go, and I started up the stairs when I remembered something. "Flora?"

"Yeah?"

"Have the gardeners across Stewart had any more problems?"

Flora shook her head. "Not since last weekend. Everything's been quiet as a mouse."

Why didn't that surprise me?

35

W HEN I CALLED BETH'S HOTEL in Augusta, the phone didn't complete a ring before Jade's voice answered briskly. "Hello?"

"Hey, Jade," I said. "This is Regina. I need to speak to Beth."

"She's resting," Jade said, very cool. "She was in workshops all day and the dinner with the sponsors is at six."

"I think you should wake her. It's important," I said, not at all comfortable with being screened like a stranger. "I just had lunch with Precious Hargrove and, trust me, she'll want to hear what I have to tell her."

She'll want to *see* it, but that will have to wait until they get back to Atlanta.

"Why don't you tell me, and I'll make sure she gets the message as soon as she wakes up," Jade said smoothly. She was loving this moment as much as I was not loving it. "Is there a number where she can reach you later?"

There was no reason to be mad at Jade. She was just doing her job. I've asked that question of Beth's callers a thousand times, and it's always a kiss-off. Maybe not a permanent kiss-off, but definitely one that's reserved for those whose calls are not automatically put through.

All right, I thought. *So be it.* I wasn't the one trying to run for governor.

"No, actually there isn't a number. I'll be out of town all weekend, so why don't you just tell her I'll call her on Monday."

"She'll call your cell," Jade said.

"I'm not taking a cell," I said, realizing it as the words left my mouth. This was not a weekend during which I wanted to be distracted from whatever was going on in front of my face.

"Not taking your cell?"

Jade couldn't have been more shocked if I had said, I'm not taking my spleen.

"I'll talk to her Monday after the meeting at Morehouse."

"Will you be checking messages?" I could hear the rising panic.

"Not until Monday morning."

"Well, how can we get in touch if we need to?"

"You can't," I said, then suddenly felt sorry for Jade, a victim of a recently instituted cultural belief that not being immediately available by phone/pager/beeper/e-mail, or the now quaintly old-fashioned fax, is tantamount to scrubbing off your fingerprints with steel wool and dropping into a mysterious demimonde where no respectable citizen of the twenty-first century would voluntarily venture.

"I'm sure Beth will be disappointed that she won't be able to reach you," Jade said, still incredulous.

"There's a way around it," I said.

"And that is?"

"Next time I ask you to wake her up, *wake her up.*"

36

W HEN BLUE PICKED ME UP EARLY Saturday morning, I was
wearing jeans and a light turtleneck sweater. He was wearing
a dark suit and tie. Out of consideration for the warm weather, he
wasn't wearing his usual overcoat, but otherwise nothing about his
appearance suggested the beach.

"I feel a little underdressed," I said as we headed downstairs.

"You're fine," he said, laying my bag in the trunk. I noticed he had
no luggage, but I guess you can travel light when you're going from
your house to your house. "I'll change when we get down there."

"Why not here?" I said as we headed toward the freeway.

He thought about it for a minute before he answered. "Part of
what I do is prevent foolishness before it gets started by being a visible deterrent."

"A visible deterrent?"

The lush green of the trees on either side of the rushing interstate
traffic was a perfect complement to the clear blue of the cloudless sky.

He nodded. "If these young hardheads see me and clock me
immediately as someone who is not going to tolerate confusion, if
they've got any sense left at all, they calm down and make another
choice. Dressing this way helps them make the correct identification
on sight. They've all seen Hollywood's idea of a big-time gangster.
Michael Corleone set the standard. All I have to do is stick with that
same sartorial model, and they transfer his power to me without me
having to lift a finger."

It wasn't just the hardheads. When I first saw him, I immediately
thought of the *Godfather* scene where Michael steps out of that big
black car to greet his former true love after having completed his
transformation from war hero to the next Don Corleone.

"Good thing for you Michael had a little style," I said. "Think if you had to go through this life dressed like Al Pacino in *Scarface*."

He laughed. I did, too. In fact, we talked and laughed all the way to Savannah. With apologies to T. S. Eliot, there is nothing cruel about April in Georgia. Whatever little piece of cold they get down here for winter had disappeared, and the heat that defines southern summers had not yet appeared. Everything that can bloom *does*, including the omnipresent pink and white dogwoods and every color of azalea in every possible combination.

We got off the interstate just past Macon and took the old state highways to the coast. Blue had played clubs in most of the little towns we passed through, and he had enough stories about his adventures and misadventures on the chitlin' circuit to fill twice as much time as it took for us to pull into Savannah and see the signs that say BEACHES and point you in the direction of the ocean.

We hit the causeway and, over the first rise, *the water*. Blue opened all the car's windows, and I could already smell the salt in the air. Blue was looking at me with a smile, and I smiled back.

"What?"

"Do you remember the sea?" he said.

It sounded so theatrical, the way he said it like that—*the sea*—but what are you going to do? The whole idea of past-life memories is already pretty over the top. A little theatricality is probably not out of line.

"From before?"

He nodded without taking his eyes off the road ahead. His face looked peaceful, unguarded in a way it never was in the city.

"No," I said. "I really don't remember anything like that."

"Did you ever want to live at the beach?"

He had me there. "Since the first time I knew there was beach."

He smiled. "That's why."

"A lot of people want to live at the beach," I said. "You think we're all being subconsciously guided by our past lives?"

"I think *you* are," he said calmly.

Something about all this was starting to make me feel weird. The *me* he thinks he knows is a woman I don't remember being. He can't help but judge me against the standard I set last time around, and, from what he's told me, I was pretty amazing. Fearless, committed, brilliant. Am I going to be competing with myself, once removed?

"You don't even really know me," I said. "You think you do because of what happened . . . what you *believe* happened before."

"I didn't mean to make you uncomfortable," he said. "I'm sorry."

"I'm not uncomfortable," I said. "I just don't want you to confuse me with that woman you knew before."

He didn't say anything to that, but I knew what he was thinking. *You are that woman.*

"I'm not her."

"I understand," he said. "Would you rather we not talk about this anymore for a while?"

That was exactly what I wanted, so, of course, I denied it. "I don't mind talking about it, I just—" I stopped.

What is that insane impetus to tell a man what you need, what you think, what you want, and then retract it the second he takes you up on it? I took a deep breath.

"*Yes.* That's exactly what I'd like."

"Done," he said, smiling.

I smiled back. *How easy was that?*

"Can I tell you something?" he said as the car headed across the last of the causeway and cruised onto Tybee Island.

"Sure."

"You can always tell me what you really want," he said. "Whatever it is, that's what I want for you, but I'm not always very good at mind reading."

"All this time travel and no mind reading?"

"What time travel?" He looked at me with a grin.

I laughed. *What time travel indeed?*

37

TYBEE IS A SMALL ISLAND THAT experienced a crushing level of commercial development after it placed itself front and center in a bid to be part of the 1996 Olympic Games up the road in Atlanta. The tiny year-round population was being forced to move as the time shares and big-chain hotels crowded out the dusty beachfront cottages and seedy mom-and-pop lodgings that had been the comfortable norm for years.

But off the main drag, bustling with new construction and weekend traffic, the island retained the charm that had drawn Blue there twenty years ago. He turned down a street that wound through a neighborhood of islanders and then meandered past the island's historic lighthouse and opened out onto the Atlantic Ocean. We pulled up in front of a large beachfront house with two sides of windows, a widow's walk on top, and a spectacular view of sea and sky that almost took my breath away.

Blue turned off the car and smiled at my obvious surprise. The ocean was less than a hundred yards away over a small rise of dunes. Seagulls and pelicans swooped and called to one another in the sunshine. For someone like me who has never gotten enough of the beach, it truly was a slice of paradise. Blue got out and came around to open my door.

I stepped out into the salty air. "*This* is your house?"

He nodded, amused at my reaction.

"You *own* it?"

"Peachy and I bought it when we were still touring."

"So you'd have a place to bring chicks?" I teased him.

"So we'd have a place to regroup. The road will kill you if you aren't careful. Then when he got married, he sold me his half and got a place in Savannah."

"Didn't his wife like the beach?"

"She was afraid of hurricanes. Savannah was as close as she could stand to be."

I followed Blue into the house, feeling like I was walking into a fantasy I didn't even know I had. Aunt Abbie's dream said blue eyes, but it never mentioned a beach house.

The house's great room looked like it had recently been featured in *Architectural Digest*. The couch and chairs were draped in those artfully rumpled white slipcovers that movie stars favor for their Malibu digs. The table at one end of the room could easily seat six people and now held a bowl of fresh fruit with a note propped against it.

Blue read it quickly and smiled. "Peachy came by to open up. He said to tell you hello and he'll be back in a little bit."

That was fine with me. I needed a chance to take all this in first. "When you said you had a place on Tybee Island, I thought you meant a time share or something," I said, gazing out the floor-to-ceiling windows that seemed to extend the living room almost to the ocean's edge. "But this—this is something else altogether!"

He laughed. "I'm glad you like it. Let me show you your room."

I liked that even though we both knew this weekend held the potential for us to take our friendship to the next level, he didn't assume anything. I followed him up a short flight of stairs that opened out onto a sort of atrium with four doors facing it. He led me through one into a lovely room and put my bag down by the door. It not only had the same giant windows that I had loved downstairs, but over the bed, it had a huge skylight that was currently framing a cloudless expanse of blue sky. Other than the bed, which was covered by a spotless white duvet and a jumble of pillows, the only other thing in the room was a huge basket of birds-of-paradise that provided all the color the room required.

I turned to Blue who was standing in the doorway. "It's beautiful."

He came over to stand beside me at the window. "I'm glad you like it."

"Are visitors allowed to walk on your beach?"

"I only own the house," he said, smiling, "not the beach."

This was an important distinction. People who forget it are usually the ones you see on TV after the hurricane, standing in front of their ruined mansions, shaking their fists at the ocean just for being the ocean, which is why they paid all that money for those houses in the first place.

"I'll take that as a yes," I said.

"If you can wait for me to change, I'll join you."

"I got nothing but time," I said, wondering what he could consider appropriate attire for a walk on the beach. "I'll meet you downstairs."

I couldn't be inside another second. Even with all the windows, I wanted to feel that breeze on my face and smell that air. I slid open the door to the back deck and stepped out of the great room and into the sunshine.

The beach was empty except for a young woman and a small boy figuring out how to fly one of those stunt kites that dips and swoops and skims the ground like it's spirit-possessed. They were tinkering with the length of the tail, and several attempts to get the huge, brightly colored kite up in the air ended in its bumping along the beach like a wounded seabird.

The little boy chased it down and brought it back carefully. The young woman tied off a piece of the long tail, and they tried again. This time, the kite lifted off as if it had wings of its own and absolutely *soared*. Against the bright blue sky, the pink-and-orange flutter of the kite looked like a tropical parrot that had wandered over from the Amazon jungle just for the day. The little boy applauded and actually did a little dance of joy. I could hear his delighted laughter carry on the wind, and it made me smile, too.

I closed my eyes and turned my face toward the warmth of the sun over my shoulder and sighed deeply. Maybe Blue was right. Maybe what I was feeling was a blood memory of another time and place on another side of another world. But how can you tell the difference? How can you distinguish between what is known to you specifically and what is known simply because you're a human being? My father gave me a book once in which the author claimed that if you went anywhere in the world and set a toddler down in front of the ocean, the kid's first response would be to open her arms as if to embrace it. I felt that way now. Safe and happy and curious about whatever was going to happen next.

"And what do you think that is?"

Blue was standing beside me holding a bottle of champagne and two glasses. I hadn't heard him walk up, but that was nothing new.

"I thought you said you weren't a mind reader," I said.

"Sometimes the magic works, and sometimes it doesn't." He grinned.

He had traded his suit for a pair of wheat-colored slacks and a white linen shirt that was a perfect contrast to his dark skin. The blue of his eyes reflected the blue of both the ocean and the sky, and I felt that panty-throwing feeling wash over me again.

"Are you hungry?" he said.

"A little."

"I'll be right back."

The kite fliers had moved farther up the beach, but I could still hear the wind whipping through their amazing *almost a bird*. Blue brought out a tray and laid the food out efficiently without making a big deal of it. There are some men who enjoy creating a perfect moment but can't let you enjoy it for reminding you how perfect it really is. They have no idea that nothing breaks the mood like somebody telling you how hard he worked to create it.

Blue popped the cork on the champagne and poured us each a glass.

"Welcome," he said.

We tapped our glasses for the toast and sipped our champagne like we had always lived this way, and maybe we had. Just not recently. He had brought out a tray of assorted cheeses, a small basket of bread and crackers, some hot mustard, and two small plates. He had added a bunch of green grapes from the bowl on the table and a half-dozen giant strawberries.

We served ourselves a little of this and a little of that, and I realized I was hungrier than I thought. Everything tasted fantastic and too fresh to have been sitting here for longer than a few hours.

"Do you have an invisible staff or a family of elves that makes sure you always have such a beautifully stocked refrigerator?"

He laughed. "Peachy looks after things for me when I'm not here. He's got the room right next to Lu's."

As if he heard us call his name, a car pulled into the driveway below us and Peachy stepped out, grinning from ear to ear. "Well, I see you Negroes made it in one piece," he said. "Welcome, Miss Lady."

"Come on up," Blue said. "I just opened a bottle of champagne."

"You ain't got to ask me twice," Peachy said, "but you gotta help me get this stuff upstairs first. I'm too old to be carryin' groceries."

Blue laughed. "What groceries you got? I thought we were taking you out."

Peachy grimaced and shook his head. "Too many tourists. I'm prepared to let you cook for me instead."

That appealed to me a lot. I never wanted to leave this deck again in life.

"And what am I cooking?"

"Seafood, man, seafood!" Peachy opened the trunk to reveal a large red cooler. "What else you gonna cook at the damn beach?"

Blue set down his glass and headed for the steps. "Be right back."

I watched them greet each other with a handshake and a hug. Peachy looked even smaller than he had at Club Zebra. Without the padded shoulders of the white dinner jacket he'd worn that night, he looked older and more vulnerable. Blue had said the death of his wife, Lillie, had been hard on Peachy. She was the true love of his life, and Peachy was a man who believed in love.

Childless by choice when Lillie said he could have babies or the road, but not both, they always traveled together. She went with him to all the holes in the wall at the beginning without complaint, and, later, when Blue stopped touring and Peachy's talent put him in demand as a stellar studio player and a valued backup musician, she was never impressed with the stars. She spent most of her time knitting backstage, unless Peachy had a featured solo, at which point she would appear in the wings where he could see her and direct his passionate playing to the object of his affections.

When she died after a long struggle with breast cancer, Peachy was inconsolable. He was better now, but her birthday was going to be a challenge. That's why we were here, and, so far, Peachy seemed to be in high spirits. He preceded Blue up the stairs, wearing a pair of old khakis and a tropical shirt that looked like it was on loan from the wardrobe department of a Cheech and Chong movie. He came straight to me, and we shared a hug that expressed our mutual pleasure in seeing each other again.

"Welcome to the island," Peachy said as Blue carried the big cooler into the house. "Do you eat seafood?"

"As long as it's cooked," I said. "I don't do sushi."

Peachy wrinkled his nose. "Don't no niggas do sushi unless they been hangin' out with white folks," he said, picking up the champagne and ushering me into the house where Blue was opening the cooler.

"Sushi?" Blue said, coming in on the end of the exchange, and raising his eyebrows in immediate disapproval.

I laughed. "I think we all agree, *no sushi!* So what are we having?"

"Depends on the chef," Peachy said, helping himself to a glass of champagne.

Blue was unpacking the cooler. Several varieties of fresh fish, a huge bag of fresh shrimp, and enough crab legs to be against the law.

"You must have met the boat," Blue said. "This stuff is *fresh.*"

Peachy beamed. "We got a guest, man. You know I'm gonna bring the best."

Blue stashed all the seafood in the refrigerator and ushered us back outside. "We were heading down for a walk. Are you up for a stroll?"

Peachy shook his head. "I've done all the strolling I can take for one day. Go on. I'll stay and finish off this champagne before it goes flat."

Blue laughed as Peachy settled into a lounge chair, put up his feet, and sighed contentedly just the way I had a few minutes ago. Maybe that was the required posttoddler human reaction to all this beauty in one place: a sigh and a smile.

"Go on and get your rest, old man. I'm going to put you to work in the kitchen as soon as we get back."

"I stand ready to be of assistance," Peachy said. "Who taught you how to cook in the first place?"

"My mama," Blue said, leading me down the steps to the path that led over the dunes and down to the beach. "Now what you got to say about that?"

"She did a fine job in that, as in all things." Peachy's laugh floated behind us.

I liked their ease with each other. They'd been friends for twenty years, and they were beyond secrets. We crested the dune, slipped off our shoes, and walked barefoot down to the water's edge. The kite fliers had disappeared, and we were the only people around. The sunlight sparkling on the waves looked like a painting, and I dipped my toes in the water. It was cool like the sand under my feet.

I looked at Blue standing beside me, and I hoped he really could read my mind because it was nothing but a big ball of absolute contentment. I owed him one for bringing me here. I turned back toward the water, and we just stood there in silence for a minute. Two minutes. Three. I could feel the stress flowing out of my body in waves. The pace of the city was being replaced by *beach time*, when standing stock-still in the surf is acceptable behavior. In fact, it's expected.

Anybody who isn't humbled in the presence of the ocean isn't looking. We stood there as if we were trying to burn the picture on our memories for this lifetime and the next one, and then, just when

I thought it couldn't be a more perfect moment, a slender black fin came into view. Then another one.

"Sharks?" I whispered.

Blue smiled and shook his head. "Dolphins."

Just as he said it, one of them leapt out of the water, twisted itself as if to catch the sunlight, and crashed back down into the waves. I had never seen a leaping dolphin before, and I was as delighted as the kid with the kite. I clapped my hands as another one rose up effortlessly and crashed back down. Just seeing them jumping like that made me so happy that I felt my eyes fill up with tears.

"Oh, my God!" I said.

I turned to Blue, and he was looking right at me.

"Exactly," he said.

And then he kissed me. He didn't touch me in any other way. He just leaned over and kissed me smack on the mouth, and I kissed him back, and it felt so good and so right that I decided to stop worrying about past lives or next lives or anything except his mouth on mine and the sunshine on our faces. When he drew back to look into my eyes, I smiled and waited for him to break the spell or complete it.

He smiled back at me. "So are you going to tell me?"

"Tell you what?" I knew exactly what.

"What's going to happen next."

"I'll write what I think in the sand and you write what you think in the sand. Then I'll read yours and you can read mine and we'll see how close we are."

I didn't wait for his reaction. I just stepped a few paces away and started writing my one-word answer to the question in the wet sand. The question of what lies ahead. The question of what we're getting ready to do. The question of what we will probably upset in the life of the other one. The question of what I'm prepared to give if he really is prepared to take it. To all those questions, I have only one answer: EVERYTHING.

In big block letters I scraped it into the sand with my toe. Blue was watching me.

"Ready?"

He nodded and as he walked over to read my answer, I did the same, although I didn't need to bother. It was like holding up a mirror. EVERYTHING, he had written in the sand in big block letters just like mine. EVERYTHING.

38

We walked all the way to the pier and back around to the lighthouse. Sometimes we talked. Sometimes we didn't. Sometimes we stopped to watch the dolphins or the large cargo tanker ships easing out of the mouth of the Savannah River and heading out toward the open sea. For the first time, I understood the real meaning of having all the time in the world. I always thought that meant a lot of time. *Hundreds* of hours, *thousands* of minutes, but it doesn't. It means that you have complete and utter possession of this one fleeting moment you're moving through on the way to the next one and the next one and the next one. And in all this world, that's all the time there is—that one perfect moment that Blue and I were strolling through. The sweetness was, we both knew it.

By the time we got back to the house, Peachy was already in the kitchen cleaning the shrimp. He had a big pot of hot water seasoned with some kind of seafood boil that was smelling so good all by itself that my stomach growled as if all that fruit and cheese I had eaten earlier was nothing but a distant memory. He had turned on the radio to a Saturday oldies show, and as we came up the stairs and slipped in the door off the deck, he was singing along all loud and happy.

" 'All you soul brothers, jitterbugs, hip cats in crazy hats, pretty girls with pretty smiles, all decked out in the latest styles!' "

Blue jumped right in:

" 'And Farmer Jim and Guitar Slim, Betty Boop and Ooh Boopa Doo, Mohair Sam from Alabam and Minnesota Fats from Hoboken Flats.' "

Peachy turned around and grinned, but never missed a beat.

" 'Breathtakin', hip shakin' cuties now, talkin' 'bout some fascinatin', devastatin' beauties now.' "

He came out from the kitchen, wiping his hands on a dish towel, and picked up a dance move that Blue slid into like they'd been practicing all week as the song wound up its complicated recitation of the delights that are awaiting those lucky enough to attend this particular "function at the junction." As a description of a perfect Negro party, Shorty Long's classic rivals Paul Lawrence Dunbar's "The Party," plus you don't have to sing it in dialect!

"Big finish," Peachy said and Blue executed a flawless turn that Peachy echoed a split second later and then hit a quick split worthy of James Brown in his prime and pulled himself up just in time to strike a pose that Blue completed.

" 'They'll all be gathering here, from far and near, for the function at the junction!' "

When the song ended, they held the pose like the professionals they were. This was showing off at the highest level, and I loved it.

"More!" I said laughing and applauding. "Encore!"

Peachy laughed and waved a hand. "*More?* That's all there is, baby. There ain't no more!"

Blue laughed, too, and jerked his thumb toward the kitchen. "I thought I was cooking, old man."

"I'm just doin' the prep work," Peachy said, turning down the radio. He was wearing a big black apron with white letters on the front that said DON'T MAKE ME POISON YOUR FOOD!

"Can I help?" I said.

"Yes, you can," Peachy said. "You can sit right here while I finish cleanin' this shrimp and tell me what the hell you see in this Negro."

"You don't have to answer that," Blue said, laughing and slipping his arm around my waist.

"You ain't in it," Peachy said. "You gotta go up to Chu's Liquor and get the Andre's."

Blue pretended to be aghast. "I got a refrigerator full of Moët and you're sending me out for Andre's? That's not going to do much for my image."

Peachy snorted. "What image is that?"

"The cool, suave, man-of-the-world brother who knows his way around a bottle of good wine."

"That's your image?"

Blue grinned. "Okay, how about a brother who has traded up from Andre's and ain't goin' back?"

"Get two bottles," Peachy said, ignoring his friend.

"Lillie is the only person who could get me to buy a bottle of that stuff."

"And the only one who could make me drink it, so we're even," Peachy said, going back to the shrimp. "Go on, now! Me and Miss Lady got plenty to talk about without you hangin' around."

Blue grabbed his keys. "Don't let him do any real cooking until I get back, okay?"

"I'll do my best."

Peachy smiled at me as Blue headed out the door. We heard the car backing out and the sound of it fading as he pulled away. I sat down and waited to see if he really did want to talk to me or he was just teasing.

"You comfortable?"

"I think I'm all right until the Andre's gets here," I said, teasing him.

He grinned at me. "You know the story about the Andre's?"

Peachy is one of those storytellers who likes to begin with a question. When you answer it in the negative, you are triggering the start of whatever tale he was going to tell anyway.

"Not yet."

He dumped some more shrimp into the sink. "Well, when my wife and I got married, we were so broke all we could afford was Andre's for the reception, so it meant something to her," he explained. "When I started making money, I'd try to bring home the expensive stuff instead—Moët, Dom P.—but she always wanted a bottle of Andre's for the memories in it."

"I'm sorry I never met her."

"Me, too. That was my baby, all right. She was down for me all the way, and that's something rare. People act like it's only rare these days, but it always was. It's always more people down for bullshit than down for love."

He went over to the sink and busied himself for a minute spraying cold water over the shrimp, and I could tell he had gotten a little choked up just thinking about Lillie. I went to the refrigerator and got a bottle of water while Peachy gathered himself together. Thinking the radio might help, I turned up the oldies again; Chubby Checker's voice boomed out the hit that changed the way people danced in America forever.

"Come on, baby,
Let's do the twist!"

"Twist it, y'all!" the DJ shouted. "You know you want to! Twist it, children!"

I looked at Peachy, and he gave me a small smile. That was all the encouragement I needed. I put down my water and held out my hand to Peachy. "I need a partner."

He hesitated for a second, but then he whipped off his apron and headed for our makeshift dance floor. From that point on, Peachy and I became twisting fools! The beauty of the twist is that anybody can do it, and it's fun or funny or sexy or silly, depending on how fast or slow you want to move. Peachy and I hit a midtempo rhythm that suited us, and we hung with Chubby to the end before collapsing, breathing hard and laughing, into two of Blue's white slipcovered chairs.

"You Negroes are going to kill me up in here," Peachy said.

"I think you can hold your own." I grinned at him.

He grinned back. "Well, as my grandmama used to say, 'If you don't hold it, who gonna hold it?' "

I laughed. "Your grandmama must have been a very wise woman."

"She was, she was, but what I want to talk about is *you*."

He had changed subjects so abruptly that I almost felt a little defensive. *Almost.*

"Me?"

He nodded. "Don't be nervous. This ain't no test or nothin'."

"I'm not nervous."

"Good." He smiled. "Here's the question, okay?"

I wasn't sure if I was being asked to agree to hear it or to respond. Either one was cool with me. "Okay."

He looked at me, suddenly serious. "Do you really like this Negro?"

Was that what he really wanted to know? "Yes."

"You know he's different, right?"

I nodded, wondering how much Peachy knew about the past lives and everything.

"Not just the eyes."

"No," I said. "Not just the eyes."

Peachy stood up and paced a little. I couldn't imagine what was making him so agitated.

"What's wrong?" I said softly.

He stopped and looked at me. "Just this. The boy been divorced three times, and I'm gettin' old. My heart ain't what it used to be. *He* might be able to survive going through all that again, but I can't."

"We're not even married yet," I said gently.

"You will be. It's only a matter of time."

The way he said it surprised me. He sounded so definite.

"How do you know?"

He looked at me like the question was so ridiculous, he had to decide if he was going to answer it at all. "I know what the love of a good woman can do for a man." He looked at me. "And I know the opposite is true, too. You can only get your heart broke so many times before you forget how to offer it up at all. I don't want that to happen to my boy. You're not like the others he was trying to make into something they were never meant to be. You might be the one he's been looking for all this time."

214

He stopped again. There was something sweet about being asked so formally not to break somebody's heart.

"He'll be safe with me," I said. "I promise."

Peachy relaxed immediately, as if I didn't need to offer him any further guarantees.

"But now you have to promise me something," I said.

"Shoot."

"Let us take it one step at a time, okay? This is all new for me."

"Which means stay out of your business, right?" He grinned.

I just smiled and turned up the radio so The Supremes could be my musical amen corner.

"You can't hurry love, no, you just have to wait."

Peachy laughed. "I hear you, Miss Ross! 'Nuff said!"

"You got to just give it time, no matter how long it takes."

" 'Nuff said!"

39

WHEN BLUE GOT BACK WITH THE Andre's, crab legs were already boiling, shrimp were frying, and the oldies had segued into a salsa show that was clearly being beamed from a Florida station. Even the DJ spoke Spanish. I had been allowed to shuck the corn, prepare a mixed green salad, and set the table for three.

Blue took it all in and grinned. "This Negro thinks he's the only one who knows how to boil a shrimp."

"Got tired of waiting," Peachy said. "What took you?"

"Tourists," said Blue, the way desert nomads might say "sand flies." "The brother in front of me bought every flavor Alize they had."

He grimaced at the name of the cognac and sweet juice drink favored by young people who want to get the taste of Kool-Aid and the buzz of malt liquor in one ill-conceived package.

I laughed. "You must have fit right in with your Andre's."

Blue winked at me, put the bag down on the table, and withdrew two of Andre's famous green bottles with the bright orange $4.99 sale price tags stuck on the front. "I had to buy these in self-defense," he said, pulling out two more bottles, both Dom Perignon, their price a secret between the consumer and the liquor store owner. If you had to ask the price of the stuff, you couldn't afford it.

"Well, pop the cork on one of each," Peachy said, "and let's eat."

In addition to the seafood feast, Peachy had steamed some asparagus, boiled some corn, and made a pitcher of sweet tea. Like Blue, he did all this with a minimum of fuss and only when we sat down to eat did he allow himself a small smile of satisfaction at a job well done. I had brought down some of the birds-of-paradise from upstairs to make a centerpiece, and Peachy nodded his approval.

Blue poured us each a swallow of Andre's and put one of the Doms in a silver ice bucket. It was sunset when we raised our glasses to toast the memory of Lillie, and the sky was streaked with bands of orange fire and splashes of gold. We had left the doors open and the gulls were calling to one another as they swooped down into the waves looking for their supper.

"Happy birthday, baby!" Peachy said as if she was sitting across the table from him, and his voice trembled just a little. "Miss you like crazy."

We clinked our glasses, downed our Andre's, and Peachy closed his eyes to send a private message to his beloved. At that moment, one of the gulls flew up, landed on the deck railing, and looked in at us looking out. Peachy opened his eyes, but nobody moved. The bird sat there for a long minute and then caught the next breeze back out over the water. I looked at Peachy, and two big tears rolled down his cheeks. Blue was watching him, but he didn't make a move in his direction.

I reached over and took Peachy's hand. "You okay?"

He nodded. "I asked her for a sign," he said softly.

"And she sent you one."

"What did I tell you?" he said, wiping his face with a napkin. "That woman was always down for me, you know? Look like she still is."

Blue was smiling now. "Do me a favor?" he said to his friend, reaching for the expensive champagne. "Next time, ask Lillie if we can let go of this Andre's and start drinking something better in her honor from now on."

"If it ain't broke," said Peachy, grinning and refilling his own glass with Andre's. "Don't fix it."

40

I T WAS AFTER MIDNIGHT WHEN we finished dinner and shared clean-up chores. The Andre's was gone, the moon was out, and Peachy was more than a little high, which was fine. If you can't get a little drunk in honor of great love lost, when can you get a little drunk?

I probably should have asked myself that question a few hours earlier, because by the time Peachy hugged us both twice, said good night, and retired to his room, I had a nice little buzz myself. Sitting on the deck beside Blue, I wanted to confess something, or promise something, or claim something, not necessarily in that order, but mostly I wanted to curl up in his arms and see if we could find a shooting star to wish on. Mostly I wanted him to hold me for a while. To let me get used to the smell of his skin, the circle of his arms, the way his mustache tickled when he kissed me.

I closed my eyes and tried to see if his mind reading was working. *Hold me,* I thought. *Just hold me.*

"Gina?" His voice was as warm as the soft night air.

"Yes?"

"Tell me what you want."

I opened my eyes and looked at him, but I felt as shy as a fifteen-year-old on a high school date.

"Do you want to go upstairs?" he asked.

Be careful what you ask for. . . .

He smiled and reached out to touch my cheek. "We won't do a single thing that you don't want to do."

"I want to do everything," I whispered, holding his hand against my face, leaning toward his kiss. "Remember?"

"Then that's what we'll do."

41

B ETH LEFT THREE MESSAGES ON Friday night, four on Saturday, and another three on Sunday. Her tone grew increasingly
annoyed, and I knew it was probably accompanied by a rise in rage at
Jade for her poor judgment in not finding out what I had to say before she let me go off God knows where for the weekend. I wondered
how she'd feel if she knew I had spent the past two days falling in love
with the one-hit wonder.

You know how sometimes after you make love everything gets
weird? I've had that experience more than I'd care to admit. For a
while, I thought it was my fault. I started believing all those frightened guys who kept telling me I was too intense or encouraging me
to *lighten up*. I wondered if I was wrong to think that sex could be
something that made everything sweeter, richer, deeper. Maybe I was
crazy to think there were things you could communicate through the
skin that you couldn't say any other way.

Well, I didn't have to wonder anymore. Making love with Blue
was the most intimate experience I've ever had with another human
being. Just before dawn, I got up and opened the big windows in the
bedroom to feel the breeze against my body. I could hear the ocean
whispering outside, and all of I sudden I did it: *I remembered the sea.*
I remembered the rhythm of it, the constant song, the power of it. I
found all that in my exchange with Blue that night, and when he
came up behind me and wrapped his arms around me, I knew he had
found something, too, and even though it had taken him a couple of
lifetimes, it had been worth the wait.

When we got back to Atlanta late Sunday night, playing games
with Beth was the last thing on my mind. I spent the night at Blue's
and told myself I was allowed to remain on "beach time" until I had

to show up at Morehouse the next morning. Freeney and I were going to screen the rough cut of the biographical video, and, after that, as promised, I would call Beth. I went home in the morning to take a shower and change, kissed Blue good-bye in the hallway, and strolled up to Morehouse with that "sure-was-good" grin on my face and not a care in the world.

Freeney met me on the steps of the old library building looking stressed. When he saw me, he waved me over anxiously, as if I wasn't moving fast enough to close the distance between us.

"What's wrong?" I said. He was a friend now as well as a co-worker, and I knew his partner was HIV positive and hadn't been well. "Is it Brady?"

"Bless you," he said, giving me a quick peck on the cheek. "But, thank God, no. Brady's getting stronger by the day. It's *her*. She's here!"

"Who's here?"

"Ms. Davis. She's already watching the video downstairs."

"She's *what*?" I headed for the conference room, where I knew he would have set up the video equipment. This was just a rough cut. Her suggestions at this point would just confuse the process.

"I wasn't expecting her," he said. "But when she showed up and I told her what we were getting ready to do, she said she'd like a look herself, so I didn't know what else to do."

I made myself slow down. Freeney was already puffing trying to keep up and what was I rushing around for? There was no problem. This was simply Beth putting me in my place for being inaccessible for two whole days. She was stamping her little feet to let me know she was displeased, and that was fine. She'd find no flaws in the video—I had made sure she was in almost every frame—and her irritation with me would pale to insignificance the minute I handed her the photograph of her beautiful little grandson.

I turned to Freeney, mopping his bald head and looking at me helplessly. "It's fine. She's entitled to see anything at any time."

Freeney looked guardedly reassured. "Really?"

I nodded. "He was her son, remember? That's why we're doing all this."

"Of course, of course," he said. "I just didn't want to jump the gun since we hadn't talked about her involvement at this level and I know Ms. Davis can be—" He stopped, embarrassed, searching for a polite way to say "a real bitch."

I put him out of his misery. "Demanding," I said. "Really *demanding.*"

He grinned at me and gave his face one more pass with that big white handkerchief. "That's it exactly."

I opened the door of the conference room and Beth was sitting there watching the monitor in the semidarkness. On the screen was a clip of Son delivering the commencement address at Morehouse last year. He was exhorting them, in the time-honored tradition of graduation speakers, to be all they could be, but in Son's mouth, it sounded like a call to arms, an invitation to excellence and the most exciting adventure possible. That was the last of the edited footage, and, as the screen turned to snow, Freeney clicked on the light.

When Beth turned toward us, her face was wet with tears. "It's lovely," she said softly, pulling a tissue from her purse and blowing her nose. "Absolutely perfect."

Freeney and I were speechless. For a test screening, tears and testimonials were high praise.

"I'm glad you—," I started to say, but she waved her hand to stop me. "No, I mean it's *perfect,*" she said urgently, her eyes imploring me to understand.

I turned to Freeney. "Can you leave us alone for a few minutes?"

"Of course, of course," he said, backing out the door, eyes wide with sympathy and surprise.

I sat down next to Beth and pulled my chair close. "You okay?"

She opened her mouth to speak, but nothing came out. Tears were still streaming down her face. I took her hand and waited. In all the rush to finish the tasks at hand and figure out what was really going on, I had almost forgotten that Beth had lost her only child when Son died. She had handled the public requirements of her grieving with class and restraint, but in the privacy of her own heart, she had never stopped missing him.

She mopped her eyes and managed a shaky smile. "I remember that day so well. He'd never been better. The students just crowded around him afterward, Gina." She shook her head sadly and dabbed her eyes again then she looked at me. "I owe you an apology."

"You don't owe me anything."

"No, I do. I know I blamed you for some of the problems between Son and me before you left, but it wasn't your fault. He had his own ideas. He wanted his own life, his own family."

I looked at her closely. *Did she know about the kid?*

"But I didn't know how to let go." Her voice trembled. "I was selfish. I wanted to keep him tied to the life I had created for him, for *us*, and I did that. I surely did that, but how he must have suffered trying to please me instead of being himself." Her voice was filled with regret.

"Don't blame yourself," I said. "Son loved you very much. You know that."

She smiled and patted my hand gently. "Yes, I know that. I also know that you think my running for governor is a really bad idea."

"We don't have to talk about that now," I said.

"I want to. I think . . . I think Son probably would have agreed with you." She smiled again. "I *know* he would have agreed with you, but . . . I think part of why running appeals to me is that it will take everything I've got, and I've got some big spaces to fill in my life, Gina, that weren't there before. It's hard to admit it, even to myself, but watching Son on that video . . ."

Her voice trailed off for a minute and her eyes filled up again, but she didn't break down. "I just wouldn't want to make a move like this without really thinking it through the way he would want me to."

I breathed a sigh of relief. There was still a chance that she'd tell the draft committee to go to hell and throw her support behind Precious!

"That's all I was trying to say the other day," I said. "I just don't want you to rush into anything that isn't in your best interests."

"I've decided to put off any decision until after the dedication. That will be Son's day, and I don't want to mix it up with a lot of politics."

"I think that's very wise."

She nodded. "Good. Then that's what we'll do."

Things were going so well, I didn't want to bring up my conversation with Precious, but I didn't have to worry. Beth had that covered. She tucked her tissue back into her pocket and sighed.

"Well, I certainly didn't mean to come in with so much drama," she said. "I was just hoping I could catch up with you and get a report on your meeting with Senator Hargrove."

She made me sound like a double agent or something. "It wasn't really a meeting. We had *tea*. She said she'd been trying to get in touch with you, but she hadn't gotten a response." I reached into my briefcase for the envelope and handed it to her. "She asked me to give you this."

Beth took the envelope and looked at the front. "It's addressed to Precious. Why would I want to read mail that isn't addressed to me?"

"It's *about* you."

"What about me?" Her voice was indignant.

I looked at her.

"All right, all right," she said, withdrawing the note and the photograph. She looked at the picture, and I knew she saw exactly what I saw: *her grandchild.*

I couldn't tell what she was feeling, but she looked at the picture for a long time, then she read the note.

"What does it mean?" she asked, her eyes flashing angrily.

"Precious thinks someone wants her to use it to get you out of the race."

"I'm not in the race."

"They don't want you to get in."

She looked at the picture again. "This is not Son's child. You know this is not Son's child."

"I don't know anything about it," I said. "But if you do have a grandson, wouldn't you want to know?"

"I would know!" she snapped. "Son never would have kept this from me."

"That's the same woman who was in the other picture with him," I reminded her gently.

"I don't care who she is!" Beth said. "And I am not going to take responsibility for a child who just happens to look a little bit like my son."

She was in deep denial, but there was no reason for me to press her. She had already agreed not to make any kind of political announcement at the dedication. That left Precious free to participate and me to write a speech that honored my friend and completed my obligation. This was a personal crisis for Beth that did not involve me beyond the passing of the photograph as requested. There was an address on the note. She could follow up on it or not. I was out of it.

"Maybe you can have your investigator talk to the woman," I said. "Then at least you'll know one way or the other."

She glared at me, obviously considering her options, then she folded the note and slid it back into the envelope with the picture. "You know what this is, don't you?" she said quietly. "This is nothing but political dirty tricks."

"I agree."

"I wouldn't have expected it from Precious, not this early anyway, but I'm not really surprised. She's already running scared."

"What are you talking about? She brought it to me to give to you."

"That's the whole point, don't you see? She's acting as if she's doing me a favor, and she's really trying to scare me out of the race with a threat like this."

I shook my head. "You're wrong. She said you were a formidable opponent and she'd rather you didn't get in the race at all, but she wasn't prepared to use dirty tricks to keep you out."

Beth smiled at me condescendingly, as if what I was saying was hopelessly naive. "What else is she going to say? 'Here, Gina, take this blackmail threat to Beth and tell her there's more where that came from'?"

She was picking up steam, working up into an outraged rant. "There's an unlimited pool of strippers in this town who will say anything they're paid to say!"

"That's the second time you've said she was a stripper."

She pulled up short, instantly wary. "Is it?"

I nodded, remembering Precious's words: *It's been a long time since anything surprised Beth Davis.* Did she know this woman?

Beth busied herself all of sudden with putting the envelope in her purse like that was a task that required her complete attention. "Well, that's what we've had to deal with before, like I said. That's who keeps making these outrageous claims and offering to keep quiet for money."

She stopped herself, having said more than she had intended to say. I looked at her, and it was clear to me that she knew a lot more than she was telling. It was also clear that this conversation was over.

Beth glanced at her watch and frowned. "Is it that late?"

That was so lame I didn't even have to pretend to believe it. "It is what it is," I said, watching her gather her things quickly.

"I've got to run. Thanks for bringing me this," she patted her purse protectively. "And pardon me for being guilty of cutting the head off the messenger. I'm used to the scams, but this one has gone too far, and I'm going to get to the bottom of it."

"Keep me posted," I said, walking her to the door of the conference room.

"Don't even worry about it," she said. "I'll put somebody on this. You just keep doing the wonderful work you're doing. Son would be so proud."

I watched her walking down the long hallway and wondered what she knew about this woman and her child. She had thrown out dirty tricks, unscrupulous strippers, and con artists as possible reasons for the appearance of the photograph. What she hadn't dealt with at all was Son staring out at her from that child's face.

42

BLUE AND I WERE GOING OUT for dinner after we stopped by to say happy birthday to Lu. Aretha had managed to score front-row tickets to the Ashanti concert tonight as her gift, and Lu and ShaRonda had been counting the hours. I was looking forward to spending the evening with my favorite landlord, but when he knocked on my door, I knew immediately this was not a social call.

"What's wrong?" I said as soon as I saw his expression.

"I'm going to have to work on my poker face," he said, kissing me lightly.

"Are you okay?"

"I'm fine," he said, "and ordinarily I wouldn't involve you in this aspect of my business, but I think I have some information you need to be aware of before I act on it."

"Sit down," I said, drawing him over to the couch. He was making me very nervous. "What is it?"

"It's possible that Beth Davis has been involved in threatening a young woman who knew her son."

"What?"

"Her cousin came to see me to ask for my help. She brought this with her."

He reached into his pocket and handed me a small photograph in a cheap, dime-store frame, but the frame didn't matter. The picture showed a man, a woman, and a small boy. It completed the trio that had begun in Freeney's dusty boxes, continued through Precious's let-ter, and was now revealing Son's other life in a moment that could not be denied.

"Have you ever seen this picture before?"

I shook my head. "Not this one, but I've seen others of this woman and one of the little boy. I found one in Son's papers, and somebody sent one to Precious with a note."

"What did the note say?"

"It said whoever sent it wondered if Beth was going to put her grandson on her campaign brochure."

"Did Precious show it to her?"

"I did," I said, with a sickening feeling that I was somehow part of this whole mess in a way I didn't want to be.

"And what did she say?"

"She denied it. She said it was probably some kind of political blackmail or a scam for money and that she'd have her people check it out."

"Her people." He spit the words out.

"What happened?"

"She sent some thugs to threaten the woman."

"Threaten her with what?"

He looked at me, and his eyes were clear and cold as ice. "They told her they'd cut her face."

43

The West End News was closed, but Blue's back office was open for business. When we walked in, there was a young woman sitting miserably at the center table, clutching her purse and looking like she'd rather be almost anywhere but here. The old guy who was usually out front making cappuccino was sitting with her, but they didn't seem to have enough in common to make for much interesting conversation. When she saw Blue walk in, she visibly relaxed.

"I thought you had forgot all about me," she said, in a manner that was more flirtatious than the moment required.

"I'm sorry I kept you waiting," Blue said. "Can I get either of you ladies anything to drink?"

"No, thanks," I said.

"I can't drink no more coffee," she said. "I'm already too nervous."

"You don't have to be nervous," Blue said, and nodded at the old guy, who went out quietly, leaving the three of us alone.

The woman looked to be about twenty-two and was pretty, but she was wearing so much makeup it was hard to tell. It was like trying to guess a doll's age. She had on a pair of skintight silver pants, a red low-cut blouse that barely covered her breasts, and high-heeled boots with alarmingly pointed toes.

"Who's she?" she asked, jerking her head in my direction and peering at me from under a cloud of curly ringlets.

"Brandi Harris, this is Regina Burns. She's been working with Ms. Davis."

Brandi's brightly painted, carefully outlined lips curled in a sneer at the mention of Beth's name.

"Some people will do anything for money," she said bitterly.

Blue fixed her with a gaze that drew her up short.

"I'm sorry, Mr. Blue. This whole thing has got me crazy. I don't mean no disrespect," she said quickly looking in my direction. *"My bad."*

"No problem," I said. "I'm sorry for your trouble."

That seemed to mollify her. "Thanks."

"Can you tell Regina what you told me?" Blue said gently.

"Okay." Brandi sighed deeply, like she didn't know quite where to start. "Madonna, she ain't never tried to make no trouble."

"Madonna is the woman in the photograph?" I asked.

She nodded. "That's her real name, too," she added, sounding a little defensive. "A whole lot of us take stage names when we start strippin', like my real name is Sarah, after my Big Mama, but Sarah don't sound sexy, so I took Brandi. But her mom was a big Madonna fan. She didn't care that nobody else around here was feelin' no white girl enough to name their baby after her, so she did it anyway."

Linear storytelling was obviously not Brandi's strong point. I looked at Blue who remained silent, watching her face.

"I gotta have that picture back, too," she said. "She's really scared if any more of her stuff gets out, DooDoo and them will come back and hurt her."

"What did they say?"

"They said they'd cut her face if she didn't take the money and get her ass out of town."

I swallowed hard. "What money?"

"They had cash," Brandi said. "Twenty grand in an envelope. We counted it when they left, even though Madonna didn't want to. She said she wasn't askin' for no money and she wasn't takin' no money."

That pretty much blew Beth's scheming stripper theory out of the water.

"That's a lot of money to turn down," Blue said. "Why do you think she wouldn't take it?"

"Who you askin'? That's what I said! Plus, she could use that money. Everything a baby need cost more money than you think it will. She ain't strippin' no more, even though she always made big money and she still could 'cause she so pretty and 'cause she can really dance. Guys just liked to watch her move. She didn't even have to do no lap dances. They'd be tippin' her ten bucks just for shakin' her ass in their face! She had it like that."

I didn't know what to say to that, so I just listened.

"But after she met Son Davis, she quit, just like that. He met her strippin', but as soon as they started spendin' time together, he told her he wished she'd stop, so she did. I don't blame her. He was prepared to take care of her and once she got pregnant, he even bought her a house over on Larchmont. Somebody musta tol' his mama because that's where they found Madonna. At home not botherin' nobody, then here come DooDoo talkin' all that smack."

My heart sank. That was the street that had been on the note from Precious. Son had successfully hidden his family from Beth, and I had sent her right to their front door.

"Is she there now?" I asked, wondering how far Beth was prepared to go and feeling responsible.

Brandi shook her head. "I told Mr. Blue already, she gone to Macon to hide out at her mama's house, but she and her mama don't get along too good, so she can't stay there long, and she scared to come back here without some protection, so that's why I came to see Mr. Blue." She fluttered her fake eyelashes at him and smiled.

"You did the right thing," he said simply.

"I hope so," she said, still sounding worried. "She my baby cousin, and I love her and Sonny Jr., the sweetest little boy you ever gonna see, but I work for King James dancin' over at the Gentleman's Club, and I can't afford to lose my job behind this. He own too many clubs for me to be on his shit list. Strippin' is hard, but it ain't as hard as turnin' tricks."

I felt sorry for Brandi. She was young and healthy, but stripping and prostitution were the only two career options she could imagine for herself. I wondered how many smart young women were choosing between those same dead ends. Heading for the hills obviously hadn't been the solution I had hoped it would be in that last life where I gathered my girls and left the men to fight among themselves. Here we were, all these lifetimes later, still taking off our clothes for money and running from the likes of Uncle DooDoo.

"Does he know you came here?" Blue asked.

Brandi shook her head. "Not if you didn't tell him."

"Good, then don't mention it to him. Are you working tonight?"

"I'm off tonight," she said. "I got a private party to do later."

"Then go on to the party and don't tell anyone that you came here. Do you understand?"

She nodded. "You gonna take care of it, Mr. Blue?"

"I'm going to take care of it."

The way he said it would have been chilling if he had been talking about anybody but DooDoo and King James. I wanted somebody to take care of them, and Blue was that somebody.

Brandi was gazing at him with a mixture of real gratitude and unabashed hero worship, which made her look about ten years old under all that makeup. "Everybody told me you were the man, Mr. Blue. That's what they said."

"And what did you say?"

"I said, 'Well thank God there are still some damn men around.' That's what I said!"

And even though directness wasn't her specialty, she hit that nail on the head. I couldn't have said it better myself.

44

PEOPLE WHO VISIT ATLANTA AND think they've been in Georgia are fooling themselves. Macon is less than two hours away, but as we left the city lights behind us and hit the part of the interstate that's still pine woods on both sides of the road, I had that little shiver that I always have driving through the rural south. There are so many bodies buried in these woods, these rivers, these ponds. So many restless spirits looking for some peace.

"What are you going to do when we get there?" I asked.

Brandi had called to let Madonna know we were coming.

"I'm going to ask her what happened and find out what she wants."

Beth's warnings about hustlers and con artists were still ringing in my ears. "What do *you* think she wants?"

"Protection."

"Can you protect her?"

He glanced over at me like the question surprised him. "That's my job, remember?"

"So *how* are you going to protect her."

"That's not what you want to ask me," Blue said, easing around a giant truck that had to be doing seventy-five.

"It's not?"

"That's a *detail* question, and you know I can handle those details alone."

He was right. I didn't really want to know the details. What was I trying to ask him? I tried again.

"How about, what am *I* going to do when we get there?"

"You don't have to do anything."

"Then why am I here?"

"I don't know."

"I don't know either."

"You will by the time we get there."

We rode along in silence for a minute. There was no doubt that this was Son's child. That much was certain. The only thing that was uncertain was Beth's role. Did she know it? Did she send thugs to terrorize her grandson's mother? And if she did, *why?*

"I need to know why Beth did this."

"Don't you mean *if*?"

I looked at him, but he didn't take his eyes off the dark highway. "Why would Brandi lie?"

"Why does anybody lie?"

That was an easy one. I had done a lot of lying during my dope-fiend days, and even though at the time I always had a thousand reasons for all the stupid stuff I did, once I really thought about it, they all boiled down to one thing: *fear.*

"Because they're afraid."

"Afraid of what?"

"It doesn't matter. Pain, embarrassment, being broke, being left . . ." I could have added my own all-time favorite, *fear of running out of cocaine,* but I think he got the idea.

"What's Beth Davis afraid of?"

"Nothing."

He smiled then. "Everybody's afraid of something."

"Well, if she's afraid of anything it would be . . . loss of control."

He nodded. "That's a big one all right."

Maybe the biggest. And losing control of the myth of the perfect son she'd spent a lifetime and a career building up? Sending DooDoo to threaten somebody was probably just the tip of the iceberg. I remembered her weeping reaction to the video of Son she saw at Morehouse. I had felt sorry for her, woman to woman. Had she been playing me for a fool all the time?

"What are you afraid of?" Blue said, pulling off the interstate at the second exit for Macon and taking a left at the Burger King.

I thought about it for a minute. "Having to quit working for

Beth before I make enough to save my house." I had told him all about the weasel, of course, and he had offered me the money immediately, but I couldn't take it. Part of the lesson I'm supposed to be learning is how to be a grown-up. Being rescued by my blue-eyed knight in shining armor was pretty romantic, but it wasn't going to make *me* any stronger. Besides, Aunt Abbie had been very clear that I was supposed to be the *shero*, not the damsel in distress.

"Why would you have to quit?"

I was surprised he had to ask. "I can't work for somebody who's sending DooDoo out to scare people into doing what she wants them to do," I said. "How can I write a speech to make people love and trust her when I know she's not who they think she is at all?"

"Then who is she?"

I shook my head as he pulled up in front of a small frame house on a narrow street where the hardworking residents still found time to grow pots of geraniums on the front porch. "I don't know anymore."

Blue turned off the car. "Maybe that's what you're here to find out."

45

MADONNA'S MOTHER OPENED the door about two inches and peeked out. Her eyes were suspicious.

"Mrs. Little?" Blue said. "It's Blue Hamilton from Atlanta."

She opened the door a little wider, and her eyes flickered over me.

"I've got Ms. Burns with me. Madonna is expecting us."

She opened the door reluctantly and stepped aside to let us in. She was a pretty woman whose looks probably hadn't taken her as far as she'd hoped they would. Since there was no one person to blame for the strange twist of fate that plopped her down in Macon, Georgia, to find her destiny, she generalized her disappointment and blamed everybody.

"She's putting the baby to bed," she said. "Would you like to sit down?"

"Thanks."

She led us into the living room, and I sat down on the couch. Blue took a chair, and Mrs. Little stood in the doorway watching us. The mantel and several end tables were filled with framed pictures of Madonna growing up. She had been a beautiful baby, rosy-cheeked and wide-eyed. If the photos on display were any indication, she had skipped any adolescent awkwardness and been an equally beautiful teenager. There were pictures of her in leotards at the bar and in costume for what looked like ballet recitals. Looking at that little girl in the pink satin ballet slippers, I'll bet you a five-dollar lap dance never entered her mind. It didn't strike me until later that there were no pictures of Madonna with her son.

I felt Mrs. Little's eyes on me, and I offered her a smile. She didn't return it.

"You work for Beth Davis?"

"Yes, I—"

"Well, she should be ashamed of herself. Her and her precious son—*rest in peace*—have been nothing but trouble for my girl since day one. I told her that, but she didn't listen, and now, look at this—" She gestured helplessly at Blue. "Look at who I've got sitting in my living room. You think this ain't gonna be trouble?"

Blue's voice was very gentle. "Mrs. Little, there's already trouble. That's why your daughter called me."

She snorted at that and rolled her eyes. "Madonna didn't call you. That other one, that Brandi, with her fast ass, that's who called you."

Mrs. Little was very agitated. I could see why. Unknown hoodlums had chased her daughter home, and then we show up at the front door, offering assistance. I glanced over at Blue. We had arrived in a black Lincoln, and Blue was dressed in his usual dark suit. Just his presence clearly made her very nervous.

"I see." Blue stood up slowly. "If your daughter doesn't want my help—"

"I do want your help!" Madonna walked up behind her mother. "I *need* your help. I apologize for my mom—"

"You ain't got to apologize for me," Mrs. Little said, stalking out of the room, her interim hostess duties complete. "This is your business, not mine."

Madonna's photographs didn't do her justice. Even in jeans and a T-shirt, she was undeniably beautiful. Her hair was pulled back in a giant afro puff, and her honey-colored skin glowed. Her big brown eyes carried a deep sadness. She looked after her mother but didn't try to stop her, then turned back to us apologetically.

"I'm sorry," she said again. "It's been hard on her." She extended her hand to Blue. "I'm Madonna Little, Mr. Hamilton. Thank you for coming all this way. I just didn't know who else to call."

"This is Regina Davis," Blue said.

Madonna turned to me. "You work for her?"

I nodded, feeling more ashamed every time somebody asked me

the question. We shook hands, but she looked a little uncertain about my role. No more uncertain than I was. We all sat down. On the wall behind Madonna's head was a framed color photograph of her six- or seven-year-old self in a little yellow ballet tutu with a buttercup bonnet tied under her chin. How had she ended up stripping for a living?

"Why don't you tell us what happened?" Blue said when she didn't seem to know where to begin.

Madonna's eyes filled with tears, but she blinked them back. "Where do you want me to start?"

"Tell me about DooDoo."

"Okay," Madonna took a deep breath. "Tuesday night, I was home with my son."

I had handed Beth that address on Monday after she wept for me at Morehouse. She hadn't wasted any time moving on it.

"It was after eleven because the news was on and I wasn't expecting anybody, so I looked out and it was DooDoo and one of those guys who hangs around with him. I was surprised, but I know him from before when I was still dancing, and I thought he might be looking for Brandi for a party or something, so I opened the door."

How many terrible moments for women begin with the words "so I opened the door"? We ought to make that a rule: *Whatever you do, don't open the damn door!* But she did.

"So they came in and DooDoo said I was . . . ," she hesitated.

"Take your time," Blue said.

"Should I say what he said?"

"If you can remember it."

"He said . . . he said I was fucking things up big time, and he was there to see what we could do about it. I told him I didn't know what he was talking about, and he handed me this picture of me and Junior. . . ." Her voice was trembling. "And a note." She stopped again.

"Go on."

"I told him I didn't know anything about it, and he told me if I didn't leave town and stay gone until he decided I could come back, I'd be sorry."

Blue's face was a mask. "Did he say anything else?"

She whispered the words. "He said first he was gonna cut my face and then he was gonna cut my throat."

I caught my breath. *Jesus!*

"We left that night and came here."

"How do you know Beth Davis sent him?" I said.

She turned toward me for the first time. "She hates me."

"Enough to threaten your life?"

"She already threatened to take my kid."

"When?"

"Right after Son died. I knew she didn't know about me or Sonny Jr. Son kept saying he was gonna tell her, but he never did. I think he was afraid of what she might say, me being a dancer when he met me and all, but after he died like that, I thought she'd want to know that he had left a son. That she had a grandson."

She clasped and unclasped her hands in her lap. "So I wrote her a letter and sent her a picture of me and Son and Junior and told her to meet me at the mall if she wanted to talk. I thought that would be a neutral space, you know?"

Blue and I both nodded.

"So she came and we sat right there on one of those benches outside the Gap, and she told me I was lying and there was too much at stake for her to let me and . . . and some brat mess up her plans. She told me if I ever contacted her again, she would get the state to take my baby away for being an unfit mother." Madonna looked at me.

"Son used to try to tell me how hard it was to talk to her, but I never got it. I had just seen the tapes, you know? You love her on those tapes; she seems so nice, like you could tell her anything and she would understand. But the woman who was talking to me, the real one?" She shook her head like the distance between one Beth and the other was too much to fathom. "So she handed me an envelope with some money in it. She said it was twenty grand and told me to keep my mouth shut or she'd send somebody around to shut it for me."

She looked at Blue. "I told her I didn't want her money and handed it back, but that's how I know it was her. That's the same amount DooDoo left with me the other night."

She stood up and walked over to a small desk in the corner, took out a thick white envelope, and handed it to Blue. "It's all there. I don't want money. I never asked for it, and I'm not takin' it."

"What do you want?" Blue said quietly.

Madonna sat back down. "Look, I don't know who sent her that picture or the note either. I don't care anything about politics, and I'll figure out a way to take care of me and my son without her money. I just want her to leave me alone. I'll die if they take my son, Mr. Hamilton. I've done some things I'm not proud of, but I'm a good mother. Even my mom will tell you that." She stopped and took a breath to calm herself a little, but when she spoke her voice shook a little bit. "I don't want DooDoo knocking on my door. I don't want him to come back and cut me."

The muscles in Blue's cheek rippled slightly. He stood up, walked over, and took her hand. "You don't have to worry about him anymore," he said. "I'll take care of it."

She looked at him. "Can you?"

He nodded. "Can you stay here a little while longer?"

"Yes."

"Good. Brandi will call you in a few days, and everything will be fine."

"Then I can go back to my house?"

"You can go anywhere you want to go," Blue said. "And I'm sorry for your troubles and your loss."

She stood up without letting go of his hand. "Thank you," she whispered. "Thank you."

I stood up, too. Blue looked at me and said to Madonna, "I'm going to say good night to your mother and let you and Gina talk for a minute. Would that be all right?"

She looked as startled as I felt. We looked at each other, mutually confused. Flora had said he always had a plan, and I guess he had one now. Only problem was he forgot to let me and Madonna in on it.

"My mom's probably in the kitchen."

"I'll be right back," Blue said, and walked out of the room in search of Mrs. Little.

Alone with Madonna, I had no idea what to say. She didn't either, so we just smiled at each other and sat back down. I figured I was safe with a topic every young mother can embrace.

"You have a beautiful boy," I said, wondering why there were no pictures of him on display.

"Thanks," she said. "Neither one of his grandmothers have much use for him. My mom's ashamed of me for having him without a husband, and his other grandmother . . . Well, it's their loss, that's what I think."

"His father must have been very proud of him."

"He was," she said, sounding a little defensive. "I don't care what Beth Davis says, Son loved his child!"

"I knew Son," I said. "We were friends a long time ago. I know how much being a good father would have meant to him."

"He was a good father. The best. I used to tease him sometimes about spoiling Junior, and he'd just laugh and say a whole lot of little black boys grow up mean because their daddies didn't know how to love them, but that wasn't going to happen to our son." She looked at me. "Can I tell you something?"

"Sure."

"He called me," she said softly, and I knew immediately what she meant. I knew where he was calling from for her to ask permission to speak about it.

"Everything was crazy, and he knew he wasn't going to make it, but he wanted me to promise to tell his son how much his daddy loved him." Her voice was calm now, and she looked me in the eye without blinking. "And I told him I would. That's why I can't take her money. There ain't enough money in the world for me to pretend his daddy ain't his daddy."

She stood up and walked over to the mantel and adjusted a picture of herself in a high school cap and gown. "Will you help me?"

"Just tell me how," I said.

Her hands kept busy straightening things that didn't need to be straightened. "Beth Davis keeps giving interviews saying how the worst part of losing her son was that he didn't leave any grandchildren for her to love. She went on and on about it on television a couple of weeks ago, like she didn't even know Junior was alive."

She turned back to me. "He's too little to see it now, but what's my son gonna think when he gets old enough to know that's his grandmother talking about how he doesn't exist?"

I had seen the interview she was talking about. Beth had said that her work was even more important to her since Son's death because by helping somebody else's grandbabies, she could honor those children her son never had a chance to father. It sounds corny to hear me say it secondhand, but when she said it to the interviewer, it was very moving. But if that was your grandmother talking, it would be pretty confusing to say the least.

"She doesn't really consult me on personal matters," I said, sounding inappropriately businesslike all of a sudden. "I don't know what I can do."

"You could give her something though, right?"

"Like what?" Where was Blue? I was getting more uncomfortable by the minute. We were there to guarantee her safety, and we had done that. Well, *he* had done that. *What had I done?*

Madonna walked over to the closet and took out a small blue Gap bag. "Before I asked her to come to the mall, I told her I'd bring some pictures and tapes and stuff so she would know I wasn't lying or anything." She handed me the bag, and inside were two small photo albums and two videotapes. "But she wouldn't even take it. She said she wasn't interested in seeing anything I had to show or hearing anything I had to say, and then she got up and walked away."

I tried to picture the scene. Madonna trying to make a dent in Beth's armor and Beth not about to let her.

"So I just stuck it in the closet," she was saying. "Because I was still thinking if I could get it to her . . . If she could see how happy Son was with us, if she could see what a sweet baby Junior is, maybe she'd feel differently."

I lifted out one of the tapes. FIRST BIRTHDAY PARTY, the label said, SEPTEMBER 6, 2001.

Our eyes met when I looked up, and she was clearly the damsel I'd been sent to rescue from the dragon lady who was her child's grandmother.

"Will you help me?"

"Yes," I said. "I will."

46

"I STILL CAN'T FIGURE OUT WHY Beth is doing this," I said to Blue when we were finally headed back to Atlanta. "How can she not claim her own grandchild?"

"Remember a couple of years ago," he said, back on the interstate now and cruising, "when Ralph Abernathy published a book about his life? Since Martin Luther King was his best friend, he talked about him, too, but some of what he had to say about Brother King's relationships with women other than his wife didn't sit well with the King family and some of the good reverend's movement friends. So they organized a press conference and called Ralph to task for tearing down the memory of a bona fide hero when, according to them, black kids need all the role models they can get. Do you remember that?"

"Sure," I said. "There was a big story in *Jet* and everything."

He nodded. "The thing is, they got it wrong."

"Because they didn't want anything to tarnish his memory?"

"Because a lie can never make you stronger, no matter how many times you tell it."

"But what about the importance of role models for black kids? That's a real thing, isn't it? If all their idols are shown to have feet of clay, who are they going to look up to?"

"Think about it this way. If Dr. King is a living saint, a perfect being, it gets me off the hook. I know I can't live up to all that, so I don't even have to try. But if he was nothin' but a man, with faults and flaws just like me, and he still did all those brave, unselfish things, then I can't dismiss the challenge of his life. I still have to step up, with all my doubts and imperfections, and be a *man,* just like he did. Just like Brother Davis was trying to do."

That made so much sense I wished I'd said it. "Can I quote you when I talk to Beth?"

He smiled in the darkness. "You better give me an alias if you do. I don't think I'm one of her favorite people."

"Fine with me," I said, feeling like I knew what I had to do and was ready to do it, but not tonight. We'd done enough for one night. "How about 'Sweet Thing'?"

He laughed low in his throat. "Sounds good to me."

47

IT WAS AFTER MIDNIGHT WHEN we pulled up in front of the house, and I was looking forward to curling up with Blue, but every light in Flora's place was blazing.

"Wonder what's going on at Flora's?" Blue said as we headed up the walk.

I knocked on the door, and Kwame opened it. Over his shoulder, I could see Flora and Aretha fussing over ShaRonda, who was sitting on the couch holding Lu's hand and looking shell-shocked.

"What happened?" Blue walked over to Flora quickly as Kwame closed the door behind us.

ShaRonda's eyes filled up with tears, and, from the looks of her eyeliner, she'd been crying for a while. The carefully chosen outfit she had worn to the Ashanti concert to celebrate Lu's birthday was ripped and dirty like she'd been fighting somebody in it. We had stopped by to say hello to the girls before we headed down to Macon, and they were in a flurry of getting ready for the big event, but something had obviously gone wrong. Terribly wrong.

"She's okay," Flora said. "She's had a scare, but you're safe now, baby. You're okay now."

Lu, already in her pajamas, was nodding like a silent amen corner. Aretha went and sat beside ShaRonda on the couch and handed her a tissue to wipe her eyes.

"Thanks," ShaRonda whispered.

Blue looked at Kwame, and his eyes narrowed. "Didn't you take them to the concert?"

Kwame didn't blink. "Aretha and I both went with them. And we took her home afterward. This happened after she got there."

Flora looked at ShaRonda, who was sniffling. She had skinned her knee and there was a little circle of blood on her white stockings. "You know Mr. Hamilton, don't you, ShaRonda?"

She nodded.

"Can you tell him what happened?"

The girl looked at Aretha, who patted her arm gently. "Just tell him what you told us, okay? Don't be scared."

ShaRonda looked at Lu, who was still nodding. "You can tell him."

Blue pulled a chair up closer to where she was sitting. "You're not scared of me, are you, ShaRonda?"

She shook her head, and Blue smiled a little. He had been doing this all night, and it looked like he wasn't through yet.

"Good. Who was bothering you?"

"It was my uncle DooDoo," she whispered.

Blue's expression never changed, but I know mine did. *Damn!* Was there no escaping this fool? Were we going to have to wait around until he killed somebody before we could figure out what to do?

"When we got home from the concert, he . . . he was there with three of his friends and that one named King James, and they were smoking weed and watching these nasty videos."

Blue's eyes never left her face as the words tumbled out, slowly at first, then faster and faster.

"And when I came in, he said, 'Girl, you look good! Come in here and let me show my boys how good you look!' So I went in there and waved at 'em, but when I got ready to go upstairs, one of them told DooDoo to pour me a drink. And I said I wadn't but twelve, and I didn't want no drink, and he said . . ."

She bit her lip, but she didn't cry again. "He said I'd like it better if I was a little drunk and Uncle DooDoo started laughin', and I said what you talkin' about? Like what better? And one of the other guys said, 'Leave that girl alone, King. She ain't nothin' but a kid,' and the guy said, 'I got hos out working right now ain't but ten.' Then he asked my uncle if I was a virgin, and my uncle said he guess I was."

I felt like I was going to be sick. I swallowed hard and took a deep breath.

"So, he said that was worth something, and he reached in his pocket and handed my uncle a hundred dollars, and I said what you think you payin' for? I ain't nobody's ho, and my uncle told me to shut up and go upstairs. I told him I wadn't going, and he hit me."

Her face was swollen and blotchy, and one eye was puffing up. "The others just laughing and reaching in they pockets for some money, too, even the one who said to leave me alone. I know he ain't gonna help me either, so I ran upstairs and locked my door, but I know that ain't gonna stop 'em, so I . . . I jumped out the window."

"You jumped out of an upstairs window?" Aretha said, hearing this detail for the first time.

ShaRonda nodded. "That's how I hurt my knee. They was gonna turn me out if I hadn't left. Everybody scared of 'em. That girl he was talkin' about, the one who ain't but ten? That's Neicy's cousin. She went to our school last year."

Lu's eyes widened. "Are you talking about Tiffany?"

ShaRonda nodded miserably and looked at Blue. "I thought my uncle DooDoo would take care of me, but he just took the money and started laughin'. He just kept laughin', so I ran over here."

Aretha hugged her, and she leaned into the embrace like it was all that stood between her and the abyss. Watching them, I realized it probably was.

Flora looked at Lu. "Why don't you give ShaRonda something else to put on, and I'll be in there in a minute, okay?"

"You want to take a shower?" Lu asked her friend gently.

ShaRonda nodded.

"Come on."

The two of them walked slowly to Lu's room, ShaRonda limping just a little, and shut the door behind them. Flora and Aretha and Kwame and I were all watching Blue, who was sitting so still he looked like a statue. King James and DooDoo's reach had extended into Blue's territory twice in one night. I had a feeling there wouldn't be a third time.

Finally, Blue looked at Flora. "I'll put a man out front in case these young niggas have completely lost their minds," he said. "You all right?"

She nodded. "I'll keep her here until I hear from you."

He stood up, turned to me, and took my hand. "Walk with me?"

"Sure."

"Mr. Hamilton?" Kwame stood up quickly. "I'd like to go with you."

Blue looked at him. It was a long look, but Kwame didn't flinch. I admired that, and I'm sure Aretha did, too. It's always a pleasure to watch a man you care about step up in a crisis.

"This ain't for you," Blue said quietly. "But thanks."

Kwame didn't argue it.

Blue and I headed outside. He closed Flora's door behind us in the hallway and took me in his arms. The sweetness of kissing Blue still made me weak in the knees, and I hugged him close.

"I've got to go," he said against my cheek.

"I know. Be careful."

"Careful as I can," he said, kissed me again, and walked out into the night alone.

48

BETH'S SCHEDULE CALLED FOR her to return to Atlanta from Gainesville last night. At seven-thirty this morning, I rang her front bell. She's an early riser, and she answered the door fully dressed in dark pants and tunic. She looked surprised, but not disappointed to see me.

"You're out early."

"May I come in?"

"Of course," she said. "I just put on a pot of coffee."

I followed her into the kitchen. The house was quiet, and as we walked through the spotless, formal living room, I wondered how Beth could rationalize doing business with the likes of DooDoo and King James.

She took down two mugs and poured us each a cup of coffee. "What's up?"

"Tell me about your grandson," I said.

She put her mug down. "Did you find something else?"

"I talked to his mother."

"You did *what?*"

"I talked to his mother. She's hiding out because the guys you sent to her house threatened to cut her throat."

She stood up quickly and walked to the window. Outside in the branches of her magnolia tree, three bright red cardinals were chasing one another. Her silence surprised me. I had expected her to have a lie ready. An intricate denial commensurate with the severity of the accusation, but she didn't say a word. She just watched the birds. Fine with me. I had come here for an explanation, and I was prepared to stay until I got one.

"This is not a game, Gina."

"Don't patronize me," I said. "How in the hell did you hook up with these thugs in the first place?"

She turned back to me. "It's not hard to find people to do whatever you need done in Atlanta. You should know that. I sent Jade back to the old neighborhood to ask around. She came back with the names of some brothers who could get the job done."

"How can you call those hoodlums *brothers*?"

Her smile was more of a sneer. "You're not in much of a position to be self-righteous, are you?"

"What do you mean?"

"What do you think your landlord does in addition to collecting your rent?"

If she thought sniping at Blue was going to distract me from the task at hand, she couldn't have been more wrong. "Tell me about your grandson," I said again.

"I don't have a grandson," she snapped, her voice ice cold. "But I'll tell you this. I'm not going to have my Son's legacy be that he was one more black man who couldn't keep his pants zipped up. Is that what you want? Haven't we got enough stories like that? How many times does the curse of Jesse Jackson have to strike before we figure it out!"

"That's not the point," I said, "and you know it."

"That's exactly the point," Beth snapped, then stopped herself and took a deep breath. "Don't you see, Gina? This means they win. This means everything they say about our men is true. That they lie. That they stick their dicks into anything that moves. That they can make a baby, but they're incapable of raising one." Her voice was filled with rage and bitterness and disappointment. "I worked all my life to prove to everybody that was just a bunch of racist *bullshit*, and I could prove it because my son was none of those things. *Do you hear me?* Whatever they said about our men, I could answer, 'Not my son!' "

"Son wanted to raise his child," I said quietly.

She sneered at me, and her face was full of the pain of her loss. "Well, it's just a little late for that, isn't it?"

"Is it?"

"Yes, it is. Listen, Gina, my work is not about one kid whose mother thinks I owe her something. My work is about changing the lives of thousands of women and their sons. You're interested in some kind of soap opera, and I'm interested in changing the world."

"Well, I guess you and DooDoo and King James have your work cut out for you," I said, getting up to go. There was no reason to continue this conversation, but Beth isn't one to leave loose ends dangling.

"I'm sorry you're upset, Gina," she said, "but there's a lot at stake here, and I can't afford any confusion."

"What kind of confusion are you talking about?" I asked, wondering suddenly if she was getting ready to threaten me, too.

"The dedication is only a week away. I've seen the lovely video; Mr. Freeney says you've done a fine job with organizing the papers, and I know the remarks you're drafting for me will be perfect, but . . ." Her voice was all edges. "If you don't feel completely comfortable, I'm prepared to pay you what I owe you and call it square between us. I'm sure Jade and Mr. Freeney can do whatever else needs to be done."

She was watching me, giving me a way out if I couldn't stand the things she was prepared to do to get what she thought she wanted.

"That won't be necessary," I said. "I'll finish what I started."

She nodded slowly. "I'm glad you're prepared to be professional about this. Just remember, my personal life, and Son's, are no longer your affair."

"I see."

"And don't worry," she said. "Nobody's going to cut anybody."

I thought of Madonna's frightened face, and suddenly I remembered something. I reached in my purse and drew out the envelope bulging with Beth's get-out-of-town money. I dropped it on the kitchen table.

"I think this belongs to you," I said. Without waiting for her to pick it up, I walked out of the kitchen and through the perfect living room, let myself out the front door, got in my tacky little rental car and backed out the driveway before she could stop me.

There was nothing she could do about what I had in mind, so there was no point in wasting time talking about it with her. So Beth is trying to change the world, huh? Well, so am I. One little brown baby at a time.

49

THERE IS NOTHING EXTRAORDINARY about the video that Madonna wanted Beth to see. It is a little out of focus sometimes, like all amateur videos. The framing of the shots could be better, and the audio is often nearly unintelligible. There is a lot of laughing and even a loud, undeniably off-key rendition of "Happy Birthday." Of course, there is cake and ice cream. Of course, there are parents and games and several tiny, bewildered, not-quite-toddlers trying to figure out what the hell is going on. Of course, there are friends around to share the moment.

And, of course, the proud parents stand on either side of their tiny son, encouraging him to blow out that one brave candle and getting instead only a delighted grin until they blow it out themselves, laughing, and everybody applauds, and Son scoops up the birthday boy and kisses him and grabs Madonna and kisses her, too, and they all laugh again and cut the cake.

I watched it twice, then picked up the phone. Precious answered on the second ring.

"This is Senator Hargrove. How can I help?"

"Regina Burns. How are you, Senator?"

"Just fine, thanks."

"You remember when you promised to tell me the story of how Beth Davis got you into politics one day?"

"I remember."

"How about we make this the day?"

50

AFTER I TALKED TO PRECIOUS, THE next person I needed to see was Freeney. He was the one who would be in the video booth working with the technician. If I was going to make this work, I had to have Freeney's help. Precious had agreed immediately, but her job wouldn't be on the line. His would.

Freeney was on the phone when I stuck my head in his office door. He waved me in.

"Yes, yes, of course," he was saying. "Certainly. Absolutely."

Sometimes I think half of Freeney's job is agreeing enthusiastically. He's good at it.

"Oh, yes. That sounds perfect. Just perfect. Yes. I will. Let me know what she says. Bye, now."

He turned to me with a wide smile. Miss Ross, his perpetually napping calico cat, was curled up in her usual sunny corner of the oriental rug. She opened one eye when I first came in, but hadn't moved since.

"Is this a bad time?" I asked, borrowing a line from Blue.

"Don't be silly! Sit down."

I took my favorite chair, the rocker. We had done a lot of work together over the last six weeks, and he was as happy as I was to be in the home stretch.

"Everything okay?"

"Couldn't be better," he said. "The mayor has confirmed and Channel Two is definitely sending a crew."

It suddenly dawned on me that what I was getting ready to do had the potential to backfire big time. Was I prepared to take responsibility for asking somebody to risk his job? It was my destiny that required the fighting of the dragon, not his.

Freeney saw my face change. "What's wrong?"

"Nothing's wrong," I said, "but I want to tell you something that has to stay just between us for now."

"Of course, of course," he said, getting up immediately to close the door into the hallway, although there is no random foot traffic in the archives. If you're not coming to see Freeney, you're not coming at all. "What is it?"

"Son Davis has a child," I said. "A boy about a year and a half old."

A strange expression flickered across his face. "How do you know?"

"Someone sent Precious Hargrove a photograph and . . . ," I hesitated. How much did he need to know? "I met the baby's mother."

His eyes widened. "Oh, my! What are you going to do?"

"I'm going to introduce him to his grandmother."

He jumped up suddenly, came over, and hugged me like I had just told him he was getting a big raise and twice as much staff as he used to have. "Bless you! Bless you! Bless you!"

He just kept saying it over and over and hugging me. Miss Ross raised her head and gave us a baleful look for interrupting her nap, but Freeney paid her no mind.

"Bless you! Bless you!"

Finally, he calmed down and pulled himself together.

"I take that to mean you think it's a good idea?"

He sat down, but he was still practically bouncing off the seat. "I think it's a fabulous idea!"

"But I haven't even told you how I'm going to do it yet."

"You're going to do it. That's what counts. This is just what I hoped would happen, and now it has!"

What was he talking about? "What you hoped would happen when?"

He took out his handkerchief and wiped his face, then grinned at me, a little sheepishly, but no less delighted for that. "When I sent that picture to Senator Hargrove."

I almost fell out of my chair. "You sent it?"

He nodded, folded his handkerchief neatly, and put it back in his pocket. His face was serious now. "I had no choice. I've kept too many secrets of my own."

"How long have you known?"

"Since before you came," he said. "I had just started going through the papers from his office, and I found that picture, of the three of them."

I nodded.

"Well, I knew immediately. I realized that he had secrets, and I can't keep secrets anymore. I pretended to be somebody else for years. Scared my family would find out I was gay. Scared I'd lose my job if my boss knew. Scared somebody would kick my ass. Scared somebody would call me a 'faggot.' And then I met Brady at an archivists conference in San Francisco, and it was love at first sight for both of us."

He blushed a little, but he wanted me to understand why he had done what he'd done. "He had never been in anybody's closet, and he showed me how good it felt to be free. He begged me to come out there and live, but I was still too scared, so I came back to Atlanta. Two years, he begged me to move, but I'd only visit, so finally he said, 'If I have to move my black ass to Georgia to be with you, then that's what I'll do.' And he did. And he taught me to be myself and love myself and not give a damn what other people said."

Freeney's voice was fierce with determination. He took a minute to calm down, and then he looked at me. "One thing that made me respect Son Davis was that he wasn't scared to talk about homophobia. I respected him for speaking out. . . . So when I saw that picture and realized he had a secret life, too, I decided to honor the life he'd been hiding, for whatever reason he was hiding it. There's no good reason to pretend to be somebody you're not, but what could I do?"

Miss Ross jumped into his lap, demanding attention, and he rubbed her throat gently. "So I sent the picture to Precious and hoped *she'd* know what to do with it so that child could claim his daddy, and she gave it to you!"

Now it was my turn to grin. I hugged Freeney, being careful not to disturb Miss Ross. "Thank you for that," I said, "Thank you for Son."

"He was a good man," Freeney said. "He just didn't have time to make it right."

"Which is why we're going to help him," I said, taking out the birthday video Madonna had given me. "Now here's what we're going to do. . . ."

51

PRECIOUS AND I HAD BEEN WORKING on her speech all afternoon. The story she told me about her initial encounter with
Beth was a moving, first-person narrative, and I intended to open her
statement with it and then segue into the rest of her remarks. It was
almost seven o'clock by the time I left her house and started home. I
hadn't heard from Blue for two days, but I wasn't worried. I knew he
had work to do just like I did.

I stopped in at the West End News to pick up a paper, and, when
I came out, I bumped smack into Brandi, who was having her hair
done next door. She stepped back, apologizing immediately.

"Oh, I'm sorry! *My bad!* I just got so excited when I saw you!"
She laughed and touched the side of her hair. "I hope that fool didn't
cut a plug out the way I jumped up so fast. She probably thought I
had lost my mind." Brandi stepped back, waved at her stylist through
the window, and held up one finger to indicate she'd be right back.

"Were you looking for me?" I asked, surprised at how much
younger she looked without all the makeup.

"I just wanted to say thanks, you know? For helping me and my
cousin. Mr. Blue sent somebody to pick her and Junior up yesterday,
and they are totally psyched about you inviting them to the big
doin's this Sunday."

"Aren't you coming, too?"

She looked embarrassed. "I can't go up there. Half them young
niggas done seen my titties at one club or another. If they see me out
and about, it might shake 'em up a little."

What she was saying reminded me of the scene in *Gone With the
Wind*, where the town's most successful madam is trying to make a

contribution to the war effort, and the proper slave-owning confederate ladies refuse it on the grounds that her money is tainted. That always cracks me up. She earns her money having sex, and they earn their money breeding people, and *her* money's no good.

"They need shaking up," I said. "Please come. Madonna's probably going to need some moral support."

"You're right about that," Brandi said. "She's already nervous as a cat!"

All Brandi knew was that Madonna and her son had been invited. She didn't know they had agreed to play a major role in the proceedings.

"Come as my guest," I said, looking through the window at her stylist, who was watching our conversation with increasing exasperation. Time is money to a beautician. On Friday night, too? Brandi was playing a dangerous game keeping the woman waiting. If she wasn't careful, she was going to find herself facing the weekend with a half-done head.

"Okay," she said excitedly. "I'll be there. And can you do one thing for me?"

"Sure."

"Tell Mr. Blue thanks for putting that money in for the dancers."

She had lowered her voice conspiratorially, although there was nobody nearby.

"What money?"

She looked surprised. "He didn't tell you?"

I shook my head.

"Well, I don't mean to be talkin' out of school, but I know it had to be him. Who else gonna think to do somethin' like that?"

"Like what?"

"When we got to work last night, there was a new guy there, a big guy, but real cool. Real polite and all, just like Mr. Blue."

I knew exactly who that was: Blue's combination driver, bodyguard, and special assistant. He never had much to say, but when he did, everybody listened.

"He told us King James and DooDoo had sold their interest in the club and it would be closing for a couple of days. Then he apologized for any inconvenience to us—that's how he said it, too, any *inconvenience* to us—and gave us each an envelope with one thousand dollars in it!"

"One thousand dollars *each?*"

She nodded enthusiastically. "Cash money! All twelve of us. You know how much that is altogether?"

She laughed and shook her head in happy disbelief. Her stylist tapped a hairbrush against the glass and frowned.

Brandi turned to me apologetically. "I gotta go before this girl goes off and starts on somebody else's head before she hooks me up. Thank Mr. Blue for me, will you? I don't know what we woulda done without him." And she ducked back into the beauty shop.

The neighborhood was humming with Friday night energy. Women were hurrying home with bags of groceries and holding hungry children by the hand. Men were stopping at the barbershop or the dry cleaner's. The line at the liquor store was still short enough to be jovial, and through the window of the florist shop, I could see a young man counting out the money for a bouquet of long-stemmed red roses.

I smiled and started home with Brandi's words ringing in my ears. *I don't know what we would have done without him.* I do, I thought, and trust me, *with him* is better. Much better.

52

W HEN I TURNED DOWN OUR STREET, there were a few people out puttering in their yards, watering their azaleas, pruning their dogwoods. Some of the vegetable gardens were already showing tiny little tomato plants, the beginnings of blooms on the bell peppers, the fuzzy leaves of summer squash. I was admiring a line of pink dogwood trees in front of a house across the street when I heard the first tentative notes of our neighborhood saxophone player. He was still working on "My Favorite Things," and he still wasn't giving the real Coltrane any serious competition, but this time, I could actually hear the melody beginning to emerge. He had slowed it down and found the fingering for at least every third or fourth note, and it was close enough so that I actually found myself singing along with him under my breath as I walked.

> *"When the dog bites,*
> *When the bee stings,*
> *When I'm feeling sad,"*

Blue's voice joined me out of nowhere.

> *"I simply remember my favorite things*
> *And then I don't feel so bad!"*

I turned around, and he was standing right beside me, smiling that smile and twinkling those beautiful, incongruous, otherworldly, past-life, ocean eyes. The dogwood trees were shedding their petals in a shower of four-pointed pink blossoms, the sky was lilac in the twilight, and Coltrane was taking a breather. The silence truly was golden.

"Welcome home," I said, smiling back at him, respecting the position he occupies around here and resisting the impulse to throw myself into his arms. "I missed you."

"I missed you, too," Blue said, offering his arm.

I took it, and we strolled on toward home as if there wasn't a big Lincoln creeping along a few feet behind us. "Everything okay?"

His smile was genuine. "Everything's fine."

Coltrane began his second set, but it wasn't a tune either of us recognized, so we couldn't sing along.

"I have a message for you," I said.

He raised his eyebrows slightly.

"Brandi asked me to tell you *thanks*."

I didn't have to say for what. We both knew she meant for creating a place where she could go to the twenty-four-hour salon and walk home safely at whatever hour. For creating a few city blocks where I can walk home alone in the twilight and allow myself to fall so deeply into the beauty of the moment that I don't even notice a man coming up behind me, and *it's okay*.

"She said she didn't know what they would have done without you."

He smiled slowly as we turned up the front walk and his driver pulled the car into its usual spot at the curb. "And what did you say?"

I stepped inside the blue door and turned to face him in the small foyer. "I said, 'You don't have to worry about that. He's not going anywhere.' "

He grinned and pulled me close. "You got that right," he said. "You sure got that right."

53

THE MORNING OF THE DEDICATION, I woke up in a panic at four A.M. What if I wasn't doing this for the right reasons? What if I was just trying to get back at Beth for her past sins against me, real or imagined? What if I wasn't being a friend to Son at all? What if I was just adding one more name to a list of imperfect black men who weren't who they pretended to be? What if I wasn't saving a damsel and slaying a dragon at all, but just adding to some mess somebody else was going to have to straighten out later?

It didn't make any difference to me who ran for governor of Georgia anyway. I can't even vote here. All I came to do was make enough money to save my house, and now I'm about to lose a third of that by biting that hand that's supposed to feed me before Beth writes that final check. *And how much do I really know about Blue Hamilton anyway?*

I tried to ease out of bed, but Blue was awake, too. He was *always* awake.

"What's wrong?"

"Just a little nervous about today," I said. "Go back to sleep."

He was already up. "Want some coffee?"

I hesitated.

"Maybe a nice hot cup of sake?" he grinned.

"You know I don't like sake."

"Coffee it is," he said, kissing me as he headed for the kitchen.

There's something so familiar to me about being up this early, leaning against the kitchen counter, waiting for the coffee to be ready so the serious business, whatever it might be, can be conducted before the rest of the world is even aware that the deal has been struck.

My parents were always up early like this, plotting something with people who arrived after dark and left before the sun came up. I yawned and relaxed a little.

"What's bothering you?" Blue set out two mugs.

"I just hope I'm doing the right thing," I said as the smell of coffee warmed up the small room.

"What was your other option?"

"What do you mean?"

He shrugged. "When you start wondering if you did the right thing, what other choices do you think would have been better?"

My mind ran through them, starting with *I could have told Aunt Abbie to keep her postmenopausal visions to herself* on through *I could have told Precious politics wasn't my thing.* I could also have told Blue I didn't believe in past lives and told Madonna her kid wasn't my responsibility. I could have pretended I didn't see DooDoo at the junior high school or King James driving away from the newsstand. Pretended I didn't see how scared Brandi was. Looked away from ShaRonda's torn stocking and turned off the birthday party video and taken Beth's check to the bank and my black ass home. *But then who would I be?*

Blue was watching me with the mind-reading look on his face, so I didn't say anything. I didn't have to. He smiled and handed me a steaming mug of strong coffee.

"You know you're doing the right thing."

"Do I?"

"Pretending you don't know something when you do know it, *and you know you know it,* is as good a definition of crazy as I've ever heard, and you are . . . a lot of things—" he said that really slow to make me blush, and I obliged him "—but crazy is not among them."

I laughed. "Can we go to the beach if they don't arrest me?"

He grinned at me. "We can go if they do arrest you. I'll post your bail."

"Good," I said, suddenly feeling more sexy than scared. It was too early to get up. "You know what?"

"What, baby?"

"I have a few more questions to ask you about this past-life thing," I said, standing up and heading back to the bedroom.

"Oh, yeah?" he said, setting down his coffee and falling in step beside me. "That's quite a coincidence."

"Why is that?"

"Because I think I have a few more answers."

54

The Martin Luther King Chapel dominates one end of the Morehouse College campus. Named in honor of the college's most famous graduate, the red-carpeted chapel seats a thousand people comfortably and is blessed with state-of-the-art audio-visual capabilities. The biographical piece that had made Beth weep when she saw the rough cut in that small conference room would be even more moving on the giant screen that dominated the back of the stage.

Freeney had ordered banks of white flowers for either side of the podium, where the dignitaries would stand to speak about Son's contributions to the college; his skill at fund-raising; his tireless mentoring; his anti-male-violence workshops. The four people who would speak briefly, including Precious Hargrove, represented the broad range of Son's constituencies. After their remarks, the biographical video would be shown on the big screen, and Senator Hargrove would return to the stage to introduce Beth. That was what the program said anyway.

Beth arrived with Jade in tow. She looked radiant and regal, wearing a dark purple tunic and pants, with a kente cloth shawl across her shoulders, and she greeted me with a smile that came from the heart. The auditorium was already filling up, and her eyes were shining with pride in Son's accomplishments and her own possibilities. I hoped this day would expand those possibilities and help her to embrace them.

She pressed the final check for my services into my hand as we stood up front watching the crowd arriving. "I know I've told you this already, but I want you to know how much I appreciate the speech you did for today. Jade is learning, but there's something about the things you write for me. It's what I want to say, *but better*. It's my best self talking, and I like her."

"I know," I said. "Me, too."

I slipped the check into my pocket, but, happy as I was to have it, I didn't have time to think about finishing up my business with the weasel right now. There was too much going on! The college president came over to say hello, and his wife needed a change in seating for one of the dignitaries, and the Glee Club has lost a soloist to laryngitis, and someone almost knocked over the scale model of the new Davis Communications Center, and Freeney had a last-minute attack of nerves that Brady addressed by walking him around the building and reminding him that getting fired wasn't the worst thing in the world because then they could move to San Francisco like they had some sense.

Then Aretha came over to tell me that Madonna's mom had shown up after all and that Sonny Jr. was adorable and that they were all waiting in the holding room like I had asked them to do. Kwame escorted Precious to her seat in the front row beside Beth. Finally, Flora hurried in with Lu and ShaRonda. The newest resident of our building, ShaRonda had moved in with Flora after her uncle disappeared, and she was thriving. She saw me and waved, and I waved back.

Blue came in by himself and took a seat on the side aisle near the back door. He grinned and inclined his head in my direction, but before I could go over and compliment him on his choice of seating just in case we had to make a quick getaway, the Glee Club took a collective deep breath and sang the program into life.

" 'Guide my feet, while I run this race.' " They sang like angels.

Standing beside me in the tech booth at the back of the auditorium, Freeney leaned over and whispered in my ear as we turned our attention to the stage, "San Francisco, here we come!"

55

WHEN THE LIGHTS CAME UP AT the end of the video, people rose to their feet in a spontaneous standing ovation. I used the opportunity to slip back down front and take Precious's seat next to Beth as the senator walked up onto the stage.

"You okay?" I said, touching Beth's arm lightly, feeling suddenly protective.

"I just miss him so much, Gina. I just miss him so much!" she whispered as we sat back down. She slipped her arm through mine like we were schoolgirls, and I could feel her trembling.

Precious took her place at the podium and looked out at the crowd. "Son Davis was my friend," she said. "And I can tell you one thing. He would have *loved* to see all of you here today to honor his life and his work."

The crowd applauded themselves, proud they had worn their Sunday best to honor one of their own.

"Because that's why we're here today, to honor my friend, our friend, Son Davis. The video we just watched told you *some* of the reasons why." She paused and smiled again. "I'm going to tell you the rest."

Beth looked at me with a small flicker of confusion. *"What is she talking about?"*

"Don't worry," I whispered. "I wrote this for her."

Beth squeezed my hand gratefully and turned back to Precious.

"Son Davis was a man with very high standards, especially for himself. He was raised that way by his mother, who devoted her life to making him a good man."

The audience applauded warmly, and I could feel Beth relax even more. Precious's earlier remarks had recalled the first time she had seen Beth speak and how moved she was by a sudden realization of her own potential. That was the day, she had said proudly, that she decided to run for political office. She didn't know how she was going to do it, but Beth had made her see that she could do anything she put her mind to. Everyone expected her introduction to be more of the same kind of praise song. Everyone but me.

"But somewhere along the way, Son started thinking being a good man wasn't enough. He started thinking he had to be better than good. He had to be *perfect*."

You could have heard a pin drop.

"Maybe he felt that he owed perfection to his mother, to repay her for her sacrifices. Maybe he felt that he owed perfection to those who believed in his mother because of his shining example as a perfect son. Maybe he thought he owed perfection to the students of his alma mater, who wanted to walk in his footsteps. We don't know. How can we ever know? But what we do know is that his feeling that he was less than perfect led him to begin to lead two lives: the one he showed the world, and the one he thought wasn't good enough to show us."

There was some murmuring now. Beth pinched my arm, *hard.*

"What do you think you're doing?" she hissed.

I ignored her and kept my eye on Precious.

"But he was wrong. For one of the very few times in his life, he misjudged us. Because there was no reason for him to hide anything. We weren't looking for perfection. We were looking for the *possibility of perfection*, and that possibility is always most beautifully present in the faces of our children and then, if we are very lucky, in the faces of our grandchildren."

She turned to Beth and, from the stage, addressed her directly. "Sister Davis, I think all of us were moved a few weeks ago during a television interview when you spoke of your sorrow over the fact that your beloved son did not live long enough to have children of his own."

The audience gave a collective sigh of sympathy.

"But sometimes the Lord works in mysterious ways, and someone else saw that interview, too. Someone who had agreed to keep silent, to make Son's secret her own."

Beth's grip on my hand was a vice.

"Someone who had been struggling with serious questions of honor and responsibility. Someone who wanted to respect the wishes of one who sacrificed everything but who also understands a mother's love and a woman's grief."

I stole a sideways glance at Beth. She knew every eye in the place was on her, so she couldn't do anything but return Precious's gaze with an unblinking stare and wait for whatever was coming next.

"And that someone is here with us today, but before I introduce her to you, I want to share another little video with you. This one isn't as well produced as the first one. Sometimes it's out of focus and a little fuzzy, but I think you'll be able to recognize our honoree today among the celebrants at a very special birthday party."

Beth tried to jerk her arm from mine, but I held on for dear life. "Let me go!" she hissed, but I shook my head.

Then suddenly, behind Precious on the giant screen where Son's *official* face had been overseeing the proceedings, another face appeared. The face of a proudly smiling young father celebrating his laughing son's first birthday. The face of a loving partner with an affectionate arm encircling the waist of the woman he loved. The unguarded private face of a man whose misguided desire to please his mother had made him withhold from her the sweetest gift he could have given, her only grandchild.

Unable to free herself and flee, Beth had no choice but to sit still and watch the screen. And as she did, I watched her. At first, she was so angry at me, at Precious, at being exposed so publicly, that her face was like stone. Her jaw was tight, and her eyes were hard and cold. But now on the video, the assembled guests were singing to the birthday boy, and as they finished the song, his father grabbed him and tossed him high in the air, both of them laughing, so happy, so alive, that the idea that one of them was gone, that this child would never again see his reflection in his father's eyes, was so overwhelming that when Freeney froze the frame, the poignant image seemed to burn itself into all of our brains at the same time, and any idea that this little family could ever be anything less than perfect seemed not only absurd, but cruel.

In the stunned silence as the picture faded from the screen, I looked at Beth's face, and it was wet with tears. Precious stepped back to the podium.

"Sister Davis," she said gently. "May I present your grandson, Theodore Davis Jr.?"

She nodded toward the back of the auditorium, and every head in the place turned to watch the lovely young woman and the little boy with his father's smile walk up the long middle aisle. Aretha had helped Madonna find a lovely pale green dress that fluttered around her as she walked. She looked like an angel, and if she was afraid, you couldn't see it on her face.

I kept my eyes on Beth, who was still clutching my hand. She looked at me, and the pain on her face was so profound I was afraid she wouldn't survive it.

"Why?" she whispered. "Why couldn't he tell me?"

It was the question that contained all the rage and confusion and anguish and guilt that had made her do things she never should have done. It was the question that she had to force herself to ask, not so she could answer it, but so she could accept the fact that there was no answer. Only a small boy who had lost his father and a mother who had lost her son.

"He's telling you now," I said softly. "Maybe he's telling you now."

She looked at me like she wanted to believe me, if she only could, and then the applause began. Slowly at first, a little tentative, and then louder and louder. As Madonna and Sonny Jr. made their way up the aisle, each row they passed stood up and cheered. They had come to honor a fallen soldier and had found themselves witnesses to the kind of revelation and reconciliation that are always at the heart of what we mean when we say *family*.

Madonna was just a few rows away from us now, and Beth turned to me in complete panic. "I . . . I don't know what to say. What can I say?"

"Don't worry," I said. "Your remarks are already at the podium."

She looked at me, and her smile was equal parts gratitude and relief. "And will it be my best self talking?"

I smiled back and realized I was crying, too. "Absolutely."

She hugged me then and took a deep breath. "Good. Then you'll excuse me while I say hello to my grandson?"

Always theatrical, she stepped into the center aisle to face them and, as if on cue, Sonny Jr. released his mother's hand and ran as fast as his little fat legs could carry him into his grandmother's arms. As she scooped him up into a long overdue embrace, I could hear her whispering over and over, *Thank you! Thank you! Thank you!*

It wasn't until she took Madonna's hand and the three of them joined Precious on the stage while the crowd went wild that I realized it wasn't Beth's voice at all. *It was mine.*

56

B LUE WAS WAITING OUTSIDE THE auditorium exactly where I'd asked him to meet me. His proud smile told me everything I needed to know, but I wanted to hear it anyway.

"So how'd we do?"

"I couldn't have done it better myself."

I laughed. "High praise from an emperor."

He laughed with me. "That was last time around. This time I'm just your humble servant."

"Good. Then let's go!"

He hesitated. "Aren't you going to stay for Beth's speech?"

"You mean the one where she says she won't be running for governor because nothing is more important to her at this time then getting to know her grandson?"

He grinned. "Yeah, that's the one."

I grinned back. "I don't have to hear it. I *wrote* it."

"So where are we going?"

I looked up at him and saw the rest of my life looking back at me through his eyes. "D.C."

He looked surprised. "Why D.C.?"

"Aren't you the guy who said that if you were patient and lucky, I'd learn to trust you and maybe even fall in love with you again so we could continue our journey together through time and space and many lifetimes like we were supposed to?"

"That's what I said all right," he said, pleased I had quoted him so exactly.

I took his arm. "Well, then, I think it's time for you to meet my aunt."

About the Author

PEARL CLEAGE is the author of *What Looks Like Crazy on an Ordinary Day . . .*; *Mad at Miles: A Black Woman's Guide to Truth;* and *Deals with the Devil and Other Reasons to Riot*. Also an accomplished dramatist, Ms. Cleage lives in Atlanta with her husband.